D1525126

Resolute Love
(Consequential Love Series #1)

By

Elaine M. DeGroot

Anne -

Enjoy Garrett + Leigh's story!

Elaine M DeGroot

Publisher's Note:

This is a work of fiction. All names, characters, places, and
events are the work of the author's imagination.

Any resemblance to real persons, places, or events is
coincidental.

Solstice Publishing - http://www.solsticeempire.com/

Resolute Love, Consequential Love Series #1 is dedicated to my dear friend, Lynne Vermillion. She and I were classmates through US Air Force Officer Training School and Communications Officer School. Over the years we communicated on an annual basis with Christmas cards. We enjoyed one assignment location together. When she retired from the Air Force, we saw more of each other. She acted as my editor during the early drafts of *Resolute Love* and the second book, *Challenged Love* of the *Consequential Love Series*. Unfortunately, she died in 2019 and will never see this story in print. Thank you, my friend. You helped me achieve my dream.

Prologue

The phone rings to voicemail. "Hi, this is Garrett. Leave your name, number, and a message. I'll call you back as soon as I'm able."

"Chief Martin, here. Hate to tell you this, but Jonas Klein escaped and disappeared! I have a bad feeling he's looking for payback from you. Call me as soon as you can."

Chapter One

The snow continued falling; the thick curtain of white visible through the windshield stretched out forever. Without Garrett's four-wheel-drive Jeep, the road conditions would soon be impassable. No ice covered the highway, so he continued on his way. Ever watchful for snowdrifts and errant drivers losing control, he handled the Jeep with ease as he drove toward his future.

A recent decision regarding his path forward brought him home to Minnesota. The Air Force and his promising career with the Office of Special Investigations, the OSI, lay behind him; a fresh start as a Special Agent with the Minnesota Bureau of Criminal Apprehension, the BCA, lay ahead of him.

Too bad he couldn't leave behind the memories that drove his separation from the Air Force: the memory of his partner, Tess, being downed by a bullet and his failure to protect her. Try as he might, he was incapable to stop the barrage of memories from reaching the tragic end of Tess dying in his arms.

A slight pull of a snowdrift on the Jeep dragged Garrett back to the present. Focusing on the white road, he squinted against the bright glare of sunshine off the new fallen snow. A check of his jacket pockets located his sunglasses.

"Much better, now I can see."

A snow-covered two-lane highway running through the forested hills of northern Minnesota stretched out before him. Inches of snow could fall in a matter of hours up here. When he left the resort on the North Shore of Lake Superior, the sun shone brilliantly, and clear skies greeted him. An hour into his trip brought him to four inches of blinding snow and the promise of a hellacious blizzard once the wind picked up.

Garrett had calculated five hours to reach Brainerd, but this front swooped in from Canada earlier than expected. The snow would delay his arrival by hours. Since he wouldn't report to his new job for two weeks, the delay didn't concern him. After a quick stop at the Brainerd BCA office tomorrow to meet his boss and co-workers, his to-do list consisted of one thing—buying a house. Once he reported for work, he wanted no distractions; his new life would be set and moving forward.

"What the…?"

Ahead a car sat on the shoulder, a cloud of exhaust pumped out of the tailpipe. A car parked on a desolate stretch of road, miles from the nearest town, brought two possibilities to mind: a breakdown or a medical emergency. Either way Garrett assumed the driver needed assistance. Leaving anyone in such a dangerous place, let alone during a snowstorm, never occurred to him. No other vehicle had passed by since he drove through the last town at least twenty minutes ago.

"Damn, another delay."

Parking the Jeep behind the car, he activated the four-way flashers. Based on his years of law enforcement, a hint of apprehension flowed over him. No telling what waited for him in the car. A figure with long, gray hair slumped over the wheel, so possibly an elderly person suffered a stroke or heart attack. A shred of luck stayed with the driver, being able to stop the vehicle on the shoulder rather than plummet down the embankment on the other side of the road. Leaning into the biting wind, he approached the vehicle while snow swirled around him.

"Do you need assistance?" Garrett called out when he rapped on the window.

The door flew open as he reached for the handle; the sharp corner clipped his forehead. The force of the impact sent him reeling backwards on the snow-covered roadway. While he struggled to maintain his balance against the wind and the slippery road, a wave of nausea hit, but his combat-honed instincts took over. One hand covered the bleeding gash in his head and the other reached for the SIG Sauer 9mm pistol in his shoulder holster.

"Stop reaching for your gun!" a hauntingly familiar voice called out in a harsh, vicious tone. Jonas Klein got out of the stranded vehicle. Tossing a gray wig on the front seat, he aimed a revolver at Garrett's chest. "Bet the last thing you expected was me turning up in Podunk, Minnesota. Wouldn't you agree, Dane?" Garrett's last name came out as nothing more than a sneer.

Regaining his footing in a wide stance, Garrett stopped reaching for his gun and glared at the other man with sheer loathing and hatred in his eyes. "Klein. Thought you'd be making all kinds of close friends in a federal penitentiary by now. What happened? Did you miss me too much?"

"Miss you? Don't be ridiculous. I promised to kill you, and I always keep my promises, especially those made to Air Force OSI agents."

"Hate to disappoint you, but I'm not OSI or Air Force anymore; I'm a civilian now."

"Doesn't matter. You destroyed my life and my future, so I will kill you."

"You're delusional, Klein," Garrett countered as he sought a way out of this unforeseen predicament. Keeping Klein talking provided time to devise an escape plan. "By becoming a criminal, you screwed up your life, not me. But when you killed my partner, I did destroy your future by doing my job. Obviously, someone didn't do their job, or you wouldn't be here. How'd you escape custody?"

"A connection here and some money there bought an effective distraction during my transportation to an administrative holding facility. Do you realize how knowing the right people helps accomplish anything, to include tracking down a former agent of the OSI?"

"By the right people you mean people willing to break the law. So, how'd you find me? I can imagine the difficulties involved in your hunt, what with you being on the run and all."

"How? A lot of money bought me surveillance equipment and operators needed to track you down, but the simple matter of patience proved most difficult for me. Although anxious to avenge my losses, I embraced my baby brother's opinion of my impatience screwing up my plans. So, I waited but not for long. People speak freely when they're among friends. Do you realize your former OSI co-workers remain concerned with your welfare? They believe…ah, what was her name?" With a finger tapping his mouth, Klein searched his memory. "Ah, yes, Tess. They believe Tess's death damaged you in terrible ways, and they still worry about you. Touching, don't you agree?"

Garrett tensed at Klein's mention of Tess. A vision of his hands wrapped around Klein's neck urged him forward, but the reality of a handgun aimed at him restrained any action. By pretending to lose his balance, he shifted farther away from Klein.

Klein flaunted his tracking skills. The man who'd taken him down became his prey, and his ego demanded indulging in this victory a little longer. Failing to realize how far Garrett had moved away, he continued bragging about how he orchestrated the successful interception of his quarry on this remote Minnesota road. "With the proper questioning technique, resort receptionists can be exceptionally talkative and free with information concerning their guests. After identifying your vehicle, I hid a small tracking device on your Jeep and *bam*!" A bullet dug into the snow short of Garrett's feet. "Here I am!"

A natural reaction to the gunshot moved Garrett backwards from the bullet's impact. The movement served him well, by adding extra space between him and Klein.

The sound of a motor in the distance captured Klein's attention.

The distraction allowed Garrett time for a glance at the embankment behind him. Way too steep, he thought. There'd be no climbing up with Klein armed and above him. The pine trees at the bottom offered cover if he reached them. The embankment represented the only option for survival. If he kept his bearings, he might find a way back to the Jeep. With surprise on his side, escape might be possible. Could he reach the bottom without being killed? He hoped so because inaction left him a dead man.

"What's your intention? Shoot me and leave my sorry ass out here, or drag me somewhere else and ensure I suffer for arresting you?"

"As much as I'd enjoy watching you suffer for your part in the loss of everything I held dear, I doubt I have the time. Necessity dictates I leave the country soon. Traveling with you in tow would be burdensome, so your death happens here. But I can still enjoy myself." Klein grinned with utter joy reflected in his eyes, as he waved his revolver at Garrett. "I waited for this day too long; all the while I dreamt of ways of killing you. I decided watching you bleed to death, writhing in pain and agony, would provide me immense satisfaction. However, such a scenario requires uninterrupted time, and a motor sounds in the distance. Can't have some unsuspecting driver disrupting our reunion now, can we? So, I must shoot to kill and...how did you so elegantly put it? Ah, yes, 'leave your sorry ass out here.' Wolves live hereabouts, right?" Garrett's nod started Klein laughing. "Wolves and crows can feast on your body and come spring you'll be nothing more than bones and a distant memory."

A wicked laugh punctuated his words. He raised the revolver and brought Garrett into his sights and aimed for the heart.

When Klein announced his intentions, Garrett twisted to his right. The shot came seconds too late. Searing pain ripped through his left shoulder when the bullet hit. The pain didn't slow his dive toward escape. The impact with the frozen ground shook through his body. He rolled to the side of the road. Momentum tossed him over the edge and down the embankment. As he tumbled out of control, curses and gunshots pierced the silence. The heavy snowfall covered his descent. Klein's anger in the failed kill spiked the hysterical rants he called out after Garrett.

"Damn you, Dane! I will find you! You hear me? I will find you and kill you!" He continued shooting blindly down the embankment in hopes of hitting his prey.

Garrett's tumble ended with a sickening crunch when he crashed into a large pine. He struggled to stand and remain conscious. Once up, he stumbled for the tree line and disappeared into the darkness of the towering pines. Behind him, Klein's rants and gunfire echoed in the stillness. With survival in mind, Garrett forged ahead in search of shelter and assistance. A short distance into the trees, he discovered a snowmobile trail and followed the path from the cover of the woods. With any luck, help would show up before he collapsed.

Klein considered following Garrett down the embankment but decided against taking any unreasonable chances. His clothes didn't suit the severe Minnesota cold or the heavy snowfall. He appreciated how a Southern boy such as himself wouldn't stand a chance of surviving in this blasted weather. He turned back to his car as a sheriff's department vehicle drove up and parked behind Garrett's Jeep.

"Is there a problem, sir?" the sheriff's deputy called out after exiting his vehicle.

"Ah, yes. I happened upon this Jeep running with its flashers on, but no one's here. I searched for the owner, but I had difficulty seeing anything with all the snow." Klein secreted his gun into a pocket of his coat. He couldn't afford drawing attention to himself, so he kept away from the deputy and Garrett's Jeep.

"I'll handle everything from here, sir. Appreciate you trying to help, but you should return home or wherever you're headed. The wind will pick up soon, and we'll experience blizzard conditions within the hour."

"Yes of course, deputy. I hope you find them." Klein returned to his vehicle and drove away. The evening before he sat glued to the TV screen as a news alert aired on the hazard of blizzards; perhaps Mother Nature would finish his work. The Jeep would be towed away, eliminating Dane's transportation, perfect! As the car warmed, he decided to stay in the nearest town, blend in for a few days, and listen for the tragic news of Dane's demise. After a brief celebration of his accomplishment, a warmer location would beckon him on.

***

The snow-covered world presented dangerous conditions, so the need for shelter spurred Garrett forward. Without protection from the bitter cold, freezing to death loomed as his immediate reality. With every inhale of frigid air, sharp pain jolted him. The tumble down the embankment damaged some ribs, he decided.

The monotony of movement—tromp forward, fall, stand up, and repeat—helped him ignore the pain and focus on his goal of survival. Picking himself up became a greater struggle after each fall, while the hip-deep snow and underbrush slowed his progress.

Hours later, he spotted a light. Or did his imagination create a false beacon of hope? Moments before total exhaustion, he broke into a clearing and collapsed in a heap. The cold settled deep in his bones as his eyes closed.

Chapter Two

Leigh gazed through frosted windows at the falling snow. Why did she need time away from family and friends to contemplate all the changes in her life? Granted, she needed time for de-stressing, but northern Minnesota in February? Hardly thought this one through, it'd serve her right getting snowbound.

At least her family's cabin kept her comfortable and toasty warm. Most people wouldn't consider this a cabin, but her family always referred to it as such. They could live here year-round, but they would miss the activities available throughout the year in Minneapolis-St. Paul, the Twin Cities of Minnesota.

Wandering through the rooms, she marveled at how the cabin mirrored the conveniences and comforts of their home in Eden Prairie, a suburb of the Twin Cities. Four bedrooms ensured family members their own room, with an extra bedroom for the ever-present guests. Both bathrooms sported elaborate porcelain tiled floors, custom vanities, jetted tubs, and expansive walk-in showers. The open design of the living area encouraged lively parties and participation in meal preparation. At her mother's insistence, the kitchen boasted top-of-the-line appliances and upgraded finishes. Heaven forbid her cooking and entertaining should suffer.

Meal preparation influenced Leigh's early years. Once tall enough to reach the countertop, she assisted her mother in the kitchen. Over the years, their time cooking together fostered an intimate relationship. The relationship fractured four years ago when Leigh broke up with her boyfriend and family friend, David Walker.

Why her mind took her down such a distant path surprised her, dwelling on the past wasn't in her plans for this week. At twenty-eight years of age, her focus should be on a promising future and the new career she desired. Accomplishments in her work with investments provided success but little satisfaction. After her close friend, Deb, suggested she use her passion for photography as a career, Leigh decided she needed such a change in her life.

A stay at the cabin allowed her time to plan the move to a new career without parental interference. In the past, she dreamed of being a professional photographer, so she jumped on Deb's suggestion. Thanks to her skills as an investment advisor, a tidy sum sat in her bank account and provided financial security during this transition period.

Since she arrived at the cabin, animals and scenery dominated her photography. If her focus settled on animals, birds, and scenery, a sizable investment in better equipment lay in her future. A variety of wide-angle lenses and filters held priority position on her shopping list.

Her mother referred to camera accessories as toys and never understood her daughter's love of capturing moments of time with photographs. An ongoing confrontation with her mother over the career change plagued her, but she didn't care. The excitement of photography recaptured her imagination and provided for her enthusiasm each morning.

Flurries began before dawn, and the snowfall turned heavy by noon, with no signs of stopping. If the wind picked up, a blizzard was a certainty and guaranteed being snowed in. Stories of people freezing to death in blizzards flashed in her memory. No way would she be a victim of the storm, so she stayed inside. Plenty of firewood sat stacked a short distance from the back door.

Thankful for her foresight in bringing a case of favorite wines on this sojourn, she selected a bottle for the evening. On a cold night, nothing beat settling under a quilt in front of a warm fire and drinking a flavorful glass of wine. Well, cuddling with a good-looking guy under the quilt would be more enjoyable, but experience proved the good-looking guys brought only trouble and rarely personalities worthy of her trust. She didn't need a guy to survive, did she?

A loud growl from her stomach turned her thoughts to supper and how a bowl of hot soup would chase away the evening chill. As she passed the fireplace on the way to the kitchen, she noticed the firewood holder contained two logs. Shoot! Supper would wait until she replenished the wood. The cold, snow, and wind outside called for snow boots, parka, hat, and mittens. Plunging into the wintry night, the diminished light of dusk greeted her. A sound in the distance caught her attention. A wild animal probably ran through the yard.

Hoping for a glimpse of whatever animal decided to visit, she looked out over the backyard. At first glance, she didn't spot anything until she caught sight of a dark mound at the far end of the yard. The dark mound was new and indiscernible at this distance. Curiosity won out over caution, so she tramped through the snowdrifts, determined on solving the mystery presented.

As she neared, Leigh realized a person had crashed into the yard, not an animal—a person lying motionless in the snow. An urgency to help sped her faster through the snow toward the still body.

"Oh my God!" she cried out after spotting deep red snow near the figure. Panic mode ruled her thoughts and actions, as she dropped to her knees.

Chapter Three

A startled gasp escaped when she rolled the person over and realized this was an injured young man with a bleeding wound on one shoulder and another on his head. To ensure his survival, she needed to move him into the cabin, but how? Too many random thoughts bombarded her, one after the other and none of them helpful. Silencing the panic, she said a hurried prayer for strength and assistance in getting him out of the cold weather. Blessed peace and tranquility engulfed her manic thoughts.

"Can you walk?" The words echoed in the emptiness as she shook the man with frantic energy, more concerned with rousing him than further hurting his injured shoulder. "You have to help me; I can't move you by myself. *Wake up!*"

His eyes snapped open. Oh my! The color of his eyes was a mesmerizing combination of blue and brown, the most unusual hazel ever created. Snowflakes clung to long lashes framing his eyes. Many a woman must have lost her good senses in those eyes—definitely bedroom eyes.

Her stomach did a flip, and butterflies fluttered around in her stomach. No, not butterflies, more akin to dragons in flight, big-hot-heavy dragons.

***

After breaking out of the woods, Garrett remembered collapsing and surrendering to exhaustion and pain. The sensation of being rolled over and a woman's frantic voice breached his clouded senses followed by none-too-gentle shaking. Damn! The shaking ratcheted up his pain. How could he stop her and let the cold chase away his aches and pain? If he ignored her for a while longer, perhaps she'd go away.

"Wake up!"

That did it; forcing his eyes open, Garrett became eternally grateful he opened them. The woman shaking him looked angelic. Blue eyes peered down at him, and a cute nose sat above the most kissable lips ever. A Nordic style winter hat covered her head, but wisps of hair fell free in a halo of gold around her face. By reaching up, he could bring the angelic face close enough for a kiss.

"Come on! Get up! I can't leave you out here, and I need your help." Leigh broke from the trance she entered with the first glimpse of his eyes. Those remarkable eyes opened and raked over her face. When they stopped on her lips, she lost herself in dreams of kisses and more.

With reluctance, Garrett surrendered the idea of a kiss and struggled to stand. The woman wrapped an arm around him, and after a few attempts they achieved an upright position. They lurched through the snowbanks, falling over often before they reached the house. She threw open the back door, and they collapsed inside with Garrett on the bottom and the woman stretched on top of him.

Although layers of winter gear separated them, he enjoyed the sensation of her body against his and her weight on him. With his arms around her, he decided this unknown woman had been built for this exact position, because she fit against him, everywhere. Within his pained and near delirious thoughts, he claimed her as his, a perfect match in all the right places. As a result, he held her longer than necessary and crushed her against his body. Their eyes met, and the room sizzled with heat as an unexpected attraction ignited between them.

"We need to remove your wet clothes," Leigh whispered in his ear, before scrambling to her feet.

With a kick of one foot, the outside door slammed shut, and she extended her hands to him. Assisted by her, he hefted himself off the floor with a grimace. While removing her winter gear, she appraised the man standing beside her.

Snow encrusted his clothes. He must be soaked, she thought. A strong jawline behind a few weeks' worth of whiskers caught her attention. She estimated his height at over six feet. The weight she experienced, as she rolled him over, hinted at a trim physique under layers of winter clothes. Again, she lost herself in his mesmerizing eyes. A slow blink on his part broke her revelry and brought her back to the moment.

Shivers ravaged his body and spurred her into action. After pulling off his gloves, she grasped the front of his jacket and drew the snow-encrusted zipper down from his neck to his waist in a slow, jerking motion. Striptease music popped into her head and her knees shook. Heaven help her through this. She assisted him out of his jacket, being extra careful with his left arm and shoulder which bled from what looked to be a gunshot. A gasp escaped when a shoulder holster and gun appeared.

"Don't worry, I'm licensed for this." He drew the weapon, set it aside, and accepted her assistance in removing the holster. When he pulled the stocking cap off his head, snow dropped on them both. "Sorry 'bout that." A sheepish smile crept over his face.

Tingles ran up and down her spine at the sound of his voice: deep, a bit soft, and with the slightest hint of an accent she couldn't quite place. Brushing at the snow on her head, she returned his smile with one of her own.

"Don't worry, it's only snow."

She reached for the buttons on his shirt at the same time as he did. Fingers fumbled together, and their eyes met again. Leigh's cheeks flushed at the contact.

Garrett didn't miss her blushing but said nothing.

Shocked by the iciness of his hands and fingers, she clasped her hands around his.

The sensation of her hands holding his and warming him with her body heat brought him immense enjoyment. The unexpected warmth of her breath on his fingers ignited shivers down his spine.

"You're so cold. You might have frozen to death."

"I'm fortunate you were outside." Understanding the accuracy of her statement, he thanked God she found him.

She dropped his now warmed hands and returned to unbuttoning his shirt. The chill of his body cascaded toward her as she eased the shirt off his shoulders. When she guided his left arm out of the sleeve, he winced. Leigh tried not to stare at the well sculpted chest in front of her but failed miserably.

"Let me grab you something to, ah, wrap around you before we take off your jeans," she mumbled, before retreating into the main part of the house.

Garrett admired the little sway of her hips as she bustled away. In appreciation for her sensuous movements, he sported a half-smile on his lips. Should he continue stripping off his clothes? A temptation for sure, observing the blush on her cheeks again would be worth the effort. He doubted she would appreciate finding him naked in the entry upon her return, so instead he kicked off his boots. His soaking-wet jeans clung to his cold legs, and his body shook from being chilled by the brutal cold.

Leigh grabbed a quilt from the back of the couch and clutched the bulk against her chest. Her thoughts focused on the gorgeous man in the entry. What she wouldn't give to experience him touching her, kissing those lips, laying beneath his body without multiple layers of clothes separating them…whoa! Where did those thoughts come from? She didn't know anything about him, yet lustful thoughts rampaged in her head. Having him here presented a challenging situation if her mind generated those kinds of thoughts minutes after finding him.

The wind howled and whipped the snow around, so she expected a blizzard by morning. A blizzard meant being stuck here together, the two of them, for a couple of days. The control over her raging emotions needed to become a priority or no telling what might happen. Best return to him before he collapsed in the entry. Upon her return she found him still in his jeans, but without his boots. He leaned against the wall, his face pale and grimacing in pain. All his discarded clothes sat in a growing puddle of water.

"Sorry I took so long." Holding out the quilt, she turned her head. "Can you strip the rest of your clothes off on your own or will you need a hand?"

"I think I can manage. We'll find out, won't we?" A sharp intake of air and a groan punctuated the pushing of wet jeans over his hips. He gave up trying to bend over. Oh, yeah, he cracked some ribs. "Turns out your assistance is needed."

Leigh turned her head and immediately lost her breath at the sight of broad shoulders and lean muscles everywhere. A light dusting of pale hair showed on his chest and drew her eyes downward. Wow! The ridiculous question of how so much gorgeousness fit into one body pinged in her head. A slight cough brought her back to the need at hand.

He stared at her with apparent interest and humor if the twinkle in his eyes and the half-smile on his lips were indicators. "I'll hold the quilt, while you remove the rest of my clothes." He captured the quilt from her fingers.

An involuntary jump happened when his fingers brushed hers, while intense need rolled through her— desire?

He held the quilt with one hand while the other worked his shorts off his hips. "Can you pull those off?" The quilt shielded his more private parts from her view.

"Sure." Kneeling in front of him, she eased the jeans and shorts down his legs and over each foot.

Her hasty glance up shot through him and generated an instant vision of her kneeling before him, without a quilt between them. His imagined vision caused a strong physical reaction. He wrapped the quilt around his body in an attempt at preventing the woman before him from understanding, without any doubts, how she affected him.

"Let's put you to bed and clean up those wounds." Leigh supported him as they walked to the guest bedroom. The darkness of the room ended when she flipped the light switch. She chattered away with nervous energy. "The cell service is dismal here at best, usually non-existent. My dad considers the lack of connectivity one of the many charms of the place. You can escape from everything, but it also means we can't call in any medical care for you." With the covers pulled back on the bed, she turned to him, curiously anxious over being alone in a bedroom with him. "Can you climb in by yourself, or will you need my help?"

The thought of her help in bed turned his mind down the same path as before. With a shake of his head, he cleared his thoughts.

"I'm sure I can climb in by myself, thanks." A huskier voice than normal answered her question.

His reaction to this woman almost scared him...almost. He couldn't remember a time when a woman stirred such thoughts and reactions in him, if ever. They were foolish thoughts with a crazed killer after him, but still everything happened for a reason.

She left the bedroom, allowing him time to unwrap the quilt and climb or fall into the bed. A fleeting thought of joining him in bed crossed her mind. Hoping he accomplished the maneuver without too much pain, Leigh returned with a variety of supplies and some warm water.

His eyes stalked her every move. When she stopped moving their eyes met and held.

She found speaking difficult, after staring into those mesmerizing eyes of his, now devoid of any blue and warmed to a dreamy brown. Her stomach lurched as the dragons took flight again.

"You're covered in bruises, and that's a bullet wound in your shoulder, right?" Garrett nodded; his eyes remained locked on hers. "I never saw one before, let alone cleaned one." Using a dampened washcloth, she dabbed at the dried blood surrounding the wound. "The bullet went through. At least I won't be digging for a bullet like they do in all the western movies."

"Thank God for small miracles. Do you have something for a dressing?" He tried not to flinch at the pain her efforts inflicted on him.

"Well, you're still bleeding a little, so I thought these would work well." Leigh held up two thick pads of material. "They're designed for super absorbency."

"Those aren't what I think they are, are they?" Garrett asked, dreading the expected affirmative response.

"If you thought a maxi pad, you're correct. Since they're designed for heavy overnight flow, they should hold up until the bleeding stops. Is anything wrong?"

"As long as my friends never find out about my having feminine hygiene products taped to my body, all's good." Resigning himself to the inevitable, he admired her ingenuity.

Leigh busied herself with wrapping the maxi pads in place, both front and back. The sooner she finished, the sooner his chest would be covered by the bedding and her attention wouldn't be so distracted.

"I should have introduced myself earlier; I'm Leigh Ramsey. This is my family's cabin."

"Pleased to meet you, Leigh. I'm Garrett Dane. Sorry I invaded your privacy."

"Since you brought up your sudden appearance, how did you find your way here, shot, and so badly beaten on?"

"Ambush."

"Would you care to provide a more thorough explanation?" She pressed tape on his chest, anchoring the makeshift bandage in place.

"I was on my way to Brainerd. In two weeks, I start working for the Bureau of Criminal Apprehension."

"So, you're in law enforcement?" Leigh turned her attention to the wound on his head; blood oozed from the jagged gash above his right eye.

"Yeah, I joined the Air Force right after high school graduation and worked in Security Forces for four years. With the security experience behind me, I qualified as a special agent with the Air Force Office of Special Investigations and worked with them for six years. Recently, I separated from the Air Force and came home to Minnesota. Before leaving the Air Force, I applied for a vacancy with the BCA, they hired me, so here I am." He winced as she rinsed the head wound.

"Sorry if this hurts," she apologized as she continued working. "Go on, you didn't say what happened to you."

"I came across a car on the side of the road, with the driver slumped over the wheel. My assumption of an elderly person in trouble proved incorrect. When I reached the car, intent on offering assistance, I committed a rookie mistake and leaned down by the door; it opened and caught me on the head. The driver turned out to be an acquaintance of mine, Jonas Klein. Needless to say, he didn't need any assistance."

"If he was an acquaintance, how did you end up shot and in my backyard?"

"An acquaintance as in the subject of a criminal investigation I worked on before I separated from the Air Force. He escaped custody and came looking for me."

Something in the sound of his voice struck her as a mystery he didn't share. "Why would he come looking for you?"

"In his mind, I'm the one who destroyed his future, so he swore he'd kill me. Today he attempted to follow through on his threat." A distant look remained in his eyes.

"This weather should keep him away and give you time to heal." Leigh placed a hand on his right shoulder, overwhelmed by the need to touch him and offer some hope.

"You're probably right. Since he's from the South, this weather will challenge him." The lightness of her hand on his shoulder distracted him from thoughts of Klein. In his imagination, her hands touched, stroked, and massaged every inch of his body. In the gentle touch, he sensed her compassion.

Leigh yearned to hold him in her arms and help him forget the ugliness of his day. "I'm fixing us some supper, and you should rest before we eat." Patting his shoulder one last time, she tucked the covers around him and walked out the door.

Her departure left a chill in the air. An intense desire for nothing further than holding her close and losing himself in her blue eyes and those luscious lips surprised him.

How could he be drawn to her so soon after meeting? Shock? Stress from the situation with Klein? No, something else called to him, something wild, primal, natural, and instinctive. The time for considering his rampant thoughts would come later after he recovered from the earlier shock of his day, he decided. Nestled in the heavy, warm covers, he fell fast asleep minutes after closing his eyes.

Chapter Four

Leigh's nerves sat on high alert, and her emotions followed suit. Did she believe his story? Yes, he oozed honesty when he spoke. The strong, lustful yearnings she experienced for him concerned her. An overwhelming need drew her to Garrett. Remembering how enticing he looked wearing only a quilt, she decided being alone with him wouldn't be a bad thing. She gave her head a slight shake to clear her thoughts of him, alone in a big bed. Now her focus should be on supper preparation and bringing firewood into the cabin. Garrett Dane wouldn't be leaving anytime soon.

After bringing in enough wood to last a couple of days, she hung up her snow-covered clothes. As she turned around, Garrett's clothes lying in a puddle of melted snow snagged her attention. These would be needed tomorrow, so she carried them to the laundry room. The bullet holes and blood on his jacket and shirt captured her imagination. He lived a life foreign to her; danger clung to him because of his work. Could she handle being a part of such a lifestyle? Leigh, really? You just met him, and you're letting your imagination run wild, she admonished herself.

Rummaging through pockets, she discovered sunglasses, a wallet, and an extra magazine for his gun. The gun sat on a shelf in the entry, along with the holster he wore around his broad shoulders. The thought conjured her memory of his delectable naked upper torso. A shake of her head failed to evict the image. Apparently, her last date occurred too many months ago since she responded to a stranger with lust-filled thoughts minutes after meeting him.

The jacket and shirt weren't salvageable, so they landed in the trash. She tossed the remaining clothes in the washer and started a cycle before carrying his things to the bedroom. In case he slept, she slowly turned the doorknob, inched the door open, and released her breath when she discovered his eyes closed and his breathing regular. She crept into the room and set his personal items on the chest of drawers. The gun, holster, and extra magazine fit in the drawer of the nightstand.

He murmured something and rolled to his right side, grimacing with the effort. Placing the back of her hand on his brow, she ensured he no longer suffered a chill and showed no sign of a fever. With reluctance, she pulled back her hand, but not until she ran her fingers through his hair. A slight moan from him anchored her in place—he remained in pain. In case he called out, she left the door ajar, so any cry would reach her as she prepared their supper.

Back in the kitchen, she heated the soup and placed a selection of crackers, cheeses, and pickles in baskets and dishes. A sudden heart-wrenching cry from the bedroom shocked her. The box of crackers she held dropped to the floor, spewing broken saltines and crumbs across the kitchen floor. Not giving the mess a thought, she raced down the hall.

***

Dreams of gunshots, Klein's threats, and a tumble down an embankment haunted his sleep. The terror of today vanished in a heartbeat replaced by the recurring nightmare of his last Air Force mission. Now he pursued Klein through a garbage-filled alley with his partner, Tess. When she directed him to a parallel route, he refused to follow her direction until she ordered him. Buildings blurred by as he raced in the dark, driven by the need to reach her before…three gunshots echoed in his head.

"*No!*" Garrett cried out. He thrashed against the bedclothes. "Tess. *Tess*! No. *No!*" Trapped in his nightmare, he held a dying Tess to his chest. Tears rolled down his cheeks. The ending never changed from the tragic outcome. Tess had died and would always die in his nightmare.

Leigh sank to her knees beside the bed, and her heart broke for the anguish on Garrett's face. She caressed his brow; her fingers fell light and soft on his skin. With gentle care, she ran her fingers through his hair and tucked soft strands behind his ear. She whispered assurances, unsure if he heard her or not. Minutes later his breathing calmed and his thrashing against the bedclothes ceased. His eyes fluttered open, and their eyes locked.

"You called out," she murmured. An inner voice demanded she find out who Tess was, but she ignored the nagging desire for an inquisition.

"Must have been during my nightmare." He couldn't share the full story behind Klein's arrest, not yet. His eyes searched her face for something. What exactly he searched for he couldn't say, but he sensed whatever he found held something important for him: forgiveness, understanding, or maybe salvation?

As she leaned closer toward him, her eyes focused on his eyes at first, dropped to his lips, and returned to gaze in his now icy-blue eyes. "A nightmare? Well, you can tell me the details when you're ready. By sharing, it might go away. For now, you should focus on getting healthy and other important things."

Her voice trailed off so soft and hushed he almost missed her last words. When her eyes moved back to his eyes, the pink tip of her tongue moistened those luscious lips. The movement of her tongue along her lips caused a distinctive and unexpected response by his body. He nearly reached out to touch her lips but watched as her eyes focused on his lips again.

"Other important things? Such as?"

"Such as this." Leigh brushed her lips gently against his.

Without hesitation Garrett responded, drawing her closer, and deepening the kiss. His tongue played along her lips, mirroring her own tongue's action, but demanded entrance. She opened to him, and their tongues tangled as he had in the bedclothes. Their kiss heightened a mutual awareness of feelings running amok between them. With reluctance, Garrett broke off the kiss, held her shoulders, and gazed into her eyes.

"I didn't expect a kiss; however, I wouldn't mind another one. This isn't a doctor-patient thing, is it?" he asked.

"I'm no doctor." With her hands on either side of his face, she gave him a wicked smile before leaning in for another seductive kiss. Surfacing for air, she added, "Supper's ready. I'll bring in our food." After a quick kiss on his forehead, she hustled out of the room.

He stared after her with a ghost of a smile on his lips. How interesting, he thought, as he replayed in his head what happened. She made the first move, and he followed her lead with enthusiasm. Almost being killed by Klein had taken a radical turn for the better.

How did she reach the kitchen? Leigh had no idea. The kisses they shared set her head spinning and her heart racing. While she busied herself with their supper, more than once she reached up and touched her lips, remembering the possessiveness of his lips on hers. She put the supper dishes on a tray to carry into the bedroom. For now, she dismissed her questions regarding Tess, who visited him in his nightmares.

Garrett pulled himself into a sitting position as Leigh set the food on a nearby table and settled the empty tray across his lap. After placing a bowl of soup, some cheese, and crackers on the tray, she sat in a chair beside the bed, so she could eat and talk with him.

"This hits the spot; tomato soup is my favorite." He crushed all his crackers into the red liquid to make a thick reddish sludge. Then he dug into the soup. "Are you sharing the pickles?"

"Sorry, forgot I brought them in. Too fascinated with how you fixed your soup." She gave him some pickles and nibbled on a piece of cheese. "I'm washing your clothes, at least the things not destroyed by bullet holes and blood. My brother might have some clothes here that will fit you; I'll look through his closet later."

"I appreciate it, thanks."

They ate in silence for a short time. Garrett held an internal debate over staying with Leigh and getting stronger versus tracking down Klein. His concern for her safety forced him to voice his fears.

"I can't stay here too long; my being here may put you in danger. You need to believe what I said concerning Klein wanting me dead. He won't care if he hurts anyone else."

"He won't be out in this snowstorm, so you can stay here for a few days and heal up. Until the weather settles, we can't leave the cabin anyway."

"The wind does sound wild outside, and I doubt he's ever experienced a blizzard. In case we're wrong in our assumptions, please keep your eyes and ears open for anything unusual. Promise you'll wake me for anything out of the ordinary."

"I promise. Now, you should sleep. I found some pain relievers for you, too."

Leigh handed him two pills, and he took them while she collected the dishes. He got rearranged in the bed with her assistance and regretted being unable to follow her out of the room.

Never had Garrett been so tired and worn out; his body hurt everywhere. He relaxed, sank into the pillows, and soon fell back asleep. The needed rest escaped him because a high-spirited, blue-eyed vixen led him into an erotic dream sequence driving his heartbeat to a blistering rate. His unconscious mind sifted through the signals Leigh sent him over their shared supper. Oh man, he received her signals loud and clear, especially through her kisses. In his dream, they moved well beyond kisses.

Leigh returned their dishes to the kitchen, washed them, and cleaned up the kitchen. Her thoughts traveled to what Garrett said about Jonas Klein. Surely the man wouldn't be so consumed with hatred he'd venture out in a blizzard? To be on the safe side, she verified all the doors and windows were locked before doing anything else.

Checking the dryer, she found his clothes were dry. Before taking them to his room, she checked her brother's closet and discovered a shirt and sweater she hoped would fit Garrett. Luck presented itself in the form of a winter jacket as well.

She would do one last check on him before she went to bed. With all the clothes piled in her arms, she walked to the guest room, now Garrett's room in her thoughts, located opposite her bedroom.

Her parents' bedroom at the end of the hall shared a wall with her bedroom. Their bathroom shared a wall with the guest room. Her brother's bedroom sat beside her room and opposite the second bathroom. She envied her brother's bedroom location for the greater distance from their parents. He never agreed to trade rooms with her, birth order had privileges.

Garrett slept with no thrashing around as before. She placed the clothes on a chair and checked on him. The wound hadn't bled anymore and a hand on his brow proved no fever raged through him. He looked restful, and she hoped his nightmare would allow him an evening off. Before she realized what she intended and unsure of what force led her on, she bent over and grazed his cheek with a light kiss.

"Sleep well." She crossed the hall and entered her bedroom. The time for sorting out her surprising feelings for him would come later. In the still of the evening, her thoughts drifted to him. When sleep claimed her, dreams of the stranger who stirred feelings deep within her soul claimed her as well.

Chapter Five

Leigh jerked up in bed, panicked. Did something scrape against the exterior of the house, or did she dream the sound? The thunderous pounding of her heart required a couple deep breaths before it slowed down. Wait for the same sound again, she counseled herself. There! The sound of someone creeping outside the house! Because the threat of Klein searching for his quarry existed, she needed to wake Garrett.

Slipping out of bed, she tip-toed across the darkened hallway, and entered his room. Once inside, she knelt by the side of the bed and touched his arm as she whispered his name.

"Garrett! Someone's outside! Garrett, wake up!"

In response to her urgent words, he lurched up and grimaced at the pain when his ribs protested the sudden movement.

"Ah, damn..." He clenched his teeth against the pain. When it eased, realization dawned on him, Leigh had abruptly woken him. "What's up? What happened?"

"A noise outside woke me. Do you think Klein found you?"

Reading fear in her eyes, his first impulse sent his arms out to hold her shaking body. "I doubt it, but a quick look should give us answers. Where did you put my jeans and gun?"

"I'll bring your jeans to you. The gun's in the drawer of the nightstand beside you."

Frigid cold snaked up his legs when his bare feet landed on the wood floor. The covers fell away from his naked body. Unconcerned with his nakedness, he tugged the drawer open in search of his weapon. The familiar weight of the SIG soothed him. After he checked the mag and chambered a round, he turned as Leigh rounded the bed with his jeans clutched to her chest.

Grabbing the jeans from her, he thrust his legs in them with a ragged inhale against the pain. The room tilted and rolled when he stood to raise the waistband over his hips. Once the room righted itself, he zipped up the fly front, and his eyes sought Leigh in the darkness of the room. He imagined her blue eyes wide with fear from the terror he brought into her life. Anger steeled his nerves, and a practiced focus took charge of his actions.

He crushed Leigh against his body. "Don't worry, we'll be fine. This is what I do." His voice sounded taut with anger. "Stay here."

With a shake of her head, she argued against his order. "No, I'm sticking with you."

No time for arguing with her, he relented. "Okay but stay behind me." They moved out the door and into the hallway. "Where do you suppose the sound came from?"

"Outside my window." A slight quiver showed in her arm as she pointed at the dark room across the hall.

"We'll go in, and maybe I can catch sight of something." Leading her into the room, he motioned for her to kneel by the far side of the bed. With a lift of the curtains, he took a surreptitious look at the yard. After a few moments, the curtains fell back in place, and he returned to her side. "Nothing outside now. Let's try another window."

The calm tone of his voice comforted her.

"A window in my parents' bedroom overlooks the backyard." She indicated the room at the end of the hall.

Again, Garrett led the way, with Leigh trailing behind him. Moonlight filtered in through sheer curtains covering the windows. As he approached a window, he directed Leigh down and behind him.

The longer he watched at the unknown threat outside, the more frightened she became. Imagining what he saw by his movements proved impossible for her. When he turned back to her, lines creased his forehead.

"It's not Klein, but there are two shady-looking characters outside. Often the way suspects move or what they wear provides a means of recognizing them even though they're wearing masks. To ensure I don't attack a family friend, you should check them out before I move on them."

Leigh's eyes widened at his words. Chewing on her lower lip, she listened as he spoke in a hushed tone. He couldn't stop from noticing how delectable she appeared with all her womanly curves accentuated by a skimpy flannel nightshirt and her silky golden hair tumbling around her shoulders. While he assessed her kissable lips and long slender legs, reality struck him: she presented a different type of danger to him—formidable, but more than likely entertaining and rewarding.

"Are you ready?"

"Yes." Approaching the window with reluctance, she took a deep breath and peeked out. "Raccoons! Nothing but a couple of raccoons!"

The fury in her eyes, when she turned on him, should spur a wise man into an apology, but a half-smile on his lips and a shrug of his broad shoulders was his only response. The audacity of the man!

"You scared me half to death! 'They're wearing masks.'" Quote motions with her fingers highlighted her glare. "This is *not* funny! Don't you dare laugh." She struck out at him and caught him in the ribs resulting in a grimace. "Serves you right."

An attempt at continuing the glare ended when her eyes locked with his. The depths of feelings reflected in them mirrored what she felt in her heart. With her hand flat against his bare chest, she experienced an undeniable draw to him, comparable to metal drawn toward a magnet.

"Sorry, warped sense of humor." At least he had the decency to act a bit ashamed along with his minimal apology.

He set aside the gun and drew her into his arms. When their eyes met, he lost himself in the glittering promise within her blue eyes. Bending slightly, he brushed his lips against hers, and Leigh responded by leaning into him. Garrett ran his hands in her hair and brought his lips back to her mouth for a proper kiss. His hands moved to her shoulders, down her back, and further still until he cupped her buttocks with each hand.

A small moan escaped when she nestled closer and brushed his erection.

In answer, he released a deep growl and deepened their kiss. His tongue grazed her lips. With her sigh, he gained access to the warm depths of her mouth.

Accented by more moans, their tongues danced a flirtatious tango.

A shiver raked through her, as his hands slid under the hem of her nightshirt. The warmth of his hands ignited nerve endings throughout her body. Hands skimmed up and forward, tracing a path of heat along her sides, over her ribs, and to her breasts. Whimpers answered as he palmed each breast and thumbed her nipples.

Her head rested on his shoulder. Delighted with his attentions, she desired more. Somewhere in the back of her mind, her conscience shrieked—*stop!* At the echo in her head, she remembered where they stood. If they continued this in her parents' bedroom, the memories would haunt her for years. A shudder overcame her, and she stepped back.

"What's wrong?" Garrett's confusion sounded in his voice.

"This is my parents' bedroom. We can't continue this in here." When she looked around the room, another shudder passed through her.

"Right." Comprehension broke through his lust-filled consciousness. "We should go to bed anyway; morning will be here in a few hours," he whispered.

"You're right, we should go to bed. Come with me and bring your gun; you may need some protection," Leigh responded in a throaty invitation. She clasped his hand in hers, intent on leading him to her bed.

Garrett stopped dead in his tracks and pulled Leigh back to face him. "Protection! Leigh, I don't have a condom. This happened so fast, I didn't think anything through. If you hadn't stopped me, we would have had unprotected sex. I'm so sorry, I didn't mean—"

Leigh placed a hand against his lips.

"Don't worry. I'm on the pill and free of any social disease, so you needn't be concerned. I suspect you have a clean bill of health. Right?"

Unable to answer verbally, because her hand covered his mouth, he nodded.

"I don't keep a supply of condoms with me either, so here's my proposal. We do this as is because I'm not in favor of abstinence tonight. Understand?"

Another nod answered her.

"Come along." Both her hands clasped his as she led him into her bedroom.

Stopping by her bed, she graced him with a brief smile before pulling her nightshirt over her head. The soft material sailed across the room and landed in a corner. She stood naked before him, and her beauty took his breath away. Before he did or said anything, she grabbed his jeans by the waistband, drew the zipper down, and tugged them past his hips. With a glint in her eyes, she knelt before him, pulled his pants off, tossed them near her nightshirt and directed her complete attention to the hardened length before her.

This woman surprised him; she was desirable and unpredictable! During this generous mood of hers, he'd accept all she offered and bestowed on him.

Her attention focused on his throbbing erection freed from the confines of his jeans. First, her tongue played against the tip and tasted his length to the base, and then she took his full erection into her mouth. She sucked and tormented him with her tongue.

His senses went haywire, as her tongue traced the length of his erection. When she took him in her mouth, his knees almost gave out. The moment she increased pressure with her teeth, he sensed a desperate need to stop her.

"Leigh." Her name came out as no more than a deep rumble.

She looked up at him and smiled.

He drew her up for a long kiss, leaving her breathless and moaning for more. His kisses trailed down her body. He ached to make love to her, so he lowered them to the bed. The thorough exploration of her body with kisses and caresses focused his attention, as he settled over her.

Pure instinct drove her responses to his touch. Moving to an internal quest for fulfillment, her body wiggled and rubbed against him. The actions of her body urged him to initiate the act she craved.

He entered her warm moistness with slow, incremental pushes until he filled her. When her muscles clenched about him, fast and urgent movements drove him deeper within her. She moaned at the ecstasy drowning her senses and screamed out his name as her world shattered. The sound of his name rocked his control, and he followed her into a shared euphoria.

Holding her close, he arranged the covers over them. Deep within his soul, he realized she was now his to love and protect. The fact they met a few hours ago didn't matter. He pulled her in closer, wrapped a protective arm around her, and placed one last gentle kiss to her temple.

She purred from his attentions. "That definitely got you out of trouble for the raccoons." Her eyes closed, and she fell asleep, exhausted, and happy.

A chuckle deep in his chest was his reply. In the darkness of the room, he drifted off to sleep, content and happy for the first time in months.

Chapter Six

The morning dawned with a howling north wind and the sound of snow pelting the window. An old-fashioned blizzard raged outside the cabin.

Leigh awoke toasty warm thanks to the delicious hunk of male flesh curled beside her and draped over her. Her thoughts rambled over all the events of the day before. So much had happened in less than one day because of one guy: the guy in bed with her, the guy who had fallen into her backyard, and the guy she was falling in love with. She stretched and turned on her side, transfixed by the sight of him sleeping beside her. How much he meant to her after less than twenty-four hours amazed her.

The tender exploration of his body by her fingers began without thought and ranged over broad shoulders, a muscled chest, narrow hips, and on to a growing erection. Thrilled at the velvet texture under her hand, she stroked and fondled the hard length. The hardening response to her touch fascinated her, so she squeezed and increased her speed. When a drop of fluid developed on the tip, she devoured his muskiness with a kiss. The heavy-lidded look in Garrett's eyes sent her desire for him skyrocketing. After a quick smile, she moved closer and touched her lips against his.

They made love in the dawning light, paying close attention to each other's responses, and learning individual preferences and mutual desires. Once concluded, Leigh collapsed against his chest, spent, and satisfied.

"Garrett," she gasped, "this is habit-forming in a good way."

She raised her head and threw him a wicked look.

He let out a low, rumbling chuckle and hugged her close.

"I agree, but I need a shower."

After a kiss and a smile, he got out of bed and left for the bathroom.

Admiring his backside as he walked away, she pulled the covers to her chin. Once the sound of running water reached her, she hustled to the bathroom.

***

Garrett stepped into the tiled enclosure. Multiple jets forced out hot water and steam swirled, as he let the hot moisture work its magic on his beaten body. Angry shades of black, blue, and purple showed on his bruised torso and legs, the result of his fall down the embankment. Washing his hair and body proved a challenge in his battered condition, so he thought standing under the water would be enough. A hand caressed his back, and he flinched with surprise.

"Easy, I thought you might need a hand or two." The fingers on both of her hands wiggled at him before she grabbed the bottle of shampoo. "Wet your hair and lean over."

Her voice warned off disobedience, and he offered none. She flexed her fingers in his hair, building up the lather, and massaged his head from front to back.

Garrett closed his eyes and enjoyed the sensuous touch of her fingers on his scalp and in his hair, while trying not to think of her luscious naked body. He could submit to this for hours, but she stopped and directed his head back into the flow of water. In moments, the shampoo rinsed out.

She turned him away from her and grabbed the soap. After a rich lather developed in her hands, she washed his body. Her hands slid down his back and over his butt. She caressed him, washed him with gentleness, and trailed the soap suds down his legs. After finishing with his feet, she snatched up the shower wand. She rinsed him while running her hands along his skin to ensure all the soap rinsed away. Once she finished his back, she turned him, so he faced her.

"Time for a frontal assault," she said in a raspy voice.

A wicked smile settled on her face. and her eyes sparkled. With soap in hand, she built up another fragrant lather. Blue eyes locked on hazel ones, while her hands caressed his neck and shoulders.

The closing of Garrett's eyes signaled his surrender to her massaging exploration. A moan escaped when her nails scraped against his nipples and hardened them to dark-brown nubs.

Much to her delight, a soft moan sounded. Bubble-filled hands massaged across his stomach. When her hands slid over each hip, he flinched and emitted a long hiss.

"Sorry!" Leigh examined a large bruise on his right hip. "What hit you?"

"To escape Klein, I dove down an embankment along the road. I must have hit every rock, tree, and stump along the way to the bottom. This bruise probably came from the huge tree I crashed into at the end of my fall." He reached for her, put a hand on either side of her face, and gazed into her eyes. "You saved my life, Leigh. Freezing to death was my immediate future, but you found me. Thank you."

He claimed her lips for a soft kiss; his hands framed her face. As he backed off, his thumbs brushed against her cheeks before his hands dropped to his sides.

Her eyes remained closed for a moment before they opened and caught his gaze. A faint blush warmed her cheeks as she realized she reacted to his kiss like a dazed schoolgirl.

"You're welcome. Now, let me finish with you."

Their eyes locked in another heated moment before he closed his eyes and enjoyed her hand massage.

Lathering up the soap again and with a gentle caress, she washed his bruised hip. A swift glance up confirmed his eyes remained closed and his breathing remained slow and easy. She placed one soap-lathered hand on his manhood, which jumped up to her touch.

Garrett's eyes flew open, and a groan escaped.

She washed all parts of his body. A reckless grin broadened with her self-indulgent actions. She ended with his legs but moved her hands back up to caress his butt.

"Time for the final rinse. Ready?" Leigh gave his backside a light pat.

He nodded his head, lost in the mischievous glint in her eyes.

While he stood under the flow of water, Leigh grabbed the shower wand. Intent on rinsing all the soap from his body, she sprayed water on him from head to toe. Taking full advantage of the situation, she stroked his body as she guided the water down toward his feet, more fondling than anything occurred.

His erection grew larger as her hands continued exploring his body. When a wet hand wrapped around his erection and stroked, his hand stilled the motion of her hand.

"I believe you're next, but we need to work together." His voice sounded hoarse and gruff.

Garrett drew her under the spray of water and switched places with her. He poured shampoo into her waiting hands. As she lathered her hair, he ached for the time when he could massage her scalp and run his hands through her hair. She nodded to him, indicating she was ready for a rinse. He employed the shower wand and directed water over her scalp and down her hair, ensuring all the lather rinsed out. Once satisfied, he put the wand up and directed her under the flow of water until her body glistened everywhere.

After she washed herself, he used the shower wand and rinsed her body. As he sprayed the water, her hands trailed over the wet areas. The erotic vision of her washing herself was one he'd never forget.

Frustration and desire to touch spurred him into action. Surrendering the shower wand, his right hand chased suds away from all sorts of interesting places. He took custody of the shower wand one last time for a final rinse.

With regret they ended their shower encounter and turned the water off. They remained in the shower and waited for their racing heartbeats to slow.

Garrett opened the door and guided her to the plush bathmat. As he wrapped an over-sized, soft towel around her, he kissed her bare shoulders. Then he grabbed a towel for himself. Leading her to the bedroom, his desire for her battled with thoughts of going slow to learn more about her.

"If we don't dress soon, we may never wear any clothes today." Garrett grabbed his jeans and departed for the other bedroom.

"Perhaps I prefer not wearing clothes today," Leigh muttered as he walked out the door.

Chapter Seven

With thoughts of future sexual activities, she rummaged through her drawers in search of the perfect lingerie. The final decision resulted in matching bra and panties encasing her curves in lace. When she viewed her reflection, a sexy and desirable woman returned her gaze. Satisfied with her selection, she pulled on corduroy jeans and a flannel shirt under a warm sweater and completed the look by tossing her loosely braided hair over her shoulder.

Once dressed, she hurried out to the large open area encompassing the eat-in kitchen and family room. A naughty daydream of Garrett seeing her in the lingerie and his response caught her imagination as she gazed out the kitchen window.

While she made coffee, memories of the night before bombarded her. Remembered sensations of him touching her body, the anticipation of him fulfilling her sexual hunger, and his satisfying her needs with delightful and unexpected methods cascaded over her. Closing her eyes, she imagined the tingles of energy when he filled her, the pleasure gained from her complete surrender to him, and how her body responded in alarming ways. A sudden wetness between her legs surprised her.

Meanwhile, down the hall, Garrett discovered his personal items and clothes Leigh left for him. Dressing proved a challenge, but after multiple tries and bearable pain, he succeeded with putting on jeans and socks. Not spotting his boots, he figured they must be in the entry where he kicked them off. With a shirt and sweater in hand, he departed the bedroom and wandered down the hallway toward the aroma of fresh brewed coffee. The bandages needed replacement before he finished dressing.

He paused when he caught sight of Leigh staring out a window at the white blur of snow. A smile broke across his lips as he remembered how she responded for him, the passion in her eyes when she climaxed, and her soft sounds of contentment during their lovemaking. Thank goodness she wasn't a shy woman,

Thoughts of how Leigh filled an emptiness in his heart crossed his mind. Bad timing, he thought. A crazed killer on my trail and a new job with an undercover assignment ahead of me. Jeez! Everything happens for a reason, but why now? Because Leigh belongs in my life, perhaps to stay? Dang! Where did that thought come from? While he processed the varied thoughts, desire for her flared in his chest. Unsure of how this would play out, he pushed the thoughts away and entered the kitchen.

"The bandages need to be redone. They got ruined in the shower; I think I stayed in too long."

Garrett's voice from behind startled her memories away. The smoldering desire reflected in his eyes made her stomach do flips and stirred her emotions higher.

"Of course, give me a minute to grab what I need. Why don't you sit over there?"

Directing him to a counter stool, she hurried off to the bathroom and returned in moments with supplies for tending his wounds. After redressing them all, she helped him ease into the borrowed shirt and sweater.

"I appreciate the use of your brother's clothes." He caught her hand as she turned away, wanting to draw her into his arms.

"No problem, I'm glad my brother left things here. Do you need anything for pain?"

Searching his face for signs of discomfort, she marveled at the color of his eyes and accepted being forever lost whenever she gazed into them. The color of the sweater highlighted the brown of the hazel coloring, and the blue had disappeared. A touch of his brow reassured her of no sign of a fever.

"Everything hurts; only one thing eased my pain last night." His hands circled her waist and drew her against him. One eyebrow rose.

A warm smile answered him, as she slapped his wandering hands away.

"Breakfast before further explorations into your alternative pain management methods."

With a light breakfast prepared, they sat together at the counter. The location afforded them a superb view of the blowing snow and the ever-increasing size of the snowdrifts.

"The snowplows won't be out until the wind dies down. This road won't be cleared for a few days," Leigh predicted while staring at the whiteness outside. She sipped her coffee and resisted the urge to lean into him.

"Do you keep a snowmobile or two here?" Garrett munched on peanut butter toast.

"There should be two in the shed, but we'll need to dig them out."

"Any chance of a snowblower sitting around?" Now he stood at the patio door overlooking the backyard and gazed at the massive snowdrifts. "With this amount of snow, I can clear a path with one in less than an hour, otherwise we may be here for a long, long time."

The hopefulness showing on his face made her laugh.

"Yes. The snowblower's in the garage." A brilliant smile accompanied her announcement.

"Awesome, I'll dig out a snowmobile and head for a nearby town."

Garrett joined her at the counter. The smile he flashed at her sparked intriguing thoughts and images. What inspired this intense sensual response whenever he came close? Not caring, she vowed to enjoy these long dormant emotions for as long as he stayed with her.

"Only one error in your plan. Change the number of snowmobiles being dug out from one to two, because I'll ride with you."

"No way! With a killer after me, being around me won't be safe." Garrett took one of her hands in his and looked into her eyes as he spoke. "I won't let Klein hurt anyone else."

Concern and sincerity blazed in his eyes, now an icy blue. But she wouldn't be dissuaded.

"Don't you understand why my being with you makes sense? If Klein's looking for you, he might come here after you leave. Being all alone when he turns up doesn't sound safe to me. Besides, a couple traveling together may throw him off your trail."

"Point taken." He returned to the patio doors and stared out at the swirling snow; his brow furrowed. When he reached a decision, he turned to her. "Okay, we'll travel together. How far is the nearest town?"

"Are we talking any town or a town with a police department?"

"How much of a difference in the distance?"

Returning to the counter, he placed an arm around her waist. The way she leaned into his embrace warmed his heart. He lowered his head for a kiss. When he deepened the kiss, she followed him into a whirl of emotion. Her eyes closed as she lost herself in the passion of the moment. He pulled away from her with reluctance.

"Leigh, the town?"

"Huh? Oh! The nearest town is fifteen minutes away but only consists of a couple of houses and a bar. The closest town with a police force is Pine Ridge, almost thirty minutes away, maybe a bit faster on the sleds."

"The town with a police force would be better. Once we arrive, we stop at the authorities and report Klein.

If I check with my old chief, he may know how Klein escaped and what's happening. Here's to our plan." A soft clink of his orange juice glass with hers sounded a toast to their future endeavor's success.

"Plus, you can be examined at the hospital. A proper doctor should evaluate your injuries." His eyebrows drew down together in a scowl, and his mouth followed suit when she mentioned seeing a doctor. Unwilling to accept no for an answer, Leigh built her case for a stop at the hospital. "The gunshot should be checked, you should be evaluated for a concussion from the car door bashing your head, and your ribs should be x-rayed."

"Alright. Alright. You convinced me." Garrett raised his hands in surrender with a slight grimace. "Police first, hospital second."

Prepared for a heated debate regarding the stop at the hospital, her astonishment in his quick agreement showed in her face. His yielding so easily made her ecstatic. She threw her arms around him and gave him a heartfelt kiss.

"Are you always this easy to please?" Garrett eyed her suspiciously, but he wore a smile on his lips and in his eyes.

"Not always, so don't get used to it."

With hands on her hips, she tried looking tough but failed in his eyes. In fact, he thought she looked adorable.

"I'll consider myself warned."

"Wait a minute. You said you wouldn't let Klein hurt anyone else, who did he hurt?" She wondered how forthcoming he'd be with her.

The eyes meeting hers flashed with anger.

"He killed my partner, Tess."

"The Tess from your nightmare?" She nearly missed the slight nod of his head. "Will you tell me what happened?"

"Maybe later."

His eyes still held hers. The reply didn't quite form a promise, and his gruff response relayed the hurt behind the story.

"Fair enough; whenever you're ready, I'll listen."

"Let me clean up the dishes." With his offer, he changed the topic. "Should we bring in extra firewood?"

"I brought some in last night, so we're set. A fire in the family room should warm up most of the house." She wanted the awkward moment of his past behind them as much as he did.

"What's on the docket for today?" Garrett placed their dishes in the kitchen sink and turned on the water.

"What we do is your decision, because technically you're a guest. First choice always goes to guests. We keep games, puzzles, and cards here for entertainment." Leigh handed him a dish towel.

"What games? I haven't played a game in ages." The enthusiasm he displayed over the prospect of playing board games appeared genuine.

Leigh gave him a quizzical look before responding. "My brother hates playing games. Are you sure?" When he nodded, she continued. "Well, the usual board games are available, also cards and a cribbage board. Oh, and there are books, too."

"Books? Are you bored with me so soon?"

He looked stricken and feigned hurt; she rolled her eyes in response.

"You are anything but boring."

As she left the kitchen, the sounds of hearty laughter followed her into the family room and warmed her. By the time flames danced in the fireplace, he sauntered in, finished with his chore. The grimace he made when he lowered himself to the floor concerned her.

"If you sat in the chair or the couch, you wouldn't suffer as much pain."

Worry about him sparked in her eyes. The last time anyone worried over him was during his last visit home, and his mother did the worrying. He treasured the idea of Leigh being worried about him.

"I'm fine, but don't expect me to get up too quickly."

She quirked an eyebrow and glanced at the zipper of his jeans.

"Standing, Leigh, not the other kind."

An attempt to maintain a straight face failed. The innuendo generated instant images of making love to her on the floor, proving how quickly he could get a particular part of his anatomy up. Certain she hadn't missed the bulge of an erection pressing against his jeans; he wondered if her thoughts mirrored his.

"Fine. Did you reach a decision on what to play?"

He shifted on the thick Persian rug, clapped his hands, and announced, "Yes, I decided on cards. How 'bout Crazy Eights?"

"It's been ages since I played Crazy Eights. Sounds fun."

"Strip Crazy Eights, to be precise." His concentration focused on her as he shuffled the cards.

"Strip Crazy Eights?" Her tone rose an octave. "You changed a children's card game into an X-rated adult game."

"Are you scared?" He dealt their hands. Plopping the remaining deck down, he flipped over the top card with a loud snap.

"Don't be ridiculous, no way am I scared!" she shot back at him as she grabbed her cards. "So, when does the stripping begin?"

"The game has a fast way or a slow way for play." He stared at her, and a challenge lurked in the depths of his hazel eyes.

"Fast or slow versions, huh? Pray tell, what's the difference?" She arranged her hand into suits as she spoke.

"With the slow version, a piece of clothing is lost whenever you lose a hand. The fast version requires stripping whenever you can't play a card."

"I imagine the latter version would play faster."

"The extended version adds time to the fast version without slowing the game too much."

With his eyes twinkling, she couldn't not ask. "And the extended version would be what exactly?

"If you win a hand, you put one item back on."

"I prefer the sound of the extended version."

"Okay, extended version it is. The first play is yours because I dealt."

"Prepare to strip; this looks like a strong hand."

"Time will tell, darlin'."

The endearment he used startled her. The intensity in his eyes was something she never witnessed before, not even with her ex-boyfriend, David. With a smile, she turned her attention back to the cards.

Starting the game, Leigh matched the overturned card with a diamond from her hand, Garrett followed suit. After she played another diamond, he surprised her by changing the suit to spades. She played a spade, and he changed back to diamonds.

"What?" The dirty look she gave him resulted from her confusion in his method of play. "Why didn't you play your diamond before instead of changing the suit to spades?"

"Tactical maneuver. Got a play?"

Pure mischief sparkled in his eyes. A tremor shook her body when she considered the sheer power of his style of mischief. A futile glance at her remaining cards evoked a sigh.

"No, I don't."

Before reaching for a card, she yanked off a sock. Still without a play, she drew a second one.

"Did I not explain how you strip every time you can't play? In other words, you lose an item of clothing whenever you draw a card."

A devilish smile spread across his face. The sleeping dragons awoke in her stomach and prepared for launch.

"No, you didn't explain the rules in such clear terms." Off came another sock, she glared at the new card, and swore under her breath.

"Not helpful?" he asked her, while hiding his smile behind his cards.

"Not at all." Off came her sweater, and she drew again. "Damn it!"

One by one she loosened the buttons down the front of her shirt and allowed him a flash of bare skin. In slow motion, she unbuttoned one cuff at a time. Holding the shirtfront closed, she pulled her arms out of the sleeves. A glance confirmed his total engagement in her striptease. With a flip of her hand, the shirt flew across the room. The drop of his jaw and sharp intake of breath thrilled her. Pleased with the success of her lingerie choices, she drew a card.

"At last!" She slapped down a diamond.

He took his time, checked his cards, and gazed at her.

The caress of his eyes warmed her and sent the dragons off in frenzied circles.

He reached for one card, glanced at her, and played a different one. Another diamond!

She searched her cards for a match.

"Oh, for Pete's sake!"

"No diamonds, no matching card?" With a huge amount of willpower, he kept the smile off his lips, but mischief glittered in his eyes.

Scowling at him, she stood, undid the button of her cords, and drew down the zipper in slow motion. Unable to force his eyes away, he followed her every move. The power of holding his attention overwhelmed her as she gauged his reaction to her movements. She took her time dragging the waistband over her hips and down her legs. Garrett's eyes widened when the cords cleared her panties; his appreciation of the minute-sized panties reflected in his expression and his hard swallow. Now, she realized how losing Strip Crazy Eights may not be such a bad thing.

She drew another card, flashed him a smile, and tossed down a matching card. "Clubs."

"Clubs, huh?" He dropped an eight on the discard pile. "Sorry, darlin', diamonds."

She dropped her hand of cards with annoyance. "You're not overly sympathetic, are you?"

The waggle of his eyebrows and a broad grin answered her. Reaching behind her back, she fumbled with the clasp of her bra.

"Do you need a hand?"

"I'm sure it'd be some sort of infraction of your rules," she replied through clenched teeth.

She unhooked the clasp and pulled one strap off a shoulder, while her other arm came across her breasts, holding the bra in place. Swapping arms, allowed her to pull the other strap down. In a tricky maneuver each hand cupped her breasts; the straps dangled, useless on either side.

Mesmerized by her actions, he struggled for control when she held her own breasts. Her antics produced a powerful physical response in him, straining against the confines of his jeans. Doubts swirled in his head on whether he'd survive to play his last card.

She tossed her bra on the pile of her clothes, reached for her cards, and sat straight and tall. Perfect breasts jutted out with each rosy nipple puckered and taut.

Definite concerns as to playing through his last two cards beleaguered him.

Checking out the drawn card, she smiled. Down came a diamond. "Hah! No way you hold another one." She sounded hopeful.

The predatory spark in his eyes should have warned her. The smoldering gaze moving from her eyes to her lips, over her breasts, along her long legs folded under her, and back up in reverse order should have alerted her. Upon making eye contact with her, he smiled.

"You're right, no more diamonds, but I do hold another eight." He drew an eight from his hand, showed her the card, and dropped it in play. "Diamonds." He whispered the word, as he gazed into her eyes.

With her eyes on him, she stood, hooked her thumbs in her panties and pulled them down her legs with slow deliberateness. Maintaining eye contact, she stepped out of them and kicked them in the direction of her clothes pile. She knelt and drew a card, a diamond. The card landed on the pile, while she watched for his response. "Hah! Guess who'll be stripping next."

He held her eyes as he dropped another eight on the pile, his last card. "Diamonds."

"What do your rules say for this situation? No diamonds and no more clothes, so do you win by default?"

"Oh, yes, I win."

His eyes blazed with desire…for her! Leigh never experienced such a sense of empowerment. The power she held over him amazed and excited her.

"I suppose I should claim my prize." As he said this last statement, he reached out for her. He caught her by the waist and pulled her toward him. She shivered in expectation. He mistook her shivers for a chill, so he gathered the quilt from the couch behind them.

"Here you are. I don't want you catching cold. Is this better?"

"I'll be better once you're as naked as I am. Can you remove your clothes by yourself, or do you need help?"

His smile brightened her morning as he snuggled near her. "I'd never refuse your help."

They laughed together and made love, sometimes quietly and other times as wild as the blizzard outside.

None of Leigh's previous sexual encounters generated anything commensurate with the euphoria shared with Garrett. She panted from the exertion, her heart raced, and a light sheen of perspiration covered her body. With her eyes closed, her memories of everything they enjoyed together appeared as a video running in her mind. Life couldn't get any better than this, she mused.

The realization of falling head-over-heels in love with Leigh shocked him. After a short internal debate, he rejected the idea of experiencing a simple case of lust. He yearned to discover her likes and dislikes, her past, and her dreams. The intense desire to embed her in his life surprised him. Deep within his heart, he wished for her lying in bed with him every night and waking with him each morning. Determination to earn her love overwhelmed him.

"Are you alright?" He needed to be sure his attentions weren't too rough.

She opened her eyes. "I do believe I've become partial to your ridiculous card game, but I doubt a loser should enjoy defeat with such pleasurable intensity. Your hands do amazing things." She smiled at him and stretched like a contented feline.

"You are quite the little minx." His words were softly spoken with desire evident in his eyes. "Are you ready for more?"

She pounced on him in reply.

Much later they lay together in a tangled heap. He drew her into his embrace, kissed her neck, and pulled her closer. Reaching for the quilt they discarded to one side earlier in their lovemaking, he spread the soft covering over them. Leigh dozed in his arms, so he curled beside her and fell into an exhausted sleep.

Chapter Eight

By midafternoon Garrett stirred, Leigh still cuddled with him, breathing against his chest. He slowed his movements in hopes of not waking her, got up, and gathered his clothes. In the bathroom, he washed and dressed. After tossing down a couple of pills, he walked to the kitchen.

Since Leigh mentioned wine in the chiller, he found and opened a bottle of Riesling. A quick search of the cupboards resulted in the discovery of a treasure trove of wine glasses. Selecting two, he grabbed the bottle and deposited everything on the coffee table. Back in the kitchen, he rummaged around and discovered crackers, cheese, and green olives; a selection of all his finds joined the wine on the coffee table. As he set a dish of olives on the table, Leigh stirred under the quilt.

"Darlin', are you awake?" he whispered in case she fell back asleep.

When her eyes fluttered open, she focused on him and smiled as she stretched. "I had a wonderful dream."

"You did?" He squatted near her, brushing a strand of hair from her eyes.

"We played Strip Crazy Eights, but I won this time. You didn't have a play, and only your jeans were left. Before you stripped, I woke up." A seductive pout transformed her lips.

A chuckle rumbled deep in his chest. His fingers went under her chin, he lifted her face, and his lips brushed hers in a soft caress aimed at whisking away the pout.

"Playing cards aren't necessary to have me strip for you. Why don't you freshen up and dress? Once you're ready, we'll spend time getting better acquainted with each other. I brought out some wine and snacks."

She eyed the spread of food behind him and raised her eyes back to his. "I like how you think, Garrett, among other things."

When she stood, she clutched the quilt about her. Giving him a coy smile, she dropped the quilt to the floor.

As his gaze raked over her, he fumbled with the wine bottle.

She rejoiced in his response to her brashness; turning away from him she began picking up her clothes.

Wine flowed over his hand instead of into the glass. "Damn it!" He stopped pouring and glanced at her, hoping she missed his clumsiness—she hadn't.

She laughed and, with a toss of her head, sashayed down the hallway. Confident his eyes followed her, she added a provocative sway to her hips.

Mesmerized by her movements, Garrett's eyes stayed glued on her figure down the hallway until she disappeared into the bathroom. With her near him, he lost the power of concentration. In hopes of gaining clarity, he shook his head, but his thoughts remained on the intoxicating beauty down the hall. Resigning himself to total infatuation, he found paper towels and cleaned up his mess. After straightening the room and stoking the fire, he settled on the couch with a glass of wine in his hand and lustful thoughts raging in his head.

At the sight of him sprawled on the couch in the family room, she hesitated and enjoyed the view of the relaxed, handsome man she realized she may love. The flames in the fireplace provided the only light in the room. Fresh wood crackled as the flames intensified. The similarity between the flames of the fire and the flames of their passion didn't escape her.

The folded quilt on the back of the couch and the neat pile of games, puzzles, and cards tucked in the corner of the room surprised her. She'd never met a guy who did things like cleaning up after breakfast, straightening a room, or preparing snacks. He's definitely a keeper, she acknowledged to herself.

"Thanks for straightening things. This," she indicated the spread on the coffee table, "is perfect." When she sat beside him, he handed her a glass of wine.

"You're welcome." He munched on cheese and tossed down a few olives. "No need making a fuss over me throwing out some cheese and crackers, or did the olives put my effort over the top?" He looked at her with interest, as if he worked on solving a puzzle she presented him.

"Over a two-year relationship with my former boyfriend, he never lifted a hand to help with anything, not even at his own place." She drank some wine and grabbed a handful of cheese and crackers. "Getting up the nerve to break off our relationship took me months after I decided enough was enough. Most of my girlfriends considered him quite the catch, and all our friends thought we made an ideal couple. My mom adored him, but I believe Dad tolerated him for my sake; his parents are their best friends. None of them realized how he took advantage of me. He took from me, but never gave of himself. Correction, he gave me good sex on occasion, but with sex he was only interested in his own enjoyment, never mine." A sly grin appeared as she settled back closer to him. "He never gave me mind-blowing sex the way you do."

Her comment produced a most becoming blush over his whiskered cheeks. His arm came around her, and he drew her closer.

"Mind-blowing, huh? I shouldn't set the bar so high right out of the gate. Didn't leave much room for improvement."

After eating a few olives from his hand, he offered her the rest.

She took his fingers in her mouth and sucked the salty juice from them. Her eyes held his as they both remembered their first evening together.

His other hand played with her braid, undoing the intricate weaving, and his fingers tangled in her hair.

"I like how soft and silky your hair is."

He massaged her head and fingered her golden tresses. She drained her wine glass, so he refilled their glasses.

"When did you end this relationship?" Trying to sound casual, his true interest was far from that, because he didn't want their meeting to be a rebound for her.

"Almost four years ago. I dated a few others over the years, but I lacked any luck in finding the right guy."

"Maybe the right guy should find you." An impetuous decision led him in a reckless move for her affection. "Well, it might be he fell into your life already."

Because of his career choice, he experienced plenty of bad things in his life. He longed for someone willing to share a life with him and be with him through all the dark times expected with his law enforcement career. Tess's death taught him life shouldn't revolve around your job; you needed someone to focus your energies on and to be the center of your existence. He wanted Leigh as his someone.

He turned toward her and shifted her, so she faced him, ready for a kiss. The gentle strength of his lips took her breath away. Ending the kiss, he gazed into her eyes.

She returned his gaze and marveled at the love and caring reflected in the depths of his now warm-brown eyes. She caressed his face and ran her fingers along his jawline.

"Do you experience the same draw…this desperate need?" she asked.

He nodded and raised her hand to his lips.

"I do. Everything happens for a reason, and you are the most beautiful reason ever for surviving an ambush."

She cherished his compliment. Grabbing the quilt from the back of the couch, she cuddled close to him, draped the quilt over them, and grabbed her wine.

"On the day you fell into my life, I remember thinking how I had my favorite wines with me, a roaring fire, and a quilt for cuddling under. One thing was missing from my evening—a good-looking guy. Soon afterward, I found you. Darn convenient, don't you think?" Her smile warmed his soul. "Now we're living my fantasy!"

She snuggled closer and downed her wine. He poured her more and topped off his glass.

"Fulfilling your needs, wants, and desires would be my pleasure." He sipped his wine. "This is a full-flavored Riesling. I learned appreciation for wines during a tour in Germany, and I enjoyed my fair share. Although I indulged in quite a bit of their beer, too." Lost in a memory, he broke free of it with a shake of his head. "You brought an interesting selection of wines."

"I love attending wine tastings and trying different wines. When I enjoy one, I buy a couple bottles before I leave the tasting, so I own wines for every occasion. I'm glad you enjoy wines, not everyone does."

Score a point for me, thought Garrett.

"Yesterday you said you came back, so you're from Minnesota?" The question led to her learning more of this fascinating man sitting beside her.

"Born and bred. I grew up in a small town in western Minnesota. Right after high school graduation I left for basic training. I was eighteen and dreamed of a career in the Air Force. Dreams aren't reality, though, so here I am ten years later ready for my second career." He reached for the crackers and cheese, handing her some. "How 'bout you? Why are you here alone? Don't think I'm complaining. I'm happy you're here all by yourself."

"I'm a Minnesota native, too, although I moved away about four years ago." She nibbled on the cheese and crackers, as she considered how much of her story to share with him at this time. "Graduated from the U with a finance degree and spent a year working in the Cities until I needed a change. So, I relocated for a position with an investment firm in Chicago, but the work never inspired me. Shouldn't your work excite you?" She glanced at him, encouraged by his nod. "I desired more from my work and mentioned my disillusionment to my best friend. At her suggestion I harnessed my passion for photography as a career path, I quit my job and moved home. I came up here in hopes of figuring out my next moves. Where should I live? How do I turn my passion into my occupation?"

"Photography? Do you have any of your pictures with you? Would you show them to me?" True interest sounded in his words.

"The only ones are saved on my camera. If you do want to look at them, I can grab it." Leigh appreciated his interest. He nodded in response, so she retrieved her camera from the back entry. She plopped beside him and handed over her most prized possession. "Here you go, look at the screen and advance the pictures by pushing there."

With camera in hand, he reviewed her pictures. Now and then, he cast a look at her, studied another picture, and looked at her again. "Wow! These are amazing. The emotion within each shot grabbed my attention; you captured the energy of the moment."

He handed her back the camera, his hand catching and holding hers for a moment longer than necessary.

She set the camera aside. "Thanks. No one's ever expressed a depth of understanding for my photographs before you. I'm happy you experienced the emotion of my shots." Reeling from his compliment and the charge of emotion when their hands touched, she emptied her glass and set it on the coffee table. "Is any wine left in the bottle?"

"Nope. Should I open another one?" Garrett asked, before attempting to rise.

"No, my turn!" Leigh patted his leg stopping him from standing. She whisked into the kitchen and opened another bottle of white wine. Returning to the family room with her stocking feet sliding over the hardwood floor, she almost crashed into the couch. "Alright, we'll try a Gewürztraminer from Washington State next. Please hand me your glass, so the tasting may begin."

"Yes, ma'am." Garrett held out his glass, which she filled. "Mmm, delicious. Sorry, I'm not skilled at describing fruity undertones and all those wine-tasting terms," he confessed when she raised her eyebrows at him.

She filled her glass and snuggled back under the quilt with him. "Me neither; you didn't learn about wine tasting while living in Germany?"

"Tasting for me consisted of drinking the wine and deciding whether I enjoy the flavor enough for a purchase. I'm not into fancy twirling and spitting. The only time I spit out wine is if the taste is awful."

Leigh smiled, drank her wine, and snuggled closer to him. He caressed her shoulder; she felt as contented as a petted kitten, in fact she might break into a purr if he continued.

"So, why back to Minnesota? Will you be near your family?" Leigh peered at him, marveling again at the strength of her attraction for him.

A shadow crossed his face. "No, I don't have any family. Mom and Dad died in a car accident two years after I joined the Air Force. No brothers or sisters either." He stared into the flames of the fire, lost in his past. He remembered the long trip home, dealing with funeral arrangements, and working on all the details finalizing his parent's affairs. At only twenty years old, his world had crashed in on him.

"I'm so sorry for your loss."

"The accident happened a long time ago." He came back to the present with a sigh. "Minnesota has always been home for me. Since their deaths, I returned on leave many times, traveled in different parts of the state, and took in the sights. In fact, I visited all the state historical sites, all the state parks and forests, and most of the national sites. I'm happiest when I'm here; I belong here."

They grabbed the same piece of cheese, fingers brushing with heightened awareness of one another. Dropping the chunk at the same time, their laughter ensued.

"You enjoy the last piece, Leigh," Garrett offered as he reached for the olives.

She brushed the chunk of cheese against his lips. With a quirk of an eyebrow, he accepted a portion of her offering. While he chewed, his eyes locked on hers. The pink tip of her tongue dragged across the remaining morsel before her teeth sank into it. He caught her hand and brought the last crumb of cheese to his lips. When he took the cheese as well as her fingers in his mouth, he tugged her closer. Spellbound, she stared as he sucked each finger.

"Thanks for the cheese." His voice sounded full of promises. His lips brushed across hers, a fleeting motion. Before she was ready, he set her back and poured them each more wine. Leigh chugged hers and reached for the bottle.

"Thirsty?" He arched the same eyebrow at her, an unspoken comment hung between them.

"I…ah…yes, extremely thirsty." She blushed as she poured herself more wine and drank it all. Staring at the now empty glass, she reached for the bottle.

"You should slow down, or you may not last through supper. Are you okay?" Apparent concern for her reflected in his voice.

"I'm fine." She shouldn't admit how his actions flustered her, should she? Concern still showed in his expression, and she realized she ached to tell him how he affected her. "You're…you're so different from anyone I ever met. You generate such intense feelings within me. I can't immerse myself in enough of you, and what I crave more than anything is fulfilling my sexual fantasies with you over and over again. Never have I performed a striptease or paraded naked in front of a guy. Let alone, joining a stranger in the shower, but with you everything feels so natural!"

"So right?"

"Yes, so fantastically right! Why am I comfortable doing things in front of you, when I never did those things in front of anyone else before? What did you do to me?"

"Not me. The energy between the two of us makes everything happen naturally."

He pulled her into his lap and rubbed her shoulders. They looked into each other's eyes with longing and understanding. Garrett angled his head in for a kiss, the touch of his lips soft and gentle on hers.

Leigh surrendered to her desire for him and kissed him back, running her fingers through his hair. After catching her breath, Leigh whispered in his ear, "We should adjourn to the kitchen, so we can work on supper and continue our discussion."

He gave her another kiss on the top of her head.

"I agree, as long as you remember where we left off."

Chapter Nine

Ambling into the kitchen, Leigh pulled out the steaks and directed Garrett to the potatoes. While he cleaned them, she turned on the oven and seasoned the steaks. After he placed the potatoes in the oven, they sat together at the counter drinking the remaining wine.

"How large is your family? How did they react after learning of your intended career change? Are they supportive?" he asked.

Ah, direct hit on her current quandary.

"There are only four in my family. Mom's a whirlwind of energy and all about social standing and prestige. Dad retired a couple years ago from his position as a history professor at the U and took up woodworking and gardening. He focuses on enjoying life and keeping Mom happy. My older brother, Alex, is an architect. He's married—"

"Wait a minute! Your brother's name is Alex—so your folks named him Alexander Ramsey?" She nodded. "Are you related to him? The former Governor of Minnesota, I mean." She laughed at Garrett's exuberance over her brother's name. "Sorry, I love Minnesota history and Alexander Ramsey is all over the early history being our first territorial governor and the second state governor."

"No, we're not related. Mom and Dad thought the name sounded good. I doubt Minnesota history came to mind when they decided. But with Dad being a history professor, we may never know for sure where the inspiration originated. Alex received a little grief in school when his class studied state history. When we were children, Mom and Dad took us to the Ramsey House for the Christmas tour. My brother thought the house belonged to him, after all he read his name on the sign! Somewhere in an old photo album there's a picture of him standing by it, looking all possessive."

"Cute story. Did your brother get over his disappointment?"

"He experienced short-lived disappointment, especially after a promise of lunch at his favorite restaurant." Unexpectedly, her eyebrows shot up and a frown replaced her smile.

Where did her memories take her, he wondered?

"What's wrong?"

"This is the first time I thought of that in years. At the time, we were so happy and close as a family, but somewhere along the way we lost the close-knit family ties."

He stood near her chair and gathered her hands in his. "I'm sorry for starting you down the memory trail, since your memories sadden you."

"Not your fault my family became a little dysfunctional over time." She swallowed hard and blushed. "Back to your other questions, my family's attitude regarding my career change, and if they support my decision. Supportive, yes and no. My mom finds my decision appalling. Although my dad tries being supportive, he wonders if I thought through all the aspects of the change, especially the financial angle. A discussion with my older brother shouldn't be as difficult. To summarize, they wonder if I can survive on photography alone. And why wouldn't they when I haven't figured out any details yet. What am I after? Will I be happy with my photographs published in magazines or hung in galleries, or should I do portraits and weddings?"

"The pictures you showed me were all scenery; do you prefer scenery for your photographs?"

"I do love scenery and animals."

"So, eliminate portrait and special event photography from your consideration. Being published or in galleries shouldn't be mutually exclusive options." He drank the last of his wine and checked on the potatoes. "If you want my opinion, continue taking pictures and research methods of getting published or recognized by galleries and collectors."

"You make the process sound easy." She slouched in her chair and drained her wine.

"I doubt if any of this is easy, but perhaps the figuring out part isn't so difficult." A single finger traced a slow path along her jawline. "You made a decision and acted on it, so follow through to the end." He kissed the tip of her nose. After draining the bottle of wine into their glasses, he relaxed in his chair, saluted her with his glass, and took a sip.

"Argh! You're right. You are so right, but I guess the business side scares me."

"An incentive may help you start on further plans." The hot glimmer in his eyes indicated the direction of his thoughts.

"More like a kick in the ass is needed." She smiled as his eyebrows jerked up at her response. "That's what my dad would say."

"I think I'll get along fine with your dad." Garrett sipped his wine. "I hereby offer my services for any ass kicking needed."

"Well, aren't you the generous one! Thanks, but no thanks; I can motivate myself."

"A more pleasant, perhaps intimate incentive came to mind before your interesting suggestion of ass kicking." Low, throaty tones emphasized his slight accent.

His offer sent chills down her back. The many intimate things he might do with her or to her as an incentive weren't difficult to imagine. Sudden heat built within her, so she pulled off her sweater. The hooded gaze he directed at her said he read her thoughts. She drank some of her wine hoping for a distraction, but without success.

"I'll check the potatoes again." She almost fell off her chair and scampered to the oven. With the potatoes nearly done, she changed the oven setting to broil and got the steaks ready to go in.

"How do you prefer your steak?"

"Medium rare, more toward rare than medium."

"Amazing, I prefer mine cooked the same way. This will be easy to finish up. Can you open the Cabernet?"

"I can wrestle with the cork. Should I set out different glasses?"

"Yeah, the red wine glasses in the upper cabinet." The tongs in her hand waved in the general direction of a cupboard. "They're larger than these, so each fill will last longer."

"A woman after my own heart."

Garrett opened the wine, found the glasses, and set two places at the counter. Leigh placed the steaks in the broiler and arranged butter, sour cream, steak sauce, salt, and pepper on the counter. As soon as the steaks were done, they enjoyed their first real sit-down meal together.

"Where would you set up shop?" He continued their conversation of her career.

"Northern Minnesota would be a better location for scenery and animals than the Twin Cities, but no firm decisions on where yet."

"Brainerd is a beautiful area and near some fascinating locations."

"As in, where you're going?"

"Well, yeah." Attacking his potato provided an excuse for not looking at her. "I thought you could join me...I mean, we're getting along well, at least I believe we are." He kept himself busy adding butter, salt, and pepper to his potato skins.

"I agree. I enjoy being with you, we're compatible in our likes, and share a passion for each other. You're right concerning the Brainerd area; the scenery should be gorgeous. Are you sure?" Leigh's heart flipped in anticipation of his response.

Garrett finished his potato, so moved on to his steak. He busied himself by cutting the meat into bite-size pieces. Leigh remained quiet, watching him, and waiting for his answer. When no distractions remained on his plate, he glanced up at her. The expression on his face sobered her.

"I need you to understand what I'm going to say, so I'll tell you about Tess first." His voice cracked, so he drank more of his wine.

"She had been my partner on what turned into my last case in the Air Force. We investigated a ring of thieves operating on the base and preying on military families living in base housing and the local area. Tess and I worked in concert with the local police department, sharing information, and working joint surveillance. We zeroed in on the mastermind, Jonas Klein, and his crew, but during the operation to capture them with the necessary evidence something went deadly wrong." His voice became a whisper, and his eyes closed for a moment, before returning to his story. "The perimeter collapsed, and Klein slipped through, but Tess spotted his departure. She and I took off on foot pursuit after Klein through the building and into the surrounding neighborhood. We separated in hopes of surrounding Klein; as a result, I wasn't in position to back up Tess. Klein pulled a gun and shot her in the neck, right above her vest. I apprehended Klein before I spotted her lying in a pool of her own blood. She died in my arms," Garrett concluded with a catch in his voice. He tried stopping all the remembered pain and grief before the memories overwhelmed him, but he couldn't. He ached for the loss of his friend.

"What happened with Klein?" Leigh's soft voice broke through his pain.

"The bastard stood trial for his crimes, and his only outburst during the whole thing was his oath to kill me for ruining his life." A raspy laugh sounded from Garrett. "Ruining his life, after he took Tess's. Unbelievable! I never took his threat seriously. Before I left the Air Force, Klein's prosecution ended with him convicted and sentenced to life imprisonment at a federal high security facility. At the time I separated, the decision as to where he'd serve out his time had yet to be finalized. The location where he spent his time behind bars didn't matter to me. Klein locked up anywhere gave me satisfaction, but nothing ended the ache of Tess's death."

"I'm so sorry. You don't need to tell me anything else." Leigh covered one of his hands with her smaller one. She couldn't imagine the pain and loss he suffered at the hands of Klein.

"No, Leigh, this is the important thing I need you to understand. When Tess died, I realized my life cannot consist of only the job I love. I needed something else. No, *someone* else. I imagine sharing my life with someone I can laugh with, someone who will share their days with me, someone I can love with a passion." He paused and drew a breath. "Someone like you."

Leigh sat staring at him for a moment, speechless. "I understand what you're telling me. I doubt anyone would believe us if we told them we sat here and shared our innermost fears and pain only twenty-four hours after meeting each other. I'm drawn to you so strongly; the power almost scares me. Almost."

She got off her chair and leaned into him. His arms came around her and pulled her into his chest.

"So, you'll come with me?"

"Yes, I'll go anywhere with you."

She raised her face to him. His lips crushed hers in a fierce demanding kiss, and she joined him with her own demands.

He pulled back, gave her a kiss on the cheek, and said, "We should finish our supper, before we talk further."

"Fine."

She went back to her chair and worked on her potato. Leigh sensed his eyes on her, caressing her.

They ate in silence, lost in their thoughts and feelings. On occasion, they shared a look or a glance.

"You do have excellent taste in wines." He sipped his wine.

"I'm glad you enjoy wine. Not every guy does."

Garrett assumed her comment meant her ex-boyfriend didn't share her enjoyment of wine. Score another one for me, he thought.

They finished their meal, so he refilled their glasses and carried them into the family room. He tossed another log on the fire, and returned to the kitchen, helping Leigh with the cleanup.

"One of my talents is researching information, so what if I looked into recommendations for a successful photography career?" He dried dishes for her as she tackled the washing.

"Is that a result of your being an investigator—the researching?"

"I always had a knack for research and for logical thinking, fitting talents for investigations. It's as though I'm programmed for the work."

"I welcome your help."

The warmth of her smile washed over him.

After they finished with the dishes, they moved out to the family room, now warmer from the fire.

"Because we're talking, I think we should sit apart. I experience a hard time concentrating when I'm in your arms," Leigh confessed as she curled up at the far end of the couch and tucked the quilt around her.

Garrett picked up his glass of wine and settled into a chair across the room from her. He stretched out his long legs and rested his feet on an ottoman. "Probably a smart idea, I'm not immune to your charms, either." The desire in his eyes set her heartbeat drumming in her chest.

"None of those, either!" She waggled a finger at him.

His expression oozed innocence. "Those what?"

"Those 'I want you naked and I want you now' looks. Don't you laugh at me; you know exactly what I'm talking about!"

He threw up his hands in resignation. "I'll try not to, but no promises because I don't understand what you mean."

Leigh shook her head, muttered "Smart ass" under her breath, and settled back into the pillows on the couch.

"Brainerd holds everything necessary for being a functional home base for your photography career." Garrett pressed on with his thoughts of her joining him there. "With state forests and parks nearby and plenty of lakes, all kinds of scenery and tons of wildlife will be available year-round. We can search for a storefront as your studio or a house with room that could work as a studio. The area is touristy and should provide an opportunity for wide exposure."

"A house?" Leigh choked out the question.

"Well, yeah. I'm working with a realtor in the area. I decided on buying a house, rather than renting an apartment. Is having a house a problem?"

"No, not a problem, only a surprise; a pleasant surprise." Leigh found she cherished the idea of sharing a house with Garrett, something more permanent than an apartment. "What about your job?"

"There'd be travel for some assignments, I'm sure. The BCA selected an undercover assignment for me when I report in. They're taking advantage of my being unknown in the area, and my new boss suggested I not cut my hair or shave. I'm usually not this shaggy looking."

"I find your shaggy appearance rather sexy." She winked at him and emitted a loud purr. He shook his head in reply. "The dangerous nature of your career concerns me, and I'm not sure how to manage my concern. You run the risk of being hurt or killed."

"Leigh, life doesn't come with guarantees. Everyday life is dangerous for everyone. I didn't expect to lose both of my parents at the same time, but I did." He looked out at the darkness, as if he viewed his past in the moonlight. "I regret I didn't spend additional time with them. I regret I didn't make what time I did have with them count for more. I regret I didn't talk with them every chance I got. I regret I didn't constantly tell them how important they were to me and how much I loved them." He blinked back the tears pooling in his eyes.

She recognized the heart-wrenching grief in his voice, and she longed for nothing more than to wrap her arms around him.

"The threat we face now isn't from my new job, but from my old one. Dangerous conditions exist anywhere near me, until Klein's found. Which is why I prefer you not being with me." His hand shot up, palm extended, ending her disagreement before gaining life. "Since you already voiced your disagreement with my preferences, please remember our survival requires vigilance and being careful."

"Always. Do you think it'll be long before he's caught?"

"Once we reach the authorities, he should be caught before too long. The feds will show up after the local authorities put out their alerts. Chances are Klein's hanging around and looking for me, so he may be visible." He didn't share his thoughts of offering to act as bait for the authorities in an attempt at a quick apprehension of Klein. That was a discussion for later, when and if his sacrifice became necessary.

"The wind is dying down. If the blizzard ends tonight, we can dig out the sleds tomorrow and head for town."

"So, tonight may be our last night here."

"Let's not waste any of our time; come over here!" Leigh threw back the quilt inviting him on the couch with her. "Do you remember where we left off?"

"Oh, yeah."

He drained his wine glass, before joining her on the couch. His arms gravitated around her, and he drew her against him as he lay back with her on top.

Their clothes flew across the room as they worked together, achieving a mutual state of undress. Laughter, hugs, and kisses preceded slow, passionate lovemaking. They indulged in pleasuring each other and found interesting ways of satisfying one another, until they lay exhausted on the couch.

"Leigh, I believe I love you." Garrett placed a gentle kiss on her forehead, on her nose, and lastly on her lips.

"As I love you. I rejoice in how your eyes and actions reflect your love for me, and I hope my love for you shows." She searched his eyes and took joy in the emotions reflected at her.

"Every touch, every sigh, and every moan communicate your love to me."

He kissed her and, without ending the kiss, carried her to his bed. She curled on her side and fell fast asleep. While watching her sleep, a protectiveness rose within him, something new and overwhelming. The innate truth of his feelings didn't frighten him but made him whole again. He welcomed this sudden love; this was the piece missing from his life since the death of his parents. Climbing in bed with the woman who brought his soul peace, he drew her close and followed her into a deep, peaceful sleep.

Chapter Ten

The early-dawn light entered through the open curtains in the bedroom. An icy chill rushed up his bare legs, shocking Garrett awake. With Leigh's warm body curled up beside him, he wondered why the warmth didn't reach her ice-cold feet resting against his shins. He snuggled closer to her, drawing her against his chest. A few extra minutes of sleep would serve him well.

Still drowsy, Leigh sighed when Garrett pulled her close. With his strong arm around her, she relaxed against his chest. This sleeping arrangement became more comfortable with each minute spent beside him.

As the sun came up, a brighter light filled the room and ended their ability to remain asleep. They awoke slowly; Leigh's stretching caused Garrett a definite physical reaction. The list of things to accomplish this morning was too lengthy for playing around, no matter how enjoyable staying in bed would be.

"Leigh, I should begin digging us out, so we can leave before noon." He worked his way off the bed and stood before her. "While I clear out the snow, you can pack a few things. There must be hotels in Pine Ridge."

"Yes, a couple, but if you don't put on some clothes soon, we'll be on a much later schedule." The tip of her tongue ran across her lips, as she eyed him up and down.

"I'm out of here!" He hurried to the family room in search of his clothes.

She emerged from under the covers, when he entered the room wearing only a shirt and sweater.

"Did you have a change of heart?" she purred at him.

"No, thought wearing my shorts today would provide me an extra layer of warmth." He grabbed his shorts, pulled them on, and sat on the bed as he donned socks and jeans.

Kneeling on the bed with nothing covering her enticing body, she interfered with his progress by rubbing against him and running her fingers through his hair.

"Will you keep your scruffiness? The longer hair and beard lend you a bad boy look I find erotic and provocative!"

A frown answered her. "Only until my assignment is over; you're stalling." After he left the room, the sound of a door closing told her he exited the house.

***

As she packed her bag, the rumble of the snowblower sounded outside. Through the kitchen window, she studied him maneuvering the machine and directing the white snow arc away from the path he blazed to the shed. She busied herself by putting a light breakfast together and straightening the family room.

The fun they shared the night before promised years of enjoyment and satisfaction, she thought. Their relationship changed after their mutual declarations of love. How to explain their sudden relationship to her family and friends escaped her. Running a sample announcement in her head didn't help. Hey, Mom and Dad, this is Garrett Dane. He fell into my life forty-eight hours ago, and we're in love. Oh, and by the way, he has a crazed killer after him. Yeah, the truth would go over real well.

The back door opened, and Garrett walked in, bringing the chill of winter with him. Between the red of his cheeks and the sparkle in his eyes rivaling the glitter of the snow reflecting in the sunlight, he looked glorious.

Leigh wondered how he managed looking sexier today than yesterday, but he did. He appeared more alive. She decided he must be feeling better. Her thought made her reflect on how active they'd been. How in the world had he accomplished all the amazing things he did with her, considering his injuries? By sheer determination and his inherent strength, she decided with a smile.

"It's bitter cold outside!" As he walked in, he blew on his hands to warm them. "I hope you dressed extra warm. The sleds are gassed up and ready to go." She pushed a plate toward him. "Peanut butter toast? For me?"

"Yes, for you. I'm packed and ready to go." She nodded at her bag. "I've driven this route over the trails before, so you can follow me."

He munched on his toast. "We go to the police first thing; I'm not sure how much time we'll spend with them. I plan on calling my old Air Force boss in case he has information on how Klein escaped. I'll press for a picture of him right away, so you can recognize him if you see him."

"When we're done with the police, we're off to the hospital ER. You agreed, remember?"

"Yes, I remember, but can we grab lunch before going to the hospital?" His eyes pleaded for her agreement.

Damn him! Disagreeing was impossible when he looked so adorable.

"Depending on how long we're with the police, we'll see. Can you live with the uncertainty?"

He nodded at her as he devoured his toast.

***

Leigh strapped her bag on the back of one snowmobile. After settling a helmet on her head, she dropped the visor in place and got on her sled. When Garrett sat astride the other one, she started her engine. With the roar of his engine coming to life, she gave him a thumbs up, and they charged off.

Garrett guessed the last time he snowmobiled must have been at least five years ago. The sensation of speed, the crispness of the weather, and the flashing scenery of wintry whiteness thrilled him. The snow sparkled and resembled a sheet of diamonds. Sun dogs bracketed the sun, predicting colder weather for tomorrow. The huge muskrat house on a slough hole they flew by promised a long winter. Both were old sayings his mom and dad had shared with him as he grew up; they now represented some of his most treasured memories.

Leigh enjoyed zooming across the snow. Riding the snowmobiles during her stay at the cabin never entered her plans, so she delighted in the unexpected fun. She recognized all the trails and ran them with the expertise gained from years of vacationing at the cabin. When she stopped at the crest of a hill, Garrett pulled up beside her.

"The town is over a couple of hills, through a field and across a lake. We're making excellent time. Are you doing okay?"

"Doing great! I haven't done this for years. We should buy one or two of these."

His smile brightened her day and warmed her. She appreciated how he considered what she might wish for and how he already thought of them as a couple.

"Let's go, so we can begin the hunt for your escaped killer." She took off, spraying snow behind her sled. They zipped across a lake, skirted ice houses, and shot across a field. As they crested the last hill, she veered to the right and zipped through a park. She slowed as they left the park and ran them along a wide road. With a visualization of the town's layout in her head, she guided the sled along the most expeditious route into town and on to the police station. After traveling a few additional blocks, they reached their destination.

Chapter Eleven

After dismounting, she removed her helmet and unstrapped her bag. Garrett joined her, and together they walked into the station. The desk sergeant listened to his story, with increased interest as the events unfolded in succinct terms and a forcefulness she hadn't heard before. The sergeant dismissed Garrett and made a hurried phone call.

"He's calling a detective, who'll be out soon. You can stay out here or come with me, whichever you prefer."

"If you want me to, I'll go in with you." She squeezed his hand in support.

"Mr. Dane?"

They both stood, as a tall, shapely brunette walked over to them. A wave of jealousy surged through her when the detective looked Garrett up and down, wet her lips, and flipped her hair. Leigh seethed inside; she recognized flirting when the action slapped her in the face.

Garrett walked to the detective with Leigh in tow.

"I'm Detective Nichols, Marci Nichols."

They shook hands, and he turned toward Leigh.

"Garrett Dane. This is Leigh Ramsey." He placed a hand on the small of her back.

"Ms. Ramsey." Detective Nichols shot Leigh a sharp glance and gave her a slight nod of her head. "Mr. Dane, you'll need to come with me. Ms. Ramsey can wait out here." She sent a short smile at Leigh.

"Leigh will stay with me." Garrett pulled Leigh closer. She relished his protectiveness.

"Fine. Please come this way." Detective Nichols led them into her office. She closed the door behind them and sat in the chair behind a metal desk. They sank into twin metal chairs on the opposite side of the desk. "Now what's this concerning an escaped prisoner and an attempt on your life?"

"Less than a month ago, I separated from the Air Force. I worked in the Office of Special Investigations. My last case resulted in the arrest and conviction of Jonas Klein. He swore to kill me for ruining his life."

"Well, threats are a professional hazard in law enforcement." Detective Nichols paused in her note-taking. She smiled and batted her eyes at Garrett. Leigh rested one hand on his arm, while the other fisted in her lap, and she fumed at the detective's blatant flirting.

"True, but Klein almost carried out his vow. He somehow escaped custody and tracked me down. The gash on my head and a bullet hole in my shoulder are evidence of his attack."

His words caught the detective's attention. "He shot you? Where and when did the shooting happen?"

"I'm not sure of the exact location, but it can't be far from here. I went down an embankment by the road, and I reached the Ramsey cabin on foot. I remember following a snowmobile trail part of the way. My Jeep may still be on the side of the road but snowed in for sure." Garrett took her questions in stride, maintaining a professional attitude. "This happened the day before yesterday."

"I'll notify the highway patrol and the county sheriff and put out an all-points bulletin on Klein." Detective Nichols keyed information into her computer. "What's the model and license number for your Jeep?"

"It's a red 4-door Wrangler with Georgia War in Afghanistan plates, number TVU 321. If we contact my former supervisor, he may have information on Klein's escape we can exploit."

"Not 'we,' me. You won't be working this investigation. You have no authority, and you are way too involved." She held her hand up when he opened his mouth in protest. "You're the victim here, Mr. Dane."

Garrett knew she was right, but he didn't like it.

They walked out of the police station after hours of providing statements and making phone calls. Garrett spoke with Chief Martin for a short time, but Detective Nichols took over the call. He never received the information he hoped for from Chief Martin, and Detective Nichols didn't share any information other than Klein's picture.

***

With mounting curiosity, Leigh sat with quiet interest as Garrett's case unfolded before her at the station. She recognized anger in Garrett's eyes and frustration in his voice, as hours passed. She couldn't imagine how upsetting the situation was for him. As they walked out of the station, he slammed the door shut behind them. She guessed his action alleviated some of his aggravation, but she suspected slamming a door was a far cry from what he longed to do.

"Damn! That was so irritating! She's so..." He kicked a chunk of snow in his path. The white clump flew forward, hit a pole, and burst into pieces. "...so...infuriating!"

"At least she gave us a picture of Klein, so I can recognize him." She tried focusing him on the small positive result of their morning, but she figured curtailing his fury with the situation would be impossible. "Maybe they'll find your Jeep and return it soon."

"Yeah, right." He stopped and flashed her one of his half-smiles. "Sorry 'bout my outburst; I'm not used to being on this side of a crime."

"I can't imagine what you're going through. As your reward for being so restrained with the detective, we'll grab lunch first and go to the hospital afterward." She linked her arm with his. "The diner is within walking distance, not even a full block from where we're standing."

"Lead the way." In appreciation of her efforts to cheer him up, he placed a warm kiss on one cheek. "Thanks."

At the diner he held the door open for her, and they sat in a booth with a view of the street. After ordering, they sat drinking coffee.

"So, am I still joining you in Brainerd?"

"If you want to, yes." At her vigorous nodding in response, he continued, "Since I'm not needed for anything around here, I can move forward with my BCA job. Once we arrive, we can buy a three- or four-bedroom house. The extra bedrooms would leave one for an office and another as a photography studio for you. What do you think?"

"You put some thought into this. Do you mean one bedroom for us and a spare bedroom for visitors?"

"Well, yeah. Unless you want your own bedroom?" The roughness of his voice surprised him.

She almost laughed at the apparent worry displayed on his face.

"No, only making sure we'd continue sleeping together." She ran her boot up his leg, watching his eyes widen and a warm glow ignite in them.

He picked up one of her hands and brushed the back with his lips. "You shouldn't doubt my longing for you, Leigh. I dream of you being in my bed every night and every morning."

She blushed at the deep and inviting quality of his voice.

His curious hint of an accent made every word he spoke sound flat-out sexy. "I need you in my life, but now might not be the best time. I don't want Klein getting to you. If he figured out how much I care for you, he might use you to reach me. Should he hurt you, I couldn't live with myself."

"I understand, but I want to be with you. The thought of being away from you maddens me. I'm not sure how you managed it, but I'm addicted to you." She lowered her voice. "Addicted to your body and your lovemaking abilities."

His heart beat a bit faster, and his body responded to her sexy delivery.

Before they got any further, the waitress delivered their orders.

"Wow, this is so delicious. Your omelet looks fantastic." With that observation, she stabbed a fork into his omelet, removing a mound of deliciousness.

"Hey! You should ask first or at least wait for an invitation." He jabbed his fork into her scramble and pulled out a hefty amount. He raised his eyebrows at her and smiled as he stuffed the fork in his mouth. "Mmm, very tasty."

"You shouldn't talk with your mouth full. Note to self, his table manners are lacking. We must work on them."

"I doubt if your table manners are any improvement over mine, Miss Omelet Thief."

"Ooh, so are you going to arrest me? Handcuff me? Do wicked things to me, so you can coerce a confession out of me?"

The mischievous grin she flashed at him sent his stomach in flips and his heart raced.

"Don't need a confession because of a reliable witness. Me. The handcuffs are a thought, though. Are you into bondage or BDSM?"

"No! Not at all. Don't tell me you are?" She got more than a trifle worried now. What did she really know about this man sitting across from her?

"I never tried any kinky stuff. Met a couple who participated in the BDSM scene, but I never quite understood the lure of handcuffs, whips, and paddles in sex. However, if the action interests you, count me in."

She blushed when he mentioned bondage. Now a deep pink colored her face as she shook her head in answer to his outrageous offer.

The dark blush turned into a downright attractive look for her, so Garrett decided he should cause her to blush more often.

Their meal concluded with a debate over who'd pay the bill. Garrett came out victorious, but he let her cover the tip. As they strolled back to their snowmobiles, they walked hand in hand, acting like a couple in love. For a moment, they caught the notice of a lone figure across the street.

***

Jonas Klein disregarded them. Couples held no interest for him because he searched for a single man. While in town, he maintained a low profile and stayed in the shadows. Since news of Dane's demise eluded him, he spent his time staking out the hospital and the police station. If no information surfaced soon, he'd leave this godforsaken state and the country. A hasty departure should be his priority, but the need for orchestrating Dane's death trumped everything. No one bested Jonas Klein and lived to boast about it.

He gave the couple one last glance. They chased one another in an empty lot, tossing snow at each other, until they somehow ended up on the ground. He gave his head a slight shake over the silliness of Northerners, as he walked farther into the shadows to his parked car.

***

Leigh and Garrett played a fast game of snow keep-away in an empty lot beyond the diner. In a moment of playfulness, she initiated the activity by scooping up a handful of snow and flinging it at Garrett. He retaliated with a cascade of snow hitting her back. She took off running into an empty lot, and he chased her. They ran in circles, almost playing a fox and goose game. Garrett caught her, but he tripped in the process. They fell to the ground in a jumble of limbs and laughter.

"Too fun!" Leigh laughed out the words. "What are you doing?" She watched as Garrett flung the healthy arm and both legs across the snow.

"Making a snow angel, I haven't made one since grade school." He stood, surveyed his work, and brushed off the snow covering his jeans and jacket.

"Oh my gosh! I forgot about them." She flopped back in the snow and made her own angel. She got up, evaluated her angel and Garrett's. "They're perfect together, even though yours is a one-winged angel."

"They aren't the only ones looking right together." Garrett stepped near her, wrapped a gloved hand around one of her mittens, and pulled her close.

She gazed into his eyes. They were a warm-brown color, darkened by his desire for her. She loved the color and promises reflected in the dark depths.

He gazed into her eyes, lost himself in their depths, and hoped he found a home in her love. The strength of the draw pulling him toward Leigh almost scared him, but the comfort enveloping him when he was with her won the battle. He never experienced any sensation such as this before. He needed her near him and with him, forever. Leaning down, he kissed her.

"After the hospital, can we find a hotel room?" His hoarse voice cracked in her ear.

Her desire for him skyrocketed.

"Yes, finding a room is a priority. In fact, while you're in with the doctor, I'll work on securing us a room." She kissed him back.

"Let's get this hospital thing over," He snatched up her hand and led her back to their snowmobiles.

With helmets on and the machine engines racing, Leigh led the way. They were in luck when they arrived at the ER; only a couple of people waited ahead of them.

"May I help you?" The receptionist gave Garrett a swift appraisal and graced him with a big smile.

"I need to be seen for a couple of injuries from the day before yesterday."

"Fill these out and bring them back up. Please ask me for help with any of the questions; I'm happy to assist you." Her smile grew, and she ran a hand through her hair and flipped it back.

"Okay, thanks." Garrett took the forms and clip board, steering Leigh toward some vacant chairs near a window.

"She's flirting with you," Leigh said, as he tackled the forms.

"What?" His head popped up, and he stared at her, brows furrowed, and his head cocked to the left.

"You don't have a clue, do you?" Leigh sat back in astonishment. "And she flirted while I stood right beside you, not very polite."

"Aw, come on, Leigh. She did her job of being helpful and providing customer service." His attention returned to the forms.

"I hope you're better at investigating than you are with observing." She gave a little snort and threw the receptionist a dark glare.

"Wait a minute! Are you jealous?" He confronted her. "You are, aren't you?"

"I'm only…well…possibly…" She shook her head. He quirked one eyebrow up at her and beamed a happy, sexy grin at her. "Fine. Yes, I'm jealous and insulted she flirted with you in front of me. The same as Detective Nichols."

"Detective Nichols? No way. And this receptionist could have been a guy for all I cared. That must tell you something about my devotion to you." He tapped the pen on her nose and went back to the forms.

He walked the completed forms back to the receptionist; she took them with a dazzling smile. As she reviewed the forms, he waited for her reaction when she reached the section where he identified 'gunshot' for his injury. Sure enough, when she read the bold scrawl, her eyes jumped to his.

"We reported the shooting to the police department before coming here, so you can check with them. Oh, and if you can hurry this along, I'd appreciate it. We've had a long day." He flashed a smile in hopes of getting speedier service.

"I'll do what I can." She smiled, took the forms, and disappeared into the back.

Garrett sauntered back toward Leigh and sat in the chair beside her.

"Some may consider flirting with a woman in front of me as reckless. Instead, I say you're shameless!" Leigh shook her head at him, laughter in her eyes.

"I flirted for us. The sooner we're out of here, the sooner we can be naked in a bed." He spoke in a hushed tone. She blushed and smiled.

In short order, a nurse called his name. As soon as he left, Leigh located a phonebook and worked on securing them a hotel room. He walked out when she finalized the reservation.

Standing behind her, he wrapped his arm around her waist and whispered in her ear, "The doctor said I received excellent medical care. My shoulder didn't sustain any muscle damage, no infection anywhere, no concussion, but two cracked ribs."

"After all the attention I enjoyed, I knew your muscles were fine. All those moves you made over the last couple of days wouldn't be possible with a muscle injury." She leaned back against him, savoring the warmth and strength of him being near. "I found us a room at the Aspen Inn on the edge of town. A snowmobile trail runs by the inn, and they have a shed for our machines."

"What are we waiting for?"

Chapter Twelve

In a few minutes, they arrived at the inn and parked the snowmobiles in a shed. Once past the ornate-wooden doors, the inn's charm captivated them. The beauty of the woodwork, a blazing fire in the oversized stone fireplace, the cozy arrangement of furniture, and the old-fashioned front desk complete with a bell and large book style register held them spellbound.

"Good afternoon and welcome to the Aspen Inn. I'm Edna, the owner." An older lady, her gray hair pulled into an old-fashioned chignon, wearing a double-strand pearl necklace and a cream turtleneck sweater over heather-gray slacks, stood near the desk. "Do you have reservations?"

"Yes, I called for a room, Leigh Ramsey?" She smiled at the woman.

"Ah, yes! The honeymoon suite! The Aspen Inn staff are pleased to welcome you, Mr. and Mrs. Ramsey." Walking behind the desk, she grabbed an old-fashioned key. "All guest rooms are upstairs, yours is the last room at the end of the hall. Please join us for a wine and cheese reception at five o'clock tonight, followed by supper at six. Breakfast runs from seven to nine each morning. If I can be of any assistance during your stay, please call on me." She presented the register for them to sign in.

Leigh met Garrett's inquiring glance with a shrug of her shoulders. He reached for a pen, signed them in as G&L Ramsey and received the key for their room.

"Thank you, Edna." The charming smile he flashed at her placed him in the favored guest category. "Let's go, darlin'. We should start working on those important things we discussed earlier." He patted her bottom as they climbed the stairs.

"Not so loud, Garrett!"

"When a couple stays in the honeymoon suite, I imagine most guests and the staff are aware of what happens in the room."

She giggled and raced up the stairs as he chased after her. Edna smiled as they disappeared on the next floor, deciding they acted as cute as they looked.

When they reached the room, Garrett set down her bag, unlocked the door, swung it open, but blocked Leigh's entrance into the room.

"I thought you were in a hurry to be naked in a bed?" She stood with her hands anchored on her hips and a frown marred her lovely face.

"Shouldn't we enter the room properly?"

"Properly? What are you talking about?"

In a smooth move, he gathered her in his arms and kicked her bag into the room. "This is the honeymoon suite, Leigh. Aren't I supposed to carry you over the threshold?"

And he did just that, kicking the door shut before dropping her on the bed. He loomed over her with a devilish grin on his face.

"Prepare yourself, Mrs. Ramsey."

"Please don't call me Mrs. Ramsey, that's my mother."

A sweater, shirt, and bra flew by his head.

"So, if I'm Mr. Ramsey, that makes me your dad?" He faked a shiver. "Creepy thought."

"Don't be ridiculous. As much as I love him, you're a far cry from my dad." She pulled his sweater off, and her attention focused on unbuttoning his shirt. "You are way too overdressed."

He waited until she finished with his buttons, before pulling off his boots and socks. He shrugged out of his shirt, and she attacked his jeans button and zipper. Once his jeans and shorts cleared his hips, she pulled him down to her on the bed.

"Finish removing those; I have work for you." Leigh kissed him, as her hands roamed over his now familiar body.

He pulled his clothes off and kicked them to the floor. Now free of any restrictions, he caught her hands.

"This is backwards, don't you think? Honeymooning before a wedding or a proposal." He joked with her, but deep in his heart he wished the proper order had been followed. He wondered if Leigh suffered similar thoughts.

Caught up in the thrill of the moment, Leigh considered what Garrett said. If he proposed, would she accept? Yes, without hesitation. Rather than express her thoughts, she decided on waiting for him to ask when, and if, he reached the point.

In no time, they lost themselves in kisses and stroking hands. The afternoon passed in a flurry of activities befitting a honeymoon suite, until they lay in each other's arms under the heavy covers of the king-sized bed.

"The intensity is greater each time, don't you agree?" Leigh's whisper broke the stillness of the room.

In answer, he smiled and brushed a lock of hair from her eyes; his hand continued in motion as he stroked her face in a gentle caress. Soft kisses traced across her forehead, her nose, before his lips captured hers in the most sensual kiss she ever experienced. His warm hands traced lazy spirals down her back, reached her bottom, and gave her a soft pat.

She raised her head, gazed at him, and asked, "What was that for?"

"Only a little love tap. We should clean up; the wine thing kicks off soon."

"You're right; wine tasting should be fun." Leigh's smile brightened his soul. She grabbed her bag and ambled into the bathroom.

"Oh, Garrett, come look!" Squealing in delight, she beckoned for him from the doorway. Curious over what sparked her obvious delight, he joined her. She pointed at a huge bathtub set in the corner of the room. "Look! A Jacuzzi tub big enough for both of us!"

She jumped for joy, and he laughed at her excitement over a bathtub.

"No time for exploring, Leigh. Once we're naked in the tub, our focus centers on pleasuring each other for hours on end, so we'd never reach the wine tasting. Sorry, but the tub will have to wait for another day."

"Of course, you're right, but won't bathing be fun when we have the time?" She couldn't hide her exuberance over the tub as her words bubbled out.

He chuckled in response. After a quick shower, he left her in the bathroom and dressed in the main area of the suite.

The honeymoon suite suited them, although their being here before a wedding put the proverbial cart before the horse. A homey quilt, buried under multiple throw pillows, covered a king-sized bed. A chaise lounge, sized for two and designed for cuddling or other more pleasurable activities, stretched out before a generous fireplace. Warm browns decorated the suite. The lack of a TV prompted focusing on each other, ensuring romance. He approved of this place.

After a glance at the time, he checked on Leigh's progress. He discovered her dressed and braced against the counter, applying light makeup. His gazed locked on her reflection in the mirror.

"How long can we stay?" She paused in brushing blush on her cheeks.

"Since my follow-up appointment with the doctors is scheduled for next Monday, we can stay through the weekend."

"I'll enjoy staying here." She caught his eyes in the mirror and smiled at him. "We should buy you some clothes, unless they found your Jeep today."

"Yeah, one pair of socks and underwear don't last long without washing them out daily." He stood behind her and put his hands on her waist. He breathed in her scent, committing the floral fragrance to memory.

"Are you ready?" he murmured, while nuzzling the back of her neck.

"Yes. Shall we go down?"

He offered his arm and escorted her downstairs.

Chapter Thirteen

Edna met them at the bottom of the stairs and showed them the way to the wine and cheese reception.

"Everyone, attention please. Allow me to introduce our newest guests, our newlyweds, Mr. and Mrs. Ramsey! Please introduce yourselves and make them welcome." Edna appeared thrilled at presenting them to the other guests. Applause broke out, followed by shouts of "Congratulations!"

Overwhelmed by the tumultuous enthusiasm and with a touch of apprehension over living a lie, Leigh and Garrett followed Edna into a room similar to a family room. A fire crackled in a stone fireplace, books lined one wall, and windows provided a view of the snow-covered yard. Other guests either sat in comfortable chairs and couches or hovered near the wine bar and cheese trays.

They accepted the congratulations from their fellow guests. At the wine bar they tried a sparkling white wine and moved on to the cheese tray. After selecting their cheeses, they found a quiet corner affording them some privacy.

"Wow, all those people congratulating us. Makes me feel like…a, ah…" Leigh struggled for the proper word as her gaze swept over the other guests.

"Fraud?" Garrett dryly suggested before draining his glass.

"Not quite but close. The good thing is Klein won't find you here if he checks for you at hotels."

"You make a valid point." He looked deep in thought. "You're not wearing a ring; I must be a cheap son of a bitch."

"Dang! I didn't think of rings." She moved a ring from her right hand to her left hand and turned the stone around so only the band showed. "Perfect, but apparently we didn't have a double ring ceremony."

He reached for her left hand and kissed her ring finger. "You're an amazing woman, Leigh Ramsey." The blaze of heat in his eyes sent a thrill through her body.

"More wine, we need more wine." She tossed down the rest of her wine, wrapped her fingers around his hand, and whisked him back to the wine bar. After getting refills, they decided they should meet the other guests.

"Hi, I'm Garrett, and this is my lovely bride, Leigh." He picked the older couple standing by the wine bar to begin their mission of meeting the other guests. Because the inn only had four other rooms, their mission wouldn't take long.

"I'm Bob and this is Grace." He indicated the petite lady standing beside him. "We're out of St. Cloud. I teach history courses at the college, and Grace is retired. What do you two do?"

"I used to work in financial investments, but I'm changing to a career in photography. Garrett served in the Air Force and just accepted a position with the BCA." Leigh beamed at him.

"The Air Force, huh? Did you see any action?" Bob inquired.

"Ah, enough." Garrett's discomfort spiked. "Between a deployment to Iraq and two to Afghanistan, I saw plenty."

"Was the action bad?" Bob didn't catch Garrett's reluctance to expand on his experience, but Grace and Leigh did.

"Please excuse Bob for being so nosy. You can remove the history teacher from the classroom but never away from his love of history, especially recent history." Grace tried redirecting the discussion from Garrett's military service.

"No, his questions are fine, Grace." Garrett flexed his shoulders to reduce the growing tension. "Overall, I spent most of my time on base, but I experienced a few horrendous moments. On my first tour, I served as part of the security force for convoys. Unfortunately, not all convoys made their way through without problems."

"IEDs?" Bob's eagerness for firsthand insight heightened his interest.

"Those and ambushes." Garrett pursed his lips together. "I fought in a few firefights with only minor injuries, but not everyone was as fortunate. A couple of friends didn't make it home."

"I'm sorry, Garrett." Bob's voice cracked. "I appreciate your sharing your experience with me. My students don't understand what's involved in wartime, and when I can add actual testimony, the lesson's meaning increases for them. Thank you for your service."

Garrett nodded and drained his wine glass, hoping the liquid would clear the tightness in his throat.

"Bob, now you put a damper on the whole evening." Grace chastised her husband.

"Don't worry, Grace." Garrett swallowed hard. "We have plenty of evening left for enjoyment."

"Thank you for your graciousness and your service," Grace replied, placing her hand for a moment on Garrett's arm.

"If you'll excuse us, Leigh expressed an abundance of interest in the cheeses." With a firm hand on her elbow, he guided her toward the cheese tray.

Before they reached their intended destination, Leigh pulled him aside.

"Garrett, I'm so sorry for the loss of your friends." She spoke in hushed tones and tears pooled in her eyes. "If you want to talk about your experiences, you do realize I'm here for you?"

"I suffered through a difficult time during those years, Leigh." His voice cracked, and though he faced her, his eyes focused beyond her. "My first deployment happened a few weeks after my parents died. After their funeral, I returned to my base, and my squadron requested volunteers for a deployment. The thought of letting my buddies with families go instead of me with no family didn't make sense, so I volunteered. Deep down, I didn't care if I came back."

"Oh, Garrett." She couldn't say anything else; her heart ached for the pain he experienced by himself.

"I acted like a maniac over there, taking all the dangerous assignments and pushing myself too hard. One day, my flight leader pulled me aside and asked what was up. I tried clamming up and pretending nothing was going on, but he saw through me and wouldn't give up. When I told him the truth, he sent me to visit with our chaplain." He choked out a laugh, but it held no mirth. "I'm sure she thought I embraced a death wish, and maybe I did. As far as I could see, I had no reason for living. I was alone, no family and nothing to go back to." He let out a sigh. "The chaplain guided me and worked with me, until I realized I never finished grieving the loss of my parents. She got me through one of the darkest periods in my life."

"How about your tours to Afghanistan?" Leigh's voice broke, she almost feared what she'd learn from him, but she needed to be aware of his experiences.

"Those came after I joined the OSI and met Chief Martin. He and his wife, Candace, filled the hole in my life created by the death of my parents." After drawing a deep breath, his voice became lighter, and a smile brightened his face. "On my OSI deployments, I had my head on straight. No more acting like a loose cannon."

"Thanks for telling me, Garrett. I wish you hadn't gone through all the loss and confusion, but I'm glad you found people who supported you through your loss and grief. I look forward to meeting them."

"Enough with my morbid past, let's grab some cheese and meet some other people."

With her spirits renewed by him sounding more like the Garrett she loved, she held his hand as they continued toward the cheese tray and other guests.

"Be sure to try the Vermont white cheddar; the flavor is intense." This suggestion came from an older woman standing near a short, stout man. "I'm Diane."

"And I'm her other half, Larry. Did you try the Chardonnay or the Pinot Grigio?" He drained his glass after he asked his question.

"The Pinot, right, darlin'?" Garrett took the last swallow in his glass. Leigh nodded her concurrence. "This is a 'who's your daddy' wine."

Questioning looks and raised eyebrows met his exclamation.

"Sorry." Garrett blushed as he realized they didn't understand him and waited for an explanation. "It's a saying I picked up from a close friend in the Air Force. Mike said it anytime he found something extraordinary. Of course, he had a knack for saying it, and try as I might, I never reproduce his enthusiasm."

They laughed in appreciation of his memory and explanation.

"With such a hearty description, I'll try that one next." Larry left for the wine bar.

"Off he goes, searching for the next best thing!" Diane watched her husband on his quest for the Pinot Grigio, with a smile on her face. "How long ago did you two get married?"

"Last Saturday. We stayed one night in the Cities before heading up here," Leigh squeezed his hand telegraphing the need for him to accept her explanation.

"Did your wedding happen in the Cities?"

"Yes, a small ceremony at my parents' home with a few friends and family." The look in Leigh's eyes told Garrett she described the wedding of her dreams. "Neither of us desired a formal wedding with multiple attendants and groomsmen. Plus, something so big would take too much time to schedule, and I wanted to marry him as soon as possible."

"Small weddings are more personal and intimate. Why spend thousands of dollars on one event, when the money could go toward a spectacular honeymoon or a first house?" Diane shook her head.

"We thought the same thing!" Leigh enjoyed making up their story. "We plan on buying a house."

Larry rejoined them, his wine glass half full. "You're right on the Pinot, Garrett, the flavor is delicious."

"No, Larry. You're supposed to say it's a 'who's your daddy' wine!" Diane corrected her husband. "Well, we wish you much happiness. Larry, we should get ready for dinner."

"You're right, as usual. We'll catch you later." The couple walked away, holding hands.

"They're so sweet," Leigh commented, "and they held hands as they walked away."

She sighed.

"I'll always hold your hand, Leigh." Garrett gathered up one of her hands in demonstration. "What do you say we try a couple of red wines?"

"Sounds fabulous; lead on."

"My pleasure." He escorted her back to the wine bar. "Would you prefer the Cabernet Sauvignon or the Shiraz?"

"The Cabernet, please."

"Here you are." Garrett handed a full glass to her and poured himself a glass of Shiraz. They sipped their wine, enjoying the moment. "You should try this." He offered her his glass.

She sipped from his glass, warmed by the intimacy of a shared glass. "Wow, sensational. Why haven't I tried a Shiraz before?"

"How's the Cabernet?"

"Not nearly as delectable as yours. Here, I'll share mine." As he drank, their eyes met for a moment. Unable to stop the blush from reddening her cheeks, she studied his eyes, and her thoughts fled to their actions from earlier in the afternoon.

"You're blushing! What are you thinking?" he teased her, his eyes blazing as he scrutinized her over his glass of wine.

"I'm certain you can guess what I'm thinking," she whispered to him. "Don't tease, 'cause payback's a bitch."

He chuckled in response to her challenge. "Shall we meet the other four guests before dinner?" At the nod of her head, he refilled his glass with the Shiraz, waited for her to finish her Cabernet, and poured her the Shiraz as well. With his hand on the small of her back, they joined the last of the guests, who sat near the fire.

"Hello. Thought we should stop by and introduce ourselves." Garrett took the lead with the cluster of guests. "This is Leigh, and I'm Garrett."

"I'm Tom, this is my wife, Connie, and our friends, Glenn and Mary."

The ladies waved a hello, and Glenn nodded at them.

"We're pleased to meet y'all," Garrett responded for them both.

"Now you don't sound too Minnesotan. Where are you from, Garrett?" Glenn jumped on the term used by Garrett.

"Sounds can be deceiving because I am from Minnesota. Over the years, I lived elsewhere." Garrett stood with Leigh nestled against his side. He marveled at how well her body fit his.

"The y'all tells me you lived south of the Mason-Dixon." Mary added in her observations. "What took you away from Minnesota?"

"The Air Force. Assignments took me to Texas and most recently Georgia, both well beyond the Mason-Dixon. Guess I picked up a few things while living down South."

"To include the sexiest, occasional accent." Leigh smiled to herself, having been enlightened as to the origins of his occasional accent. Her comment brought a blush to Garrett's cheeks and soft chuckles from the others.

"Did you serve in the Air Force, too, Leigh?" Connie became interested in their story.

"No, not me."

"So, how did you meet?" Tom joined in the questioning. Now all the guests fully engaged in Leigh and Garrett's story.

"Some might say we met by accident, but the how isn't as important as finding true love." Garrett pulled Leigh closer. "I couldn't risk losing her, so I proposed shortly after we met."

"How romantic!" Mary put her hands over her heart, and tears filled her eyes.

"I couldn't say no to him. I mean, look at him! What woman in her right mind would say no?" Leigh turned toward Garrett, and her starry-eyed gaze spoke of her love for him.

He choked on his wine, and the other two men laughed while their wives nodded in agreement with Leigh.

To his relief, Edna stepped into the room and announced, "Dinner is served."

They spent the rest of the evening enjoying the company of the other guests, the atmosphere of the inn, and a delicious dinner. After dinner, they said goodnight to the others and departed for upstairs.

Garrett unlocked their door and led her inside. He held her hand, shut the door, and spun her around to face him, her back against the door. Her blue eyes sparkled at him. His eyes locked on hers, his hands on her shoulders, and he stepped in closer.

"I need you, Leigh, and always will." He growled his confession, the truth reflected in his eyes. His mouth found hers for a devouring kiss before she answered him. Their kiss reflected the need they shared for each other, and the truth threaded within the stories they fabricated throughout the evening.

Her arms went up his shoulders, and she drew him closer. When he lifted her, she wrapped her legs around him. He carried her to the bed and held her close as they kissed.

"Leigh, you are my everything." His voice roughened from his growing passion for her.

She blushed, her hair tumbled over her shoulders, and she smiled at him.

"Marry me." Not surprised by his desire for her finding an outlet, Garrett's voice echoed his resolve to have her as his wife.

Her smile spread until she glowed with happiness.

"Yes, Garrett; I'll marry you."

Her arms went around his neck, and she drew him down with her as she fell backward to the surface of the bed. Their lips met in a soft, gentle kiss. They drew back from each other in surprise when the realization of what transpired hit them at the same time.

"I need a ring," Garrett announced.

Leigh burst out, "I should call my parents!"

They looked at each other and broke into laughter.

"We can shop for rings together, unless you prefer being surprised?"

"I think choosing our rings together would be lovely."

They pulled off their clothes in a hurry, climbed under the covers, and cuddled together. Throughout the evening their love and passion for each other flared to life, and afterward they slept in the afterglow filling their room and their hearts.

Chapter Fourteen

The harsh ring of Leigh's cell phone woke them. Following the sound, she found her phone on the dresser.

"Hello?"

"Miss Ramsey? This is Detective Nichols. Can you reach Mr. Dane for me, please?"

"Yes, of course. One moment." Leigh walked back to the bed and thrust the phone at him. "Detective Nichols for you."

When Garrett sat in the bed and reached for the phone, the covers fell to his waist. The sight of his naked chest drew her back into the bed.

"Dane."

"Mr. Dane, we located your vehicle. A county deputy recalls seeing Klein, but sent him on his way, before calling a wrecker for your Jeep. If you stop by the station, you can take possession of your vehicle."

"Thanks, Detective. We'll be by later today." He ended the call and reached for Leigh. "Come here, you!"

"Did they catch Klein?" She let him pull her close against his warm, hard body.

"No, but they found my Jeep, and we can pick it up today."

"Mmm, how nice." Her fingers traced circles on his chest, and she placed gentle kisses along his jaw. "We can pick it up later, right?"

"Oh, yeah, much later."

Warm hands ran along her body until he cupped her buttocks with his hands. Shifting her beneath him, he rained kisses from her stomach to each breast and continued to her mouth. His roving hands reached between her legs. He slipped one finger inside her and discovered her depths wet for him, so he settled between her legs.

Her moan urged him on. He murmured her name before deepening their kiss. Their hands traveled over each other exploring, teasing, sensing until their passion for each other spiked. Without hesitation, they became one, joined by a swift thrust. The morning exploded with their love for one another as Garrett made slow, deliberate love to her. They peaked together as one.

They lay face-to-face, looking into each other's eyes. A smile crept over Garrett's face as he waited on her return from the climax.

"What?" Leigh wondered what thoughts ran through his head.

"Contemplating what we're doing today—buying our wedding rings!" He kissed her nose. "If we shower now, we can grab breakfast here, collect the Jeep, and begin our shopping."

She stretched catlike and rubbed up against him. "You go first. I'll stay here in bed until you're done. Okay?" She raised the covers to her chin and curled up on one side.

"Sure, a cold shower is necessary after witnessing your seductive stretch." He grimaced as he entered the bathroom.

In moments the sound of water running in the shower reached her. She planned on resting a short while but fell asleep before the shower turned off.

Garrett finished his shower. He studied his whiskered face in the mirror. Years of military life conditioned him to prefer being clean-shaven; only a few times in his career did he go unshaven. His first BCA assignment required a grubby appearance, but hopefully not for long. Ending his musings, he headed to the other room. He pulled up short in the doorway when his eyes fell on Leigh asleep in the bed with the covers down around her waist.

"Damned if I suffer through another cold shower." He tore his eyes from her glorious body and searched for his clothes. "Leigh! Wake up!"

She stirred but didn't wake.

"Leigh! I'm ready for breakfast." He dressed and risked walking near the bed. "Wake up, darlin', rise and shine."

She stretched again and blinked her eyes open. She grinned up at him.

"I dreamed of our true honeymoon."

"Did your dream differ much from our pretend one?"

"Not much, except you weren't hungry for breakfast." She looked at him in a sly and devious manner before she left the comfortable bed and wandered around the room picking up items of clothing.

Even though he recognized she displayed her nakedness for his benefit or rather his detriment, she still drove him to distraction.

"Leigh, please move your pretty, naked self into the bathroom," he growled at her.

"Or what, Garrett?" She stopped gathering her things, dropped her clothes to the floor, put her hands on her hips, and stared at him.

"This."

She didn't expect the speed he showed as he crossed the room, pulled her into his arms, spun her around, and marched her into the bathroom.

"Time you got ready for the day. Hurry up, so we can eat breakfast here at the inn." As he closed the door behind him, a hot breath escaped. He marveled at the control he somehow mustered to keep from tossing her back in bed and joining her.

Leigh finished her shower shy of twenty minutes. She stumbled out of the bathroom and began donning her clothes.

Diverting his eyes away from her glorious body, he wondered if he'd ever reach the point of not itching to wrap his arms around her and to make love with her whenever he saw her naked. He hoped the time never came.

***

They walked downstairs holding hands. On the last couple of steps, they overheard Edna answering a call.

"This is the Aspen Inn. How may I help you?" A long pause before she continued. "I'm sorry, but we don't show a Mr. Dane staying with us. If you're concerned over your brother, you should check with the police department. Hello, sir? Sir? How strange." She hung up the phone and nodded in their direction as Garrett and Leigh walked toward the dining room.

"Did you hear her?" Leigh whispered.

"Yeah."

"What should we do? Do you think the caller was Klein?"

"I'm certain Klein's the only person searching for me. If you loan me your cell phone, I'll call Detective Nichols. She should be able to check on the inn's incoming calls and trace back to his phone or wherever he called from."

"Sure, here. Should we go back to the room for added privacy?"

"Yeah, our room is the right place for making this call."

They scooted back up the stairs. As soon as they entered their room, Garrett placed the call.

"Detective Nichols, this is Garrett Dane."

"Mr. Dane, what can I do for you?"

"We're staying at the Aspen Inn, and we overheard the owner receive a call from someone we believe is Klein."

"What makes you think the caller was Klein?" Skepticism dripped from her tone.

"The caller asked for a Mr. Dane. I don't believe in coincidences." Garrett paced as he spoke, the hand not holding the phone formed a clenched fist and beat against his leg. "The caller claimed to be my brother." The pacing stopped. "I don't have a brother, Detective."

"Oh. I'll see what I can find out," she promised before hanging up.

"She'll check into the call. Let's eat breakfast while she works the problem." Garrett's brusque tone reflected his agitation. He handed her phone back.

"She didn't say anything else?" Leigh followed him out the door.

"No, nothing else. When we stop for my Jeep, we'll check on what she's found out." Garrett reached his hand back for her.

"Then it has to be enough for now." Leigh put a hand in his and caught up to him. "You're having more than peanut butter toast this morning, aren't you?"

"Absolutely!" His dazzling smile made her weak in the knees. "I caught a whiff of breakfast, and it smells delicious!"

They got downstairs and entered the dining room. Only two other guests were eating breakfast.

"Morning, Tom, Connie," Garrett greeted them as he and Leigh walked through the buffet line.

"Hey! Good morning. We didn't expect an appearance by you two for a few days, what with this being your honeymoon," Tom joked, and Connie jabbed him in the side.

"Hush. You'll embarrass them," Connie scolded her husband.

Tom ignored her, chuckled, and winked at Garrett.

"We worked up an appetite with all our honeymoon activity," Leigh said with a laugh.

"And we need sustenance to keep up our strength for further honeymoon activity," Garrett added as he selected two plates for them.

"You'll regret encouraging him." Connie shook her head at them, but she smiled. "What's on your schedule for today?"

"We're picking up a vehicle and doing some shopping," Garrett replied. He held the plates as Leigh piled on food.

"Did you hear him, Tom?" Connie poked her husband again. "He's shopping with his wife!"

"Garrett, you're making life difficult for all of us other husbands. The guys and I will teach you the ropes of being a proper husband," Tom threatened.

"You leave him be. I love him exactly as he is." Leigh turned toward Tom and shot him a playful glare.

"You tell him, Leigh." Connie threw in her support for Leigh, while Garrett wisely remained quiet.

They joined the couple for an amiable breakfast. When finished, they said their farewells and went to their room in preparation for the ride downtown. All bundled up, they left the warmth of the inn for their snowmobiles in the shed.

"Why don't we drive one snowmobile this morning since I'll pick up my Jeep," Garrett suggested as they reached for their helmets.

"I agree. We'll need to sort out how we return the sleds to the cabin once you retrieve your Jeep." Leigh got on her sled and tapped the seat behind her, inviting Garrett to join her.

"The Jeep has a hitch; we can ask about renting or borrowing a trailer to haul them back." He settled behind her.

"We'll ask Edna if she's aware of a trailer available to borrow. Are you set?" Garrett's hands settled around her waist in answer to her question, so she took off for the police station.

Chapter Fifteen

After parking the snowmobile near the police station, they removed their helmets and walked inside. Garrett asked for Detective Nichols, and they waited for her to appear.

"Mr. Dane." Detective Nichols stepped out from behind the locked door. She reached Garrett and shook his hand. A mere nod of her head sufficed as her cool acknowledgment of Leigh. "Come with me, and I'll find the paperwork you need to get your vehicle out of the lot behind this building. Also, I can share some information on Klein."

"Great. We're anxious to hear whatever you learned." He grasped Leigh's hand and drew her close.

A slight frown crossed the detective's face, but she didn't say anything.

Leigh didn't miss the frown and appreciated how Garrett automatically included her.

They walked to Detective Nichols' office and took the same chairs as before. Sunlight beamed through a window behind the detective's back and blinded Leigh as she sat lower than Garrett.

"Here's the paperwork for your vehicle. No apparent damage: we checked under the snow, too. As I said, the county towed your Jeep in." She handed Garrett the papers. "I tracked the call placed to the inn. If Klein made the call, he's in the local area. By checking with other hotels in the area, we learned they all received similar calls from someone claiming to be a brother searching for you. Because you used your own name at the hospital, I also checked with them. I requested a flag be added to your record, so they'll contact me if any inquiries regarding you are received. Once the night shift reports for duty, I'll check with them. Hopefully, no one bought into his sob story and offered any information."

"I appreciate your thoroughness, thank you." Impressed with her work, Garrett complimented Detective Nichols. "I follow up with the doctor on Monday, so we're staying in town. We'll keep an eye out for Klein while we're here."

"Because of the Georgia plates on your Jeep, you should reconsider picking it up. Those plates stand out in this area. If Klein catches sight of your vehicle, he'll be after you in a heartbeat."

"True, so we needn't hurry to pick it up?"

"No. I'll tag your vehicle as remaining for a few days due to an ongoing case." She smiled at him and ran a hand through her hair and down the front of her suit.

Flirting again, Leigh fumed, while Garrett remained oblivious to the detective's attempt at capturing his interest.

"I do need my bag and cell phone from the Jeep."

"Of course. Why don't I ask someone to retrieve those items for you? In case Klein is watching from nearby?"

The woman's sweet tone grated on Leigh's nerves.

The detective made a quick call. "There, all done. An officer will bring in your things."

Not missing the stiffening of Leigh's body beside him nor her narrowed eyes and grim set to her lips, Garrett recognized Leigh's growing resentment toward Detective Nichols. The ability of being aware of her moods after such a short period amazed him. Unsure of the basis for her changing mood, he sensed he should remove her from this office and soon.

"We're distracting you from your work, so we'll wait for my things out front. Thank you for all you've done, and please keep us posted on any developments," Garrett said in hopes of departing the office before Leigh exploded.

He stood and offered his hand to Detective Nichols. She stood, shook his hand, and ignored Leigh. With a firm hand on Leigh's back, he herded her through the door with a gentle push.

His use of inclusive terms when talking with the detective made Leigh ecstatic. As inexplicable as it seemed, they existed as a couple in his mind, and the realization relaxed her. The detective might be making a play for him, but he had no interest in her. Leigh couldn't stop smiling.

"You look like the proverbial 'cat that ate the canary.' What's up?" Garrett quizzed her as they sat in the front waiting area.

"You included me when you talked with her, no matter how much she flirted with you." She planted a hasty kiss on his cheek.

"You're way too easy to please. Guess I'm a lucky guy." Although he didn't have a clue about flirting actions by Detective Nichols, his reaction brought Leigh happiness, so he achieved his new mission in life—keeping her happy.

"Your words and actions are a huge thing. My former boyfriend would never do what you did; he always flirted back. On occasion, he accepted what some women offered." A note of sadness entered her voice as she spoke. "At first, I never suspected anything, but when I figured out what he was doing…" her voice cracked. "Well, let's say I didn't appreciate his deception and betrayal. Months later I still found dating impossible; the thought of putting myself in a vulnerable position again hurt too much." Her eyes filled with tears for the remembered hurt.

"He was a fool. For my sake I'm grateful for his foolishness, but I hate how much he hurt you." Garrett leaned over and kissed her, demonstrating his deep feelings for her.

The desk sergeant smiled at them as he called out, "No hanky-panky in our waiting area! You two should get a room."

They both blushed as they settled back in their chairs. Garrett kept hold of her hand, running his thumb slowly across her palm. Within five minutes, an officer appeared and handed over Garrett's bag and cell phone. After thanking the officer, they walked out into the freezing Minnesota winter.

"I forgot how cold a day can be when the sun shines bright; the day appears warmer than the temperature reads." Leigh stood by the snowmobile and stamped her feet.

"Sun dogs were out yesterday, so I knew today would be colder," Garrett mentioned as he strapped down his bag.

"Sun dogs?"

"Yeah, those partial rainbows on either side of the sun. When I was little, my mom told me about them. Although I have no idea how scientific any of this is, they always provided accurate forecasts for me."

"Are they out today?"

He squinted at the sun. "Yes, they are. See the short rainbows on either side of the sun? Those are sun dogs." His hands locked over her hips and turned her in the right direction, helping her locate them.

"I never noticed them before. You are a wealth of knowledge."

"Wait until I tell you what the size of a muskrat house forecasts." He dazzled her with a smile and a wink before he pulled on his helmet. "Let's go and begin our ring shopping."

Leigh settled on the snowmobile in front of him, thrilled at the touch of his strong hands on her waist. Considering the location of the local jewelry store, she figured out the route they should ride. The snowmobile kicked up a trail of snow as they left the station.

***

Once at the jewelry store, they gazed at the rings displayed in the windows.

"What can you afford, Garrett?" Leigh gazed at the beautiful rings; astonishment hit her after seeing the hefty price tags on them.

"Whatever you like. Don't worry about the price." He flashed a lopsided grin.

"But some of those prices are astronomical! We should be reasonable about this rather than going into debt with the rings." Leigh reminded herself they needed a discussion of finances; with plans for buying a house, they should spend wisely. "Do you know anything we should consider when shopping for a diamond?"

"Not too much, enough to act as a jewelry salesman." At her confused expression, he explained further. "Had an undercover job in a base exchange once to catch a thief. With diamonds, you consider the four C's: cut, clarity, color, and carat, if I remember right."

"Four C's, huh?"

"Yup, it's all about the diamond. Oh, I forgot to mention something to you. I prefer a double ring ceremony, so I need to be sized for a band." Garrett surprised her as he opened the door and escorted her inside the store. "If you're marked as taken, so am I."

A broad smile conveyed her happiness with his words and the sentiment behind them.

"Welcome. How may I assist you today?" A middle-aged man dressed in a dark-blue suit with a coordinated shirt and tie greeted them.

"We're here to buy some rings." Garrett gathered Leigh into his arms. Their smiles told the salesman what type of rings.

"I'm guessing we're talking engagement and wedding rings. Are you having a double ring ceremony?"

"Yes, sir, we are," Garrett responded.

"The trio sets are over here, if you prefer, they all match. We offer a choice of yellow gold, white gold, silver, and platinum metals for the bands, and a variety of cuts and colors for the diamonds. Do you have a preference?" The salesman walked them to one section of the counter. He directed a smile at Leigh as he asked, and she responded with a shake of her head. "Why don't I leave you with these to consider in private? Take note of any catching your eye. I'll return in a few minutes." He gave them privacy for looking at the various ring sets.

"Wow! They're all so beautiful. This won't be easy." Leigh looked at all the rings and shook her head. "I'm not sure where we should begin."

"How 'bout with the diamond? Do you prefer a single diamond or a ring with multiple diamonds?" Garrett asked, while they gazed at the selection of rings.

"A single diamond, the multiple diamonds are too gaudy."

"What size of diamond?"

"I never cared for the over-sized ones. Whenever I saw women with a huge rock on their fingers, I wondered why they got one that size. If I wore a large one, I'd be afraid of catching the diamond on something and losing the stone or my finger."

Garrett chuckled at her words. "I must admit I wondered about the larger diamond rings myself. Always figured the stones must be cemented in place to keep from being lost. So, we go with a smaller solitaire. What color for the band?"

"I prefer the silver or platinum, anything but yellow gold."

"I can live with those choices, so we've narrowed the selection down a bit. Well done!" He rewarded her with a kiss.

The salesman took their kiss as a sign of decision, so he reappeared. "Can I pull out anything for you to try?"

"Yes, let's try those two, please." Leigh pointed out two sets.

"Excellent choices." The salesman set the selections on the glass before them.

Garrett picked up his favorite of the two. "Let's check out this one first."

Leigh gave him her left hand. He removed her other ring and slipped the engagement ring on her finger.

"Oh my! This ring is gorgeous. What do you think?" She held out her hand and admired the ring.

"Looks gorgeous to me."

A glance at Garrett showed his attention wasn't on the ring but locked on her. Her cheeks burned. Did the temperature go up in here?

"The ring is nice, too," Garrett added.

The salesman smiled and a short chuckle escaped him. "Why not try on the other one now?"

Leigh pulled off the first ring, but her eyes remained focused on the simple, yet elegant ring laying on the velvet lined tray. She realized no ring would be a better one. She studied the second ring as Garrett slipped it on her finger. The larger stone of the second ring didn't look quite the same as the first ring.

"I prefer the first ring over the second." She took off the second one and reached for the first set. "We should try the wedding bands, too. What do you think of this one?" She held up the man's ring for his inspection.

"Only one way we can reach a decision." He extended his left hand to her, and she slid the ring over a knuckle to the base of his finger.

"Is the band too small?" she asked.

"The size is perfect." His eyes focused on her again. "A wider one would bother me."

She raised her eyes and met his; the heat of his gaze warmed her to her toes. How did one look from him make her so flushed and ready to jump in bed with him? She decided they should end this and return to their room. "This is the set we'll buy."

She smiled at Garrett, and his desire for her threatened to burst free of any confines. He never expected watching Leigh try on rings would excite him, but the growing bulge in his jeans proved otherwise. Maybe the cold outside would cool him off, but he doubted the weather offered any relief. His blood ran hot with need when Leigh was near him. He hoped her desires would fall in line with his, and a return to the inn happened as soon as they finished here.

"I'll need to measure for your ring sizes and write this up." The salesman busied himself with the tasks at hand. "You're in luck. This set is in stock, so your rings could be ready for you in a day or two, no later than Monday. Does the timing work for you?"

"Perfect," Garrett replied, remembering his doctor's appointment fell on the same day.

"Here's your receipt and congratulations!"

"Thank you," Leigh and Garrett answered together.

Garrett stuffed the receipt in a pocket. The reality of the purchase hit him hard as he grasped Leigh's mittened hand and walked her out of the store. He proposed marriage, and she accepted. Soon they'd embark on their life together in Brainerd. His dream of loving someone and sharing his life with someone was on the verge of coming true. The thought exhilarated him, but one thing from his past needed wrapping up before they could safely begin their life together. Klein must be caught; otherwise, he presented a constant threat to their happiness.

Memories of the last few days bombarded her. She loved Garrett and soon a new chapter of her life began, one with him in it. The thought of being married to him intoxicated her. She never believed she fostered a sexy persona, but Garrett not only nurtured her sexual nature but unleashed an unlimited wanton behavior. Mere thoughts of their previous activities, of all the wonderful things they did with and to each other, brought on a quiver of expectation. Returning to the inn as soon as possible became a priority.

"Since we don't have anything else for us to do, why not head back to the inn and our room?" She straddled the snowmobile, wishing she straddled him instead of the cold machine.

"Sounds like a plan, let's go." Garrett sat behind her and drew her against him, certain she discovered how badly he favored returning to their room.

"Ooh!" A rigid erection pressed against her. "I feel reaching our room is necessary for both of us."

"Ya think? Put this machine in high gear, darlin'. Once we're in our room, we celebrate."

They took off in a blast of snow and exhaust.

Chapter Sixteen

As they entered the Aspen Inn, Edna greeted them. "Good afternoon. Looks as though you two need warming up."

"You're right, Edna, it's freezing outside." Leigh pulled off her mittens and blew on her hands, trying to warm them.

"Does the fireplace in our room work?" Garrett asked, as he pulled off his gloves and hat.

"It does. I'll send up firewood and kindling for you." Edna reached for the phone.

"Would you also send up some champagne or sparkling wine? We're doing some private celebrating," Garrett explained. He pulled Leigh into his arms and held her close.

She wondered if he did this because he loved her or because he didn't want Edna viewing the bulge in the front of his jeans, proof of how they would celebrate. Deciding his reason didn't matter, she leaned into him and delighted in the warmth radiating from his body.

"I'll prepare something a bit extravagant for your celebration."

"Perfect!" Leigh beamed at Edna.

"I'll send everything up shortly."

"Thank you," Garrett said as he turned them both toward the stairway.

They scrambled up the stairs and rushed down the hall to their room. At the door, Garrett pulled Leigh into his arms for a mind-numbing kiss.

She pulled back and asked, "Where's the key?" She nearly missed his response of, "In my front pocket," before his lips descended on hers again.

His kiss demanded her full attention. She ran her hands over the front of his jeans in search of the key. He moaned as her hands grazed his erection. Pulling her closer, he ground into her. Her eyes closed, and thoughts of the key disappeared when his hands found her breasts. She ran her tongue along his lips and gained easy access to his mouth. They stood before their door lost in each other's kiss. A not-so-subtle clearing of a throat brought them to their senses.

"Excuse me, but Edna asked me to bring you some firewood." The young man carried a bundle of wood slung over his shoulder and a deep red flush of embarrassment on his face.

"Sorry, we got carried away." Garrett retrieved the room key and unlocked the door. Leigh went in and Garrett held the door open for the young man. He pulled out his wallet and handed over a ten-dollar tip.

"Gee, thanks." The young man pocketed the money and whistled his way down the hall.

"Are you okay?" Garrett shut the door and turned to Leigh, who no longer wore her jacket and boots. "I didn't intend on ravishing you in the hallway. Proper ravishing should only happen in private and preferably in our room, but you looked so damn hot I couldn't stop myself."

"I'm fine, all the while I worried you might be in pain or would burst out of your jeans." Leigh giggled and crossed over to him. She threw her arms around his neck, rose on her toes, and trailed soft kisses to his lips. "Because drinks and whatever Edna throws together for us are coming up, no more for you. I refuse to be caught naked in front of the fire when our order's delivered."

"Believe me, I'd toss a quilt over you," Garrett offered. His eyes turned a darker brown. "Does the Jacuzzi tub play into our plans for this afternoon?"

"How astute of you. I'll prepare things in the bathroom, while you build a fire and wait on our stuff." Leigh raced into the bathroom and closed the door.

"You are aware how predictable you can be, right?" Garrett called after her. He laughed outright at her response of "Whatever."

Flames devoured the wood in the fireplace by the time a knock on their door announced the arrival of celebratory food and drink. He opened the door and found Edna with a cart.

"Hello. I selected a variety of items for you, and I see the firewood arrived." She rolled in the cart and turned to him. "I hope you find this meets your needs. Enjoy your afternoon and evening." She turned to leave the room.

Garrett reached for his wallet, and she shook a hand at him. "No tip is necessary; this is my pleasure. You are the sweetest couple who stayed here in a long time."

"Thank you so much, Edna. We're enjoying our time here."

"I always hope our newlyweds experience a successful beginning at the Aspen Inn, and we hold a memorable place in their happily-ever-after."

"You and your inn provided us a safe beginning and more. Thanks again."

He closed the door behind her and circled the cart. What he found overwhelmed him. Edna brought up chilled champagne with crystal flutes, a selection of cheese and crackers, boiled shrimp, pickled herring, smoked oysters, and ham wrapped around asparagus and cheese. A selection of mini cheesecakes as well as strawberries dipped in dark chocolate served as dessert. They would eat well.

He locked the door, pulled off his boots, and entered the bathroom. The jets in the tub rumbled, and Leigh lounged neck deep in the water with her eyes closed.

"I need you stripped and in here with me." The love and passion she held for him reflected in her now opened eyes.

"Yes, ma'am." He tossed her a salute and attacked his shirt and sweater. They came off over his head and ended in a heap. His hands moved to his jeans, undid the button, and drew the zipper down in slow motion.

"Enough already! Pull off your jeans and join me in here!"

"This is supposed to be a slow striptease; I thought my actions might escalate your expectations."

"Escalate your expectations with these." She rose out of the water, gifting him with a clear view of her holding glistening wet breasts, droplets of water hanging off each rosy tipped nipple.

"I'll see those and raise you this." He pushed everything down and freed his erection from his confining jeans.

"Come here." When he stepped closer, her hand clasped around his hardened flesh. "No way are you wasting this."

He smiled at her and dropped a kiss on her forehead. "Let me pull off my socks before you drag me in."

"Hurry up, mister." She let go of him and settled back under the water.

He found the hot water soothing, as his body sank lower into the deep water. The jets bubbled and forced water in various directions. He closed his eyes and reached for Leigh. She slid over and sat in front of him, relaxing against his chest.

"You feel amazing." Garrett ran his hands over her body, settling on her breasts. He fondled them, circling each nipple, and took each between a thumb and forefinger. He rolled and pulled on them.

Leigh remained reclined against him. She moaned. She whimpered. When she rubbed against him, he groaned.

He ran one hand down her side until he reached the thigh. His hand moved across the thigh to the apex of her legs. His fingers played in her wet curls before one finger pressed inside her.

She gasped with pleasure. Reaching behind her, she found him rock hard, so she stroked the length of his erection and imprisoned the hard flesh in a firm grasp.

With his eyes closed, a variety of feelings bombarded his senses: her hand stroking him, his finger within her warm moistness, her muscles strong around his finger, and his other hand massaging one of her soft, full breasts. Life couldn't get any better, or could it?

"Leigh, can you rise up a little and scoot forward."

"Hmm?" Incoherent, Leigh tried responding. "What?" Lost in her own world of sensations, what Garrett asked of her hadn't translated into motion.

"Raise a little and scoot forward, so I can...yes, perfect." Leigh shifted as he requested. He replaced his finger with his erection and pressed into her. They both adopted a slow up and down motion.

"Garrett. Oh my gosh!" Leigh hovered on the edge. She moved over him. "I...I...oh my..." She peaked and her cries echoed in the bathroom.

Garrett followed her with his own release and held her tight. He kissed the nape of her neck.

"Leigh, I love you so much." His declaration came as a mere whisper in her ear.

She snuggled into his chest, letting the water flow around her.

They stayed in the tub until the water cooled. Garrett turned off the jets and got out first. He wrapped one fluffy towel around his waist and held out another for Leigh.

"Here you go." As she rose out of the water, her beauty struck him again. He wrapped the towel around her and lifted her out of the tub. "Dry off and put something on. We can indulge in the feast Edna brought up and enjoy the fire."

She nodded her agreement.

After a quick rummage through his bag, he located flannel pajama bottoms and a thermal Henley. A glance at Leigh rewarded him with a view of her magnificent bare body. Mesmerized at the sight, he stared as a flannel nightshirt caressed her curves and floated in place. The sight and associated memories drew out a moan before he disappeared into the other room.

He snatched a colorful quilt off a rack and draped it over the chaise lounge before the fire. After he parked the cart within reach of the chaise lounge, he wrestled with the champagne. The cork popped out of the bottle, as Leigh sashayed past him. A single braid slipped over one shoulder and brushed against a breast as she walked. The scent of lily of the valley tickled his nose.

"Wow. This looks delicious! Edna outdid herself." She accepted a glass from him and nibbled on some cheese.

"She told me we are a sweet couple. She brought this up herself and wouldn't accept a tip." He raised his glass to hers. "To us, the sweetest couple to ever defraud the Aspen Inn."

"Stop calling us frauds!" She swatted his arm. "We didn't plot for this to happen. Edna assumed we were newlyweds, and we let her run with the assumption. The only room available in this entire town was a honeymoon suite, so we didn't cause this situation, we accepted the inevitable. Mmm, the shrimp are delicious. Ooh, herring! I love pickled herring." She piled food on one plate, passed it to him, and made up one for herself.

"Thanks. I thought we could sit together, devour a little food and drink, do some cuddling, and perhaps some talking. We'll be comfortable in front of the fire." He grinned and patted the space beside him.

Impossible to decline such a charming invitation, she joined him on the chaise lounge. "This is rather comfy." She smiled at him and settled in close to him, setting her plate on his stomach.

"Hey! I'm not a coffee table."

"No, but you'll do." She drank some of her champagne and set the glass on the cart.

They ate and drank in companionable quiet for a few minutes.

"I enjoyed today."

He imagined a smile in her voice. "So did I, in fact, today turned out being one of my best days ever."

His comment thrilled her, especially hearing she was part of his best day ever. She munched on the food from her plate as she replayed his words in her head. Her love for him continued growing as he shared insights of his life with her.

"This food is delectable. Are you still hungry?" she asked.

"I am. Are you serving?"

"Sure." She loaded up his plate and topped off their glasses with champagne.

"Are you truly happy with your engagement ring? The stone is small." Worried she chose a smaller diamond because of the cost, Garrett pressed her regarding their choice of rings.

"Yes, I love the ring, the style suits me. The moment you put it on my finger, I decided this would be the one for me."

"As long as you're sure; I can afford what we spent today and more."

She caressed his face. "I'm sure."

When he kissed her, she responded and kissed him back. He draped an arm around her and pulled her closer. He loved the touch of her beside him. Her warmth permeated into his soul. The threat presented by Klein's existence needed to be eliminated before their life together moved forward. The plan he devised presented a risk to him, so he assumed Leigh wouldn't agree with it.

"You still need to tell your folks about us. How will they receive the news?" He stared into the flames, absentmindedly running his hand over her shoulders.

"I intended to call them when we got back to our room, but we got busy, and I forgot. They'll be surprised because I haven't been dating anyone. I'm sure they'll insist on coming up right away, so they can meet you."

"Check me out, and determine whether I meet their qualifications before I marry their daughter?"

"For sure. And to verify I didn't take leave of my senses. Accepting a marriage proposal after having met you a few days prior is not something they would expect of me. They'll need to satisfy any doubts by observing I'm not being forced into this engagement and I'm not pregnant. I'm not sure how they'll do the latter one unless they insist on my peeing on a test thingy."

"The thought of you pregnant with my baby takes my breath away." When she stared at him, he blushed beneath the scruff of whiskers covering his cheeks. "Of course, babies shouldn't arrive right away. We need time for us first, but my dream family does include children. You do want children, don't you?" He held his breath waiting for her answer.

She smiled at him. "Yes, my dream family includes two or three children: the right size for a family. The boys would play football and hockey. The girls would play basketball or hockey. They would all play golf and play a musical instrument."

"Sounds as though we'll be busy driving them back and forth from activities."

"Once the oldest gets their license, they can chauffeur the younger ones." A faraway focus in her eyes held the dream of their future family.

"We never discussed religion. The denomination of church I grew up in is the United Church of Christ. Are you a member of a church?" He realized how little he knew of her, but he believed they would live a successful life together. He trusted his gut instincts, and they told him a relationship with Leigh would work.

"I'm embarrassed to admit the last time I attended church was years ago. Mom and Dad attend a Methodist church near them but on an irregular basis. Your church isn't fanatical, is it?"

He laughed. "No. A minister described the church to me one time as the denomination unafraid of pushing the envelope on current issues. Other churches wait on the results before deciding whether to follow their lead. I admire the church for its attitude. It wouldn't be deemed fanatical, but the church isn't static or stuck in the Dark Ages either, and Brainerd has one."

"Your church sounds acceptable; let's attend a service together after we settle in. We'll need to decide on who should perform the wedding ceremony for us. Any ideas?"

"Anyone able to marry us quickly and legally. Your parents' minister or a justice of the peace works for me."

"Before we marry, we must decide on many things for the wedding and reception." Her voice trailed off as she realized for the second time how little she knew of him and his preferences. "I don't know what music you listen to, what movies you prefer, if you read books, or what kind of wedding you want."

"Country, action and drama, I do, and whatever you want." He drew her closer and kissed her furrowed brow. At her puzzlement, he elaborated. "I listen to country music. I prefer action movies and dramas. I do read books, mostly mystery-thrillers; I'm currently hooked on books by Stuart MacBride and John Sandford. And, whatever kind of wedding you want, will suit me. What are your preferences?"

By turning her own questions back on her, he caught her by surprise.

"Jazz and classical music, dramas and chick flicks, and lately, I'm reading romances and books on photography techniques. My preference is for a small wedding, one like what I described to Diane and Larry the other night. Well, now we know each other so much better, my parents shouldn't object to us getting married so soon after meeting. Once my parents are informed, I'll call my friend, Deb, and ask if she'll be my maid of honor. She's my best friend, and the one who suggested I pursue my love of photography as a career. Who would you ask to be your best man?"

"I can check with Matt, my buddy back in Georgia, and ask if he's available. If he can't be here, do you think your brother would stand up with me? Is a best man required?"

"You should have a best man, if only to help support you at the altar. I'm certain my brother would be honored to be your best man, but a friend would be better. I look forward to meeting your friend and hope he can join us on our wedding day."

"Before we call our friends, we should decide on a date for the wedding, so people can work on their schedules. You should call your parents, so we can move forward with our planning."

"I'm nervous to call them. They'll ask so many questions, such as who you are, your background, and how we met. What if I can't answer them?"

He hugged her closer. "Darlin', the two most important things are you love me, and I love you. The rest will fall into place."

"You honestly believe our plans will work out?"

"I do. Call your parents tonight and get the surprise of our engagement over. The longer you put off calling, the greater the difficulty in telling them."

"You're right, but I thought this night would end in a more pleasurable way." She got up and grabbed her cell phone.

"The night's not over yet."

The promise in his voice and his spoken words thrilled her; the same promise radiated in his eyes as they darkened.

"Stay close, please? For moral support?" With a punch of the screen, the phone speed dialed her parents.

Chapter Seventeen

"It's ringing."

Leigh paced in front of the fire.

Garrett couldn't tear his eyes away from her. Her nightshirt stopped at mid-thigh, allowing him a thorough examination of her long, slender legs. The low-cut neckline afforded him a tantalizing view of creamy breasts. Due to the slight chill in the room, peaked nipples pressed against the material. Nipples weren't the only thing hardening in the room. A rearrangement of the quilt hid his physical condition from her, so no distractions drew her focus off the important phone call. Whenever she glanced at him, he smiled his encouragement for her.

"Hello, Mom? Yeah, it's me."

"Leigh, we've been worried, what with the blizzard and all."

"No reason to worry, Mom, I didn't experience any problems. In fact, something incredible and unexpected happened."

"What? Something good or bad?"

"Something better than good, Mom." She beamed at Garrett, and his nod of encouragement relaxed her a trifle.

"You and David are back together?" Of course, her mom would jump to an improbable conclusion.

The pacing stopped and Leigh glared at her phone.

Garrett recognized the instantaneous tension in her entire body. Whatever her mom said didn't sit well with her. A tight constricting in his gut spoke volumes, the call had taken a turn for the worse.

"No, Mom, David and I are not back together and never will be." Leigh spit out the words through clenched teeth.

Wanting to comfort her, Garrett shifted away from the chaise lounge, but Leigh's eyes met his. She shook her head and waved him down. With emotions rolling through him, he sat but ached to hold her in his arms.

"Mom, something's come up and I need to go. I'll call back later. Love you." With an abrupt end to the call, she turned off her phone and tossed it on a table. "Sorry, but the last thing I expected was her assuming I returned to my ex-boyfriend."

"No apology needed for her assumptions; she took you by surprise. Guess my focus will be on winning her over."

"You'll do fine. I'll call back in a half hour and try again. This time I'll be sure Dad's on the line, too. I should explain what happened...well, at least try to explain. The David she brought up is my ex-boyfriend, David Walker. Remember I told you how my mom adored my ex-boyfriend?"

A chill ran down his spine, as Garrett nodded. His conviction of everything being all right appeared premature. Damn!

Leigh continued with her story. "Well, Mom adored him, and he's the son of her best friend. David represented everything Mom expected for my future: money, prestige, power, and a place in the Minneapolis-St. Paul society. She never understood my decision to break off our two-year relationship. I explained the hurt and humiliation I suffered over the last year of our relationship, but Mom didn't believe my stories of David's sexual dalliances, lies, and deceit. She wouldn't accept how despicable her best friend's son acted toward her daughter. If she believes he's in my future, she's delusional. *Argh*!"

She flopped back down on the chaise lounge and drew the quilt over them. Strong arms wrapped around her, as she cuddled closer into him. He handed her glass back to her, and she took a long swallow.

"Did your dad believe you regarding David?" Garrett needed additional information from her in support of his quest to win over her parents.

"Yes, and he supported my decision to break up with David. But he never convinced Mom of David's faults. I believe Dad tolerated David for my sake while we dated." She devoured a chocolate dipped strawberry. "I'm sure he'll be fond of you because of how you treat me. You're different from David in all the important areas, by the way."

"Sounds promising. How long did you know David?"

"In a way we grew up together because our parents are best friends. He attended an out-of-state medical school and completed his residency away from home. Upon returning with his medical license, he joined his father's medical practice, and we began dating." She hated the look of hopelessness in Garrett's eyes, but she plunged on with her story. "Our friends and family expected we'd marry, but as marriage expectations increased among those around us, I found myself doubting our relationship's future success. The signs of his lies and indiscretions couldn't be ignored any longer, nor his tendency of taking me for granted. I confronted him with all the lies I uncovered and the many signs of his relationships with other women." She drew in a deep breath before continuing. "He threw all my charges back at me and blamed me for his indiscretions. Because I didn't meet his sexual needs, he looked elsewhere. His words and actions hurt me deeply and nearly destroyed my self-confidence as a woman."

Garrett's eyes ignited into icy-blue flames. If he ever got his hands on the guy who inflicted such pain and injury on Leigh through his selfish behavior, no telling what might happen. He scooped her into a warm embrace and absorbed her body's tremors as she fought her tears.

"He was an idiot, Leigh, with no concept of the love and compassion he tossed aside. For you, I'll gladly throttle him anytime." Soft, gentle kisses emphasized his sincerity and poured his love over her old wounds.

She let out a hard laugh at his offer to 'throttle' David for her. "I'll keep your offer in mind, thank you." She buried her head in his chest and thanked God for bringing this strong, generous man into her life.

He held her for a few more minutes, before adding, "So, I should focus on your mom and gain her acceptance. What about your friend, Deb? What will she think of our relationship?"

She rewarded him with a huge smile for his question. "Deb will believe our story is an amazing romance. She'll love how you support my pursuit of photography as a career and be super excited when she learns where we'll live. The Brainerd area will be the nearest I've been to her since college."

"Having your best friend's support will be a relief."

"What will your friend think about you getting married?" Leigh peered at him.

He fed her a strawberry while he thought of his response.

"I'm sure Matt will be shocked when he learns I'm getting married, but he'll love you once he meets you."

"I'm sorry you have more people to meet than I do." She selected another strawberry and fed him.

"Don't worry about me." He captured her hand and licked her fingers clean of the dark chocolate.

Did the heat cascading through her come from his actions or the champagne?

"Don't worry about impressing my family or winning their approval. They'll see how deeply we love each other. Besides, they'll have no alternative other than acceptance, because we're getting married no matter what they say or think!"

She reached up and kissed him. In turn, a gentle caress of her face and the shared kisses launched the dragons, building her desire for him.

"Why don't you try calling your parents again?" With the quiet murmur, he meant to encourage her, but the stiffening of her body against him spiked his concern for her.

No matter how much she dreaded going through with the call, the deed needed to be over and done. Growing dread grounded the dragons and extinguished the desire coursing through her.

"Fine, I'll make the call."

"Sit with me when you call and let me help you through this."

"Thank you, your being close will make a difference." She cuddled with him under the quilt before she tried calling. The phone rang and her mom's voice sounded.

"Leigh?"

"Hi, Mom. Is Dad home?"

"Yes, he's here. Frank, pick up the extension." Her mom didn't bother covering the mouthpiece of the phone.

"Hi, honey." Her dad's presence gave her confidence to continue. "Your mom said something happened to you up at the cabin? Are you okay?"

"I'm fine, Dad. I want to share something with both of you."

"We're listening." Her dad spoke for them both, concern still sounded in his voice.

"Mom, Dad, I needed to tell you...to let you know..." She didn't trust herself to continue, until Garrett gave her a hug of encouragement. She took a deep breath and plunged forward with all her news in one burst. "I met someone, we love each other, and we're getting married as soon as we can finalize arrangements."

Surprised by her sudden outburst of information, Garrett figured her parents entered a state of shock before she finished talking. He didn't expect a response until their heartbeats settled down, after which a relentless barrage of questions should be expected.

"Well done, darlin', you shocked them into silence," he whispered into her ear.

She glared at him in return.

"Mom? Dad? Are you still there?" Leigh panicked. Visions of her parents hanging up on her in disgust shook her confidence.

Her dad spoke up first. "Yes, we're still here. This is quite a surprise; you never mentioned dating anyone."

"Because I haven't been dating anyone. I met Garrett three days ago." She cringed at her confession and waited for a reaction. Her mom didn't disappoint her.

"Three days! What happened? Is he forcing you into this? Are you alright?" Mom's screech pierced the silence in their room.

Garrett tried hard not to laugh at the questions but failed. A deep chuckle escaped, followed by a strong elbow to his chest. No doubt Leigh didn't appreciate him finding humor in the conversation.

"Nothing's wrong. We fell in love."

"Love at first sight does not happen in reality." Skepticism filled her mom's voice. "Is he why you stayed at the cabin? You wanted to be with him?"

"No, Mom. I arrived at the cabin two days before I met Garrett."

"Honey, where did you meet, ah, what did you say his name is?" Dad, always the voice of reason, questioned her.

She glanced at Garrett, covered the phone, and asked, "How much should I tell them?"

"Might as well tell them all the facts. They'll find out sooner or later. This way we'll finish the drama over the phone instead of in person." He smiled and winked at her.

"His name is Garrett Dane. He's a kind, smart, honorable man who makes me happy. You'll like him."

"But how did you meet? The weather's been severe up north, so I doubt you got out much in the last few days." Dad wouldn't be distracted from his original question.

"Yes. How did you meet him?" Of course, Mom chimed in on this.

"Well..." Nerves took hold of her, and she second-guessed her earlier decision to tell them the whole story. Maybe this should be done in person, her voice shook as she continued. "He stopped at the cabin in need of shelter during the blizzard."

She winced as she felt Garrett's eyes on her, her eyes pleaded for his understanding. She stopped talking and hoped her parents wouldn't ask additional questions. Licking her dry lips, she raised her eyes to Garrett and hoped for his approval.

He observed her with the eyes of an investigator, trained to notice the slightest movement and nuance. He admired how she handled her parents, but when she skirted the truth of their meeting he got concerned. In time her parents would learn the whole story, and they may not appreciate the fact she misled them.

Regardless, she did a decent job of dealing with a prickly conversation. He decided she deserved a reward or at least a distraction, so he reached for one of her legs. Sliding a hand under her nightshirt, he roamed up her soft thigh toward the curls of hair at the junction of her legs.

Leigh closed her eyes and dropped her phone into the quilt as he elicited a deep moan from her. The warmth of his hand as he caressed her leg muddled her thoughts. I should stop him, she thought, but dismissed the idea as she experienced increasing pleasure from his wandering hand and fingers.

"So, you're still at the cabin?" Her dad asked one of the questions she hoped they wouldn't ask.

"Hmm?" The tap of Garrett's hand on her leg brought her back to her phone conversation. After retrieving her phone, she addressed her dad's question. "Ah…no, we snowmobiled to town."

"Snowmobiled to town? Well, I believe we should meet this person and ensure he's right for you," her mom said.

Her mom's displeasure thickened her voice. Apparently, she maintained a strong desire for Leigh's falling back into David's arms.

"Garrett, Mom, his name is Garrett, and you don't need to come up." Frustration with her mom's attitude turned Leigh's voice harsh. "I'm a grown woman who can make her own decisions."

"I believe your mother's right. We should at least meet him. What if we come up for the weekend? I should check everything at the cabin and verify no problems exist. You and Garrett can join us, can't you?"

Her dad brokered a deal, as usual he assumed the mantle of peacemaker between Leigh and her mom.

She stared at Garrett and grimaced in frustration.

He shrugged his shoulders, and a nod of his head showed his agreement with going back to the cabin.

"We'll meet you Saturday. Bye." With the call over, she relaxed against Garrett. She suspected the call with her parents would be difficult, but she didn't anticipate her mom being in such an attack mode.

"Are you okay?" Garrett asked as his hands soothed and warmed her all over.

"As long as you continue doing what you're doing, I'll be fine."

The love reflected in her eyes dazed him. He wondered what he did to deserve her. Hugging her close, he threw all his love into a deep kiss.

"Thanks, I sure needed this," she murmured against his chest.

"My pleasure; I aim to please."

"You do realize we'll probably sleep in separate bedrooms when we're at the cabin with them? So, these next couple of days may be the last times we'll be making love until after the weekend is over."

She sighed and snuggled deeper in his arms.

"No midnight trysts? No meetings in the bathroom with the shower running?" A kiss followed each question.

"Sounds like you're experienced with situations like we're in." Her eyes narrowed, and her tone sounded full of accusations.

"Nope." His kisses reached her nose. "I never did this before." His lips brushed hers. "I watch movies, and I'm trained for covert operations."

"Excellent!" She returned his kisses with enthusiasm. "I can't imagine surviving a whole weekend with you around and not making love a few times."

Strong arms went around her, and with a quick roll she found herself under him. She got lost in the depths of his eyes. They darkened to the warm-brown color she associated with his heightened passion. She watched his expression change from playful to smoldering. During their last few days at the Aspen Inn, she planned on showing him how much she loved him. Her arms went around his neck; she drew him down and brushed her lips across his.

Their shared kisses facilitated her forgetting the call with her parents and the meeting with them over the weekend. She had him and his love here and now; the certainty of their relationship made her smile and comforted her. Together they would move forward, but tonight she let him temper her worries over the past, her parents, and the upcoming weekend.

The gentleness of their lovemaking demonstrated his recognition of her need for comforting. The attitude of her mother hurt her to a greater extent than she would ever admit, and he sensed her reaction. Tonight, Leigh experienced the gentle side of Garrett Dane and learned how much she needed this considerate, tender attention.

In the failing light of the early evening, the glow from embers in the fireplace offered the only light in the room. They lay in each other's arms, neither anxious to leave the cocoon of warmth they created on the chaise lounge under the quilt. They didn't bother speaking since the end of her phone call. Both lost themselves in their lovemaking and now in thoughts of their pasts and their future together.

Leigh's thoughts wandered to having Garrett's children, and she smiled. She treasured the idea of having his children. What if he already impregnated her? Birth control didn't come with a one-hundred-percent guarantee. The idea of having his baby now rather than later didn't frighten her, and instead warmed her. She must be head over heels in love with him.

"What is your smile all about?" Garrett's question was a breath and whisper in her ear.

Should she admit her thoughts or hide them in fear of turning him away from her? He's not David, she thought. His response would include listening and understanding. "Babies, our babies. What if my birth control..." She couldn't continue.

"If your birth control what?" His eyes darkened further, and his breath caught.

"If it failed and a pregnancy happened. I thought how much I'd love having your baby." She forged ahead with her thoughts. They already discussed children, and they both wanted them. She turned to face him.

The long silence meeting her words concerned her until she gazed into his eyes; they spoke volumes to her. They sparkled. His mouth moved into a lopsided smile; she'd learned it resulted when he experienced happiness.

"I considered the possibility, too," he confessed.

"You did? When?" The last thing she expected was his thinking of pregnancy and babies.

"The first night we made love, Leigh." His voice rumbled within his chest. "Having a baby right away doesn't scare me; I actually liked the idea."

"Oh, Garrett! I love you so much." She kissed him, throwing her arms around his neck.

He broke from their kiss and looked into her eyes; tears glistened in them.

"We'll make this work, Leigh. I promise you." As if sealing a bargain, he kissed her with a passion he never wanted to end.

The flames of passion glowed within them as the embers in the fireplace glowed red-hot before them. They were content remaining in each other's arms as the day ended.

Chapter Eighteen

In the dark, he sprinted down an alley. Why? His hand clenched the SIG, never a good sign. The odor of garbage reminded him of another time. What compelled his frantic pace toward something or someone? Why couldn't he remember?

Racing around a corner, he skidded to a stop when Klein appeared. Garrett raised his gun and prepared to bark out an order when Klein turned and displayed a captive—Leigh! One arm wrapped around her waist and the other held a gun to her head. God, no! Please not Leigh! He aimed his gun at Klein.

"Drop it, Dane, or she's dead." The coldness of Klein's voice intensified his threat.

"I can't." Garrett's clipped response echoed in his head, his eyes locked on both Klein's gun and Leigh's terrified eyes.

Bang!

Garrett grappled with the covers, waking Leigh. She thought he fought his recurring nightmare.

"No! *No!* Leigh! Leigh!" Garrett called out in his sleep.

He never called out her name before; always the name belonged to his partner, his dead partner. She reached out to calm him and gently wake him.

"Garrett. You're okay, you're safe. I'm right here. It's Leigh, I'm here."

He began to still as her words broke through his sleep-induced terror. His eyes slowly blinked open.

She watched as he woke and left the nightmare behind. She smiled at him.

"See? Everything's fine. I'm here. We're still at the Aspen Inn." She breathed easier, as his eyes cleared and focused on her.

He wrapped his arms around her and held her tight. He didn't say a word until his breathing returned to normal.

"Leigh, I will stop Klein. Tomorrow, I'm getting my Jeep, and drawing him out of whatever hole he's hiding in."

"Why? What did you dream?" She leaned back in his embrace and looked him in the eyes. Icy-blue eyes stared back at her, the brown of his eyes gone, reduced to mere flecks in his irises.

"Almost the same as with Tess, I was running so fast, turned a corner, and stopped. Klein stood with his back to me, but when he turned around, he held you. He demanded I drop my gun and threatened to shoot you. I told him I couldn't." His voice sounded raspy, and he struggled to ease his heavy breathing.

"Right answer. I won't stand for you being unarmed around him." She gazed into his eyes and saw something never reflected in them before, a cold emptiness.

"A gun fired, but I woke up before I dreamed what happened."

"You can't foretell the future no matter how realistic your dreams appear unless you hold an ability for predicting the future you never shared with me?" She quirked an eyebrow at him. "You should let the police handle this."

"They still haven't found him. With no reason to stay here, he'll disappear. If he disappears, he'll be able to come for me at any time. How can we have a life together with him out there?" He entwined the fingers of one hand with hers. "If he wants to find me, he will find me. That leaves you and any children we may have in danger, not an acceptable situation. I'm serious, Leigh."

"Please let Detective Nichols work this."

"She can be a part of it, but I need to finish this."

"Why? This situation is dangerous; you don't have any idea as to when or where he might show up."

"You're right, so you should return to the cabin."

She jerked her hand from his and scrambled off the chaise lounge. The fact he thought nothing of putting himself in danger upset her, but suggesting she leave him alone against a killer made her furious.

"No, I won't leave you." She raised her chin in defiance.

He stood, straightened his flannel bottoms, and glared at her. "Yes, you will."

"No, I won't." She crossed her arms and stood her ground.

"Oh, I think you will."

"I don't care what you think, I'm not going anywhere."

"Leigh, be reasonable."

"I am being reasonable. You're the one being unreasonable."

"I am not being unreasonable."

"Yes, you are."

He sighed in response and ran a hand through his hair. He tried glaring at her, but she stood firm.

"Glaring at me won't change my mind."

"Guess what this is, Leigh."

Admiration for her strength bloomed through his chest. She loved him and wouldn't leave his side. With arms crossed under her breasts, the allure of her standing before him increased his desire for her. The stance she assumed hiked up the nightshirt, so the hem skimmed the bottom of her butt. The vision before him served as quite a distraction; his mind focused on how they should be making love in front of the fireplace rather than having a disagreement.

"An impasse?" Her low tone and glare reflected her anger.

"Yes, but also our first fight." His eyes sparkled at her.

Unwilling to stop arguing her point with him, a growing bulge under his flannel pants distracted her. "You're right; this is our first fight. Supposedly makeup sex is beyond satisfying, but we should end our fight first."

"There are rules?"

"Of course, there are rules. We'll settle this tonight. I won't leave you; I can't."

"I'm certain I'll regret this, but okay. With any luck, we can catch Klein before we meet your parents at the cabin."

"Thank you. Thank you. Thank you." She threw herself into his arms. "You won't regret letting me stay, I swear."

"I already regret agreeing with you, so you must promise you'll do whatever I say." He looked down at her. When she smiled at him, he realized his world centered on her, and she was all he needed in this life.

"I promise, as long as you don't tell me to leave again." She drew his face toward her, and her lips brushed his in a gentle caress. "And you promise me you'll never drop your gun when you're up against him. Promise me, Garrett."

"I promise."

Their tongues tangled with a forceful need, reflecting the passion they held for each other. Standing in the center of the room, their hands ran over each other. She reached for the waistband of his flannel pants and prepared to pull them down when her phone rang.

"Ignore it," Garrett growled at her.

"But it might be important."

"They'll leave a message." He trailed kisses down her neck.

"One quick look to see who's calling…ah, whatever you're doing feels heavenly." Breathless, Leigh reached for her phone. Not too far lost in pleasurable sensations, she managed a glimpse at the call display. "You should answer this."

"Mm-hmm." He continued his kisses along her shoulder.

"Detective Nichols is calling you." She thrust her cell at him.

He raised his head and reluctantly accepted the phone. "Detective, what can I do for you?"

"Mr. Dane, two U.S. Marshals arrived and are taking over the investigation."

"Their arrival doesn't surprise me because Klein had been a federal prisoner. Of course, they show up and take over the investigation. By the way, we decided to pick up the Jeep tomorrow. Thought we might drive around and be seen in the area. If Klein is still here, seeing me may draw him out."

"I don't believe your idea is practical. There's no telling when Klein might strike."

"Leigh said the exact thing." She gave him a smug look and mouthed 'I told you so' at him. "Tell you what, Detective; inform the marshals what we're planning. I suggest you place surveillance on us, but you guys do what you deem necessary. I'm not living my life looking over my shoulder and wondering when Klein will show up. This is ending with him either captured or dead, and I don't much care which one it is."

"I'll talk with the marshals, and we'll discuss our strategy with you tomorrow. Goodbye."

The abrupt end of the call said he upset her, and he understood why. If a victim ran roughshod over his case, he'd be pissed, but consideration could be made when the victim's a fellow officer.

He turned the phone off and tossed it aside.

"Now, where did we leave off?" A devilish gleam flashed in his eyes as he scooped Leigh up in his arms and dropped her in the middle of the bed.

She giggled as she bounced. "I believe initiating our first makeup sex."

He stretched out beside her. She rolled into his arms and kissed him with an intensity mirroring her love for him. His quick acceptance of her staying satisfied her, and she loved how he used 'we' when talking with Detective Nichols.

After a frenzied attack on each other, they culminated their first makeup sex. Garrett pulled Leigh close to his body and wrapped his arms around her. She nestled against him and relaxed.

"This makeup sex is great, but I prefer we skip the fighting," he whispered his confession in her ear.

She murmured her agreement as she fell asleep.

"Sleep well, I love you." He kissed her and drew her closer. In the quiet of the night, he vowed to stop Klein and ensure her safety.

Chapter Nineteen

The dawn came bright and clear. Leigh stretched and reached for Garrett but only found an empty bed and his pillow. In an instant, she woke, afraid he left for his Jeep without her. She hopped off the bed and walked toward the bathroom.

"Garrett?"

When she found an empty bathroom, panic and dismay took hold of her emotions; he promised she could go with him today. She grabbed a house robe from the closet. The door opened as she tied the belt in place. The scent of fresh coffee hit her first, followed by him walking through the doorway.

He wore charcoal-gray cords that had to be soft to the touch, and the way he filled them out made her desperate to touch. He wore layered Henley's for warmth, a black one over an off-white one. His hair shone in the light; all warm shades of blond and light brown, it touched his collar and hung in his eyes. He'd trimmed his beard from scruffy to well-groomed, looking too sexy for this early in the morning. He smiled at her as he carried a breakfast tray into the room and to a small table.

"Good morning, darlin'." His eyes sparkled a balanced hazel of brown and blue.

He kissed her on her lips, leaving her a little dazed, as she plopped down on a nearby chair.

"I thought you deserved some coffee and breakfast in bed this morning."

"What? Why?"

"Because you are the love of my life, the life I live, the life I love." He poured her some coffee, adding cream and sugar exactly as she preferred, and passed her a plate.

He poured his own coffee, grabbed his plate, and sat across from her.

"Your words touched my heart; where is the saying from?" She sipped her coffee and eyed him over her cup.

"From my heart, Leigh." After drinking some coffee, he dug into his breakfast.

She stared at him, amazed at how relaxed and nonchalant he appeared after saying the most romantic thing she ever heard. Reaching across the table, she caressed his face and kissed him.

"I love you so much." She sat back and began eating her breakfast. "When I woke and you were nowhere to be found, I feared you left for the police station without me."

"A promise is a promise, darlin'." With the half-smile she cherished in place, he reached for his coffee. "Once you're done with breakfast and ready, we'll leave. We can catch a ride from the inn."

"My goodness. You've been busy this morning. How did you manage all of this?"

"Proper planning and prompt execution. I'm an action kind of guy."

"Yes, you are an action kind of guy, but not always so prompt. As I recall, sometimes you aren't overly prompt at executing, but I'm not complaining." He choked on his coffee, and she laughed. "I'm taking my coffee with me into the bathroom, so I'll be back soon."

Still coughing, he waved her on.

***

Leigh scrutinized her reflection in the mirror.

"You're hopelessly in love with the man."

A radiant smile stretched across her face as she thought of how handsome he looked this morning, but he also appeared different. Even the way he walked into the room was different. She hadn't figured out why while she sat across from him, but now the difference hit her. He had exuded confidence and purpose. Assured of his abilities, they gave him confidence in being able to triumph over Klein.

Despite her belief in him and how safe she felt with him, she said a short prayer for their safety and a positive outcome ending this once and for all.

***

The swoosh of a door opening brought his head up. Leigh emerged from the bathroom; he forgot to breathe. Her hair hung at her neck in a loose ponytail. Tendrils of golden hair hung free about her face. The cream sweater she wore reminded him of an angora kitten, and his hands itched to pet the kitten. Maroon cords covered her beautiful legs, and she wore short black boots. He would forever respond to her—she called to him in so many ways. How fortunate she loved him because he would love her forever.

"Ready?" He hoped the cold outdoors would rein in his rampaging desire for her.

"Ready."

With one arm in her jacket, she hesitated. Her eyes focused on him shrugging into a shoulder holster. She stood spellbound by his actions, following his every motion as he picked up his gun, checked it, and slipped the dark weapon into the holster. Next, he slipped on a black leather jacket, the front hung open. A frown marred his handsome face when he glanced at her. Frozen in place, she stared as he approached her. At that moment, she realized he resembled an angel of death, so lethal and deadly. She swallowed hard. His large hands grasped her arms.

"Leigh? What's the matter?"

The warmth of his hands radiated through her. She gave her head a little shake.

"Your appearance is so different, and now I realize this is you at work. You look rather lethal, Garrett."

He raised an eyebrow at her, an unasked question hung between them.

"I mean lethal in an appropriate way for Klein or any other bad guy you go after."

He let out a short laugh and helped her into her jacket. "I never thought how a civilian might respond to me. You looked scared, and I would never intend to scare you. Are you sure you're ready for this?"

"Yes, I'm sure." She smiled at him.

He caught her hand and kissed the back of it.

"Time to go." Still holding her hand, he led her out of their room.

At the desk, Edna greeted them as they entered the lobby. "Ah, you're ready; I'll call for the car. Please have a seat while they drive around front."

"Thanks, Edna," Garrett said.

They sat together on a couch near the fire in the lobby area. With joined hands, they sat in silence, both lost in their own thoughts. The car showed up in short order, and they walked out into the bright, cold morning.

Garrett asked the driver to drop them off in the downtown area. In case Klein surveilled the police station, he didn't plan on advertising their lodgings by being seen arriving in the Aspen Inn's courtesy car. The police station sat a couple blocks away, a short walk for them. He hustled Leigh into the nearest store.

Once in the store, he scanned the displays surrounding them. They stood in the baby section of a children's clothing store. He glanced at Leigh, who wore a silly grin. She raised her eyebrows and winked at him.

She browsed through the baby clothes, held up a cute blue outfit, and said, "Check out this one, sweetheart. Wouldn't this be perfect for the little guy?"

He blushed when a salesclerk approached him and asked, "Is this for your little one or a gift?"

Somehow, he found his voice. "We're just looking, thank you." She took his meaning and moved off to assist another customer.

He stepped over to Leigh's side, while looking out the window. "Not funny, Leigh," he whispered in her ear. "Let's go. I don't see him outside. I imagine he watches both the hospital and the police station."

He led her outside, wrapping his left arm around her. She realized walking this way kept his right hand free for drawing his weapon and her away from the road—out of harm's way.

Ever vigilant, his eyes scanned the area ahead and on either side of them as they walked. He set a leisurely pace. As they neared the police station, a parked car caught his attention, so he memorized the car details and license. He spoke quietly. "A late model green Ford is parked across the way. Someone's in the driver's seat, and they're trying hard not to be spotted. Keep the car in mind. If you ever spot it again, tell me immediately." He smiled at her as though he said something pleasant or amusing.

She followed his lead, smiled up at him with a small laugh. "I understand."

When they walked into the police station, the relief she experienced surprised her. The shivers raking her body didn't come from the cold.

"We're safe in here, Leigh, and we'll be fine. Trust me?" He spoke in a quiet tone with his accent apparent. He ran his hands up and down her arms, trying to still her shivering.

"I trust you, Garrett." She lost herself in his eyes, surprised by the change in them. The typical warm-brown color had turned into an icy blue, cold and stark. He appeared more lethal now.

The desk sergeant recognized them and called Detective Nichols. She joined them in five minutes. Instead of taking them into her office, she opened the door of a larger meeting room. Three men sat around a long conference table; they all stood as the detective led them into the room.

"Garrett Dane and Leigh Ramsey, these are U.S. Marshals Kelly and Clark, and this is my boss, Chief Patrick. Please take a seat, and we'll discuss this situation."

Garrett held a chair for Leigh, and he sat beside her. He held her hand under the table, waiting for the presentation of their strategy. If he didn't agree with their plans, he'd say so and suggest changes. If they didn't ask for his input, he and Leigh would leave. Dealing with Klein on his own didn't concern him, he'd passed the point of caring how Klein met his end long ago.

Marshal Kelly started them off. "We believe Klein is still in the local area. A patrol located his car on the outskirts of town."

"From the day he attacked me?" Garrett drilled the marshal with his gaze.

"Ah, yes, when he attacked you. We learned he called all the local hotels and those in two surrounding towns asking for you. He also tried hospitals and clinics. Fortunately, Detective Nichols alerted the local hospital regarding the calls, and we've confirmed none of their workers released information concerning your treatment."

Leigh shot an astute glance at Garrett. They alerted Detective Nichols of Klein calling hotels, but obviously the marshals weren't aware of their involvement. She waited for Garrett's mentioning of the car outside the station. Won't they be surprised?

Marshal Clark cleared his throat and began speaking in a dull monotone. "We understand you're planning on driving your vehicle in town to draw Klein out of hiding. Do you still intend such a foolhardy tactic?"

"Foolhardy to you, a necessity for me, so the answer to your question is yes." Garrett spoke in a clipped manner. He waited on their response.

Marshal Clark continued. "We don't consider your plan smart. We're watching all nearby airports. He can't make a move without us finding him."

"Your watching didn't work too well last time, did it? If you were any good at watching, Klein would never have attacked Garrett a couple of days ago!" Aggravation rang in Leigh's response.

The pride he held for Leigh skyrocketed at her standing up to all the folks in the room, and he thought himself fortunate she sided with him.

"Yes, well, we're concerned with the here and now, not the past."

"If you paid attention to the past, you'd be aware of how resourceful Klein is and how he becomes invisible with ease." Garrett spoke with quiet fury. His eyes pinned Marshal Clark in place for a couple of seconds and cut to the other marshal. He dealt with marshals in the past. Most were competent, and he had worked well with them. A few were pompous fools and considered themselves God's gift to local law enforcement. He put Clark in the latter category and Kelly in the former. "Are you aware someone has this station under surveillance? A late model green Ford is parked on the street out front, and the driver tried real hard to not be seen as we walked in. I suspect the person is Klein."

By their reaction, Leigh and Garrett could tell they surprised them with news of the car. Chief Patrick made a call and dispatched forces out to investigate the vehicle. A short while later the phone rang, and the chief received an update.

"The car left before my officers got outside. We'll check any surveillance camera footage in the area in hopes of identifying the driver. Did you get a license number?"

Garrett nodded and rattled off the number. Detective Nichols wrote down the information and stepped out of the room. The marshals huddled together in one corner of the room. The chief excused himself and walked out.

Garrett whispered in Leigh's ear, "My guess is he stole the car, later today or tomorrow the police will find it wiped clean, and they'll be no closer to catching him. These two are deciding whether they'll support our plan or stick with theirs. Either way we're out of here."

He led her toward the door.

"Dane! Where do you think you're going?" Marshal Clark demanded while he moved toward them.

"We're leaving, picking up my Jeep, and going for a ride." Garrett's hand on Leigh's back guided her closer to the door.

Marshal Clark stopped between them and the door. "You're not going until we say you can."

Garrett stood toe-to-toe with the marshal; he towered over the man. His hands clenched into fists; his eyes narrowed. "We're leaving. We're getting my Jeep, and we're going for a ride. Excuse us."

The marshal got ready to say something when his partner broke in. "Move aside, Clark. We can't force them to stay."

Leigh had backed away when Garrett and Marshal Clark squared off and glared at each other. She marveled at Garrett's strength and fearlessness; her pride in him leaped higher. Marshal Clark moved aside but still glowered at Garrett as they walked past him.

They continued to the front and asked the desk sergeant for directions to the Jeep. Turned out they could go through the building and reach the yard housing it. Garrett thanked him for his assistance and led Leigh away. They found the Jeep with no problem. Garrett unlocked it, helped Leigh into the passenger seat, and climbed in himself. The engine turned over easily. With a wink at her, Garrett drove out of the yard and through the downtown area.

"We'll stop at the hospital first. If I were Klein, that's the other place I'd expect me to show up. For him the hospital is a safer location than the police station and holds less chance of him being recognized as an escaped felon. I'll need directions to the hospital." He glanced her way. She sat rather rigid and staring out the side window. "Leigh. Leigh!" She jumped and stared at him. "Sorry, I didn't mean to startle you. How do we get to the hospital from here?"

"Stay straight for two blocks and hang a left at the next street. The hospital is a few blocks down."

"What were you doing?"

"Huh? Oh, trying to keep an eye out for the car and Klein, but I can't! The scenery, the vehicles, and the people, they all go by so fast, too fast. How can I help you when I can't spot a threat as we're driving?" Tears pooled in her eyes and trickled down her cheeks. The words flew out of her mouth, and she hiccupped.

He stopped the Jeep on the side of the road. He took her head in his hands and rubbed his gloved thumbs over her damp cheeks. "Darlin', you're helping me by being with me. When we're driving, focus forward about one block, that gives you plenty of time for seeing everything. If anyone is on the side streets, they'll pull in behind us and I'll spot the vehicle tailing us."

Her tears slowed and no hiccups erupted since he stopped the Jeep. He fixed his eyes on hers as he spoke; his heart wrenched for the fear and pain he caused her. He leaned over and kissed her, a gentle, loving kiss.

"Better?"

She nodded in response.

"So, we can get going again?"

She murmured a response, which he took for agreement. He pulled the Jeep back on the road and continued to the hospital. As they drove, he pointed out things for her to focus on. She calmed, and her tears stopped. He circled the hospital covering all entrances. He pulled into the front parking lot and parked the Jeep in the rear.

"Why'd you park way out here?"

"While we walk toward the building, we can view most of the parking lot and spot anything suspicious. Do you remember the car from the police station?" At her nod, he continued. "Alright, keep an eye out for it over the next few days."

They headed for the entrance of the hospital. Because of his height, Garrett's field of vision was wider than hers. He wore his sunglasses, so she couldn't see his eyes. He led her along the left side of the lot.

"Did you notice something?" She tried reading his body language, as they walked between vehicles.

"Why do you ask?"

"You veered us left instead of continuing straight for the front entrance."

"Very observant. The green Ford from the station is parked near the far side of the lot. It'd be an excellent location for observing people entering or leaving the hospital and still safeguard a fast exit."

He moved in his typical stealth mode. Observing his jaw set and his mouth a grim line, she figured this must be his working mode. Amazed, she mentally acknowledged his transformation from her playful, loving Garrett into a lethal hunter focused on his prey.

As they neared the car, he hunched over and utilized the surrounding vehicles for cover. When they reached two rows back from the vehicle, he drew her down below the outline of an SUV.

"I need you to stay here and out of sight."

She ached to argue, but one look at his face told her she wouldn't win this one. She nodded.

"Call 911 and tell them where we are and what's happening. I'll be right back." He smiled, but with his eyes hidden behind his sunglasses, the smile lacked a sense of warmth or reassurance. Hunched over to hide behind parked vehicles, he took off toward the suspicious car.

Settling against the rear passenger door of the SUV, she dialed 911 and gave them all the details.

"Klein! Out of the vehicle!"

The force and authoritative tone of Garrett's command surprised her, yet another side of this multi-faceted man.

A booming noise sounded—a gunshot! Her heart pounded in her chest. She figured Klein must have shot at Garrett. Ready for a peek through the SUV's windows, she ducked when a second shot went off. She sneaked a peek through the windows of the SUV. No one stood by the green Ford or sat in it. Another shot sounded to her right, and she ducked below the windows.

The sound of heavy steps running in her direction caught her attention, but no one came into her hiding space. She peered through the windows for a sign of Garrett's whereabouts, when a strong arm wrapped around her waist and jerked her upright. A man held her against his chest, his breathing came hard and fast.

"You're his girlfriend, aren't you? Spotted you two walking toward me in my rearview mirror. I'm lucky you didn't move because you're my ticket out of here. I'll still get my revenge on Dane and you're helping," Klein spoke into her ear as he jerked her closer.

His rancid breath made her nauseous. She struggled against him; in response, he tightened his hold on her. In the distance, sirens screamed.

"The wailing sirens is the sound of police and U.S. Marshals coming for you. No way you're escaping." Garrett's deep voice rang out from somewhere.

Frantic, she scanned the parking lot for sight of him, but without success. Panic overwhelmed her thoughts.

What if Klein's shot hit him, and he lay on the pavement bleeding out? She struggled again, but Klein held her tight.

"It's over, Klein." Garrett's voice reached them: clear, menacing, but without anger.

Klein spun putting Leigh between him and Garrett's voice. He held his gun against her chest.

Garrett caught a glimpse of Klein manhandling Leigh. His fury spiked, and he fought off memories of his nightmare from the day before. The similarities heightened his agitation, but he remembered what Leigh demanded regarding him never being unarmed against Klein. He would save her; no other alternative existed for him. The sirens sounded closer, but experience told him this would be over before they arrived.

"No, I don't think so, Dane. I'm holding a gun on your girlfriend. Will you lose her, the same way you lost your partner?" Klein taunted Garrett, in hopes of his losing control and becoming vulnerable.

"I won't lose her. You need to release her, put your gun down, and your hands on your head." Garrett's voice came from a different direction. Klein spun again and positioned Leigh between him and the direction of the voice.

"Not going to happen. I'm calling the shots here, not you." Klein couldn't locate Garrett.

Terrified at first, Leigh calmed as realization struck; she believed in Garrett and maintained confidence in his ability to save her. She thought of his nightmare from yesterday. Unbelievably, they were living it. Would he remember what she told him if Klein insisted he drop his gun?

"Show yourself, Dane! Or else I'll hurt your pretty little thing for starters." Leigh strained against Klein's hold of her. "How 'bout I put her head through a car window, scar her up a bit for you."

"No, no!" Leigh struggled harder with Klein. "Don't listen to him, Garrett!"

"Sounds as if she cares for you, Dane. Does she love you? Are you willing to risk her life?" Klein searched the lot for a sign of Garrett's whereabouts.

"No, I won't risk her life." Three cars away Garrett stood tall with his gun drawn and pointed at Klein. "You need to let her go."

Klein laughed. "Or what?"

"Or I'll kill you."

"No, you need to drop your gun, or I'll shoot her."

"Can't."

"Why not?"

"She asked me not to."

"Doesn't she mean anything to you?"

"She means the world to me. You have damn little time left before the police arrive." The sirens sounded close about a block away. "You can be sure snipers are coming or getting into position as we speak."

"Put your gun down, Dane. I'm not telling you again."

When Klein moved his gun from Leigh's chest up toward her head, a shot rang out. Klein's hold on her loosened, so she broke away from him. She stumbled, went down to the pavement, and crawled on all fours, getting the SUV between her and Klein.

Garrett's shot struck Klein's right arm; the force weakened his hold on Leigh and spun him backwards. Leigh fell and disappeared. Using his left hand, Klein fired. The bullet impacted a vehicle on Garrett's left as he squeezed off another shot. His bullet caught Klein in the chest, and the man dropped. As soon as he fired, Garrett raced for the spot where he last saw Leigh. Hearing his steps, she scrambled into his arms. He crushed her against his chest and held her close.

"Are you alright?" He held her by her shoulders, scanning her for injuries.

"Yes, yes, I'm fine. What about you? You aren't shot again, are you?"

"No. He missed this time." He removed his sunglasses, so she could see his eyes. His smile received a smile in return. "Stay here, I need to check him. Okay?"

She nodded and leaned against the nearest vehicle for support. Her heart pounded in her chest, and her knees shook in time with every heartbeat.

Garrett stepped around the vehicle and knelt beside Klein's body. He checked for a pulse and found none. "This is for you, Tess," he whispered. He returned to Leigh as the squad cars rolled into the parking lot.

"You did all right, Leigh. I'm proud of you." He put his arms around her waist. "They'll interview us both regarding what happened. Expect separate interviews, so tell them what you remember."

"I counted on you, and you saved me." She clung to him, thankful for his strength.

"I will always be here for you."

Detective Nichols hurried to them, the U.S. Marshals on her heels. "Where's Klein?"

"Over there." With a toss of his head, he indicated where Klein lay. "He's dead."

"What the hell did you do, Dane?" Marshal Clark eyed him with suspicion.

"Protected my fiancée and defended myself." Garrett pulled Leigh closer.

"We'll need your gun." Marshal Kelly spoke up and held out his hand. Garrett handed over his weapon. "And we'll interview you both on what transpired here. Detective, your folks can process the scene. We'll conduct the interviews of Mr. Dane and Ms. Ramsey."

Detective Nichols nodded her agreement and walked away, busy giving instructions and making calls.

"We'll meet you back at the station," Garrett told the marshals as he turned Leigh toward the Jeep. He routed her away from Klein's body.

"Dane, I demand—" Marshal Clark burst out.

Garrett stopped, turned, and stared down the marshal. "In case you didn't understand me, I'll repeat myself for you. We will meet you at the station." Ice would have been warmer than his words. He didn't wait for a reply. He turned and, with his arm around Leigh, guided her away.

After he helped her into the Jeep, he climbed in, sat without saying anything, and stared straight ahead. Leigh reached for his hand. Her touch brought him back to the present.

"I am so sorry, Leigh. If Klein hurt you or worse—" His eyes closed, shutting out the horrendous thoughts.

"I asked to be with you; I needed to be here. Because of you, nothing bad happened. You saved me from him." She silently pleaded for him to believe her.

"If anything happened to you…" Without a glance in her direction, his head dropped to the steering wheel.

"Your nightmare is over, Garrett. Now we can move on with our life together without any worries." She rubbed his shoulders; tension knotted them hard and stiff. She kissed his neck. "We should leave for the police station; they're expecting us." Her voice was a soft whisper.

He raised his head and stared at her. The icy-blue color of his eyes gave him a predatory look, but when he smiled at her, her loving, caring fiancé had returned. "I suppose after this, meeting your parents will be a walk in the park."

"Real funny! At least you're smiling again; you worried me. I feared I lost you."

"You'll never lose me, Leigh. For the first time in a long time, a situation scared me. My concentration faltered because his hands were on you. When I imagined losing you, my resolve returned, and my training kicked in."

"As if you could ever lose me; you're stuck with me for the duration." She threw her arms around him and gave him a kiss to remember. "I love you so much."

"I love you, too; you're my life, Leigh."

His planned kiss was preempted by her phone sounding a tone.

With a sigh, she pulled the phone out of her pocket and read a text.

"When we're done with the marshals, is there anything else we should do or can we head for the Aspen Inn?" he asked. With a turn of a key, the Jeep's engine rumbled, and he drove out of the parking lot.

"Yes, we should complete one errand before going back to our room. The jeweler texted me and said our rings are ready! We can pick them up today, so I can wear the engagement ring this weekend when we meet my parents." Her expression showed her excitement.

"For sure we'll pick them up. Hopefully, your parents will be more accepting of our engagement, if you wear a ring on your finger." He winked at her. "You can't put your engagement ring on until we leave the Aspen Inn, unless we're confessing our fraud to Edna and the other guests." He shot a glance at Leigh.

"If we come clean with Edna, she may welcome us back for our real honeymoon."

He laughed, lighthearted for the first time in months. The anguish he lived with since Tess's death eased. He knew the key for his reaching this point sat beside him. The woman who accepted his marriage proposal and saved him from a life of despair.

"Let's go in, complete the interviews, and put this all behind us. What d'ya say?" Garrett asked as he parked the Jeep at the station.

"I say, yes, let's finish this."

Garrett hopped out, helped her out, and escorted her into the station. The desk sergeant called Marshal Kelly, who came out for them.

"Thanks for coming right in. We'll interview you separately and send you on your way." He led them to separate interview rooms. He directed his words at Garrett. "I'll interview you, and Clark will interview Ms. Ramsey."

Leigh recognized a well-thought-out plan when she heard one. If Clark interviewed Garrett in a room alone, a fight or worse would break out. She'd put her money on Garrett winning that contest. She walked into her designated room and sat in front of Marshal Clark. With a smile, she offered a greeting for the scowling man across from her. "Good afternoon, Marshal Clark, I'm all yours."

For nearly two hours, she recalled what happened in the hospital parking lot for the marshal. She answered numerous repetitive questions such as the number of shots fired, who did what, how they found Klein, how Klein captured her, and how Garrett saved her. Finally, Marshal Clark thanked her for her time and cooperation and showed her out of the room. He stopped by another room, knocked on the door, stuck his head inside, and said something about being done and taking her somewhere. He shut the door and escorted her to a break room.

"Would you care for some coffee or something else to drink?" Marshal Clark's consideration for her well-being would have been touching if not for his earlier confrontations with Garrett.

"Coffee, please," Leigh accepted with a smile.

He brought her a coffee, showed her the sugar and creamer, and excused himself. She hoped Garrett would be done soon. While she drank her coffee, a door opened in the hallway. She strained to hear the voices, listening for Garrett's. A recognizable deep rumble thanked Marshal Kelly for something, she couldn't make out what. Realizing he headed her way, she drained her coffee, grabbed her jacket, and met him at the doorway. He stood in the hallway, holstering his gun.

"You got your gun back already?"

Leigh eyed the gun in his holster. He shrugged into his jacket. As his jacket covered his gun, her concentration on it broke, and she gazed into his eyes.

"They processed it quickly as a favor to me, fellow officer type of thing, I guess. Clark didn't harass you in any way, did he?"

"No, he can be incredibly polite."

"Polite?" Garrett scoffed at her declaration of Clark's politeness.

"Well, he got me a coffee."

Chapter Twenty

Garrett held Leigh's jacket as her arms slipped into the sleeves and then waited while she arranged her hat and scarf. As she pulled on her mittens, he held the door for her. They walked through the doors together, hand in hand. Once outside, Garrett drew her into his arms.

"I've been desperate to do this for some time now." His lips crushed hers. She leaned into him, tasting him, and loving him. With reluctance, he ended the kiss. "Why don't we pick up our rings?" He spoke in a deep-husky voice and sounded so sexy she took a few moments to gather her senses and manage the short walk to the Jeep.

They arrived at the jewelry store within minutes of it closing for the day. Their salesman greeted them.

"Ah, Ms. Ramsey and Mr. Dane. I suspected having your rings ready this soon would be exciting news. Here you are."

He reverently set a beautiful box on the counter and raised the lid. The diamond sparkled as Garrett took the ring from the box. He studied Leigh for a second. Her eyes sparkled as bright as the diamond he slipped on her finger.

"You are my life, Leigh. I love you." He lifted her hand and kissed her ring finger. Her knees weakened, so she leaned into him.

"I am yours for forever and a day, Garrett." Her arms went around him. She loved this man with all her heart. She couldn't wait for the wedding ring to be added to her finger.

He returned her hug and leaned down for a kiss. He gathered up the box containing the remaining two rings. They thanked the jeweler and walked back to the Jeep.

"Let's go visit with Edna, and let her in on what's been going on, shall we?" Garrett steered the Jeep toward the Aspen Inn.

***

Edna sat reading a newspaper at the desk as they walked in. Looking up, she greeted them. "Mr. and Mrs. Ramsey! I hope you enjoyed your day."

"Our day turned out to be rather exciting. We should clear something up with you before we leave on Saturday." Garrett leaned a hip against the desk. Leigh stood near him, beaming with happiness.

"You sound ominous." She set aside her newspaper and directed her full attention at them.

"We're not newlyweds and only Leigh is a Ramsey. My name is Garrett Dane." He paused for a moment allowing Edna time to connect his name with the phone call she received from Klein the day before.

"Dane? I received a call the other day from your brother looking for you!"

"I don't have a brother. The man who called was an escaped federal prisoner, who wanted to kill me."

"He's why we didn't correct you when you assumed our status as newlyweds and Ramsey as our last name," Leigh explained with care, unsure how many details Garrett would want disclosed.

"Oh, my! What a relief you didn't register in your own name. Is he still trying to kill you?"

"No, he's no longer a threat." Garrett's words squashed any further discussion of the day's events.

"The Aspen Inn is wonderful, and we enjoyed our stay here. We hope to return as real newlyweds, since we're officially engaged now." She pulled off her mitten and showed Edna her ring. "We picked up our rings this afternoon!"

"Gracious, you had a busy day! Congratulations!" Edna admired Leigh's ring. "You got engaged here?"

"Yes." They answered her at the same time.

"Then a celebration of your engagement is called for! We'll do it tonight!"

"Edna, there's no need for all the trouble." Garrett tried reining her in.

"Nonsense! A small celebration will be no trouble at all; besides I love a party. If you'll excuse me, I need to make a few calls." Edna disappeared into her office.

"I guess we should rest before this evening, apparently we're having a party!" Leigh reached for his hand and led him upstairs.

"I don't know about you, but my conscience is relieved after being honest with Edna," Garrett confessed as he unlocked their room door and held it open for her.

"Mine, too. I'm surprised she took our news so well." Leigh tossed all her outerwear on a nearby chair.

"Not to mention, she's hosting an engagement party for us. What a lady!" Garrett removed his gloves and jacket and holster. "Shall we curl up for a nap?"

"Well, I'll curl up with you, but only if you're up to it." With deliberate slowness, she pulled her sweater over her head and tossed it aside.

Garrett raised his eyebrows. Off came her boots, socks, and cords. She stood in the middle of the room wearing exceptionally sexy lingerie; the diminutive amounts of silk and lace left most of her body uncovered. He didn't move, while his eyes ran over her delectable body.

The hot gaze from across the room made her knees tremble. Warm-brown eyes captured her attention, and she couldn't look away. As he moved toward her, he reminded her of a cougar stalking its prey. Desire for him spiked along with anticipation of the pleasures guaranteed from his touch. One hand stroked a hip; his fingers spread, reaching under the silk of her panties. She gasped.

His palms warmed her skin as he caressed her breasts. A shiver of expectation coursed through her. The slow, deliberate precision of his movements aroused her as his hands found every sensuous spot on her body. One hand traced tight spirals on a hip, stoking tension within her with each spiral. When she moaned and leaned against him, his attack on her senses intensified. Two hands roved across her skin, caressing and exploring, while a hard body ground against her sensitive, near-naked body. Seeking her lips, their tongues danced and muffled mutual groans of pleasure sounded.

Her body yearned for him, ached for him, and prepared for him. No longer capable of thought, she succumbed to sensory overload. Ah, this was torture of the best kind. He abandoned her body, and the loss of contact with him left her cold and lacking. She almost cried out, but the sensation of his arms around her stopped her cry. She melted into him as he held her close, both anxious for their physical joining.

He carried her across the room and lowered her until her back hit the quilt on their bed. His lips plundered hers. She flung her arms around his neck and pulled him closer. He wore all his clothes, and they prevented her from being as close as possible. She pulled on his sweater, but he caught her hands in his. A rumbling growl came from him as he kissed her. She nipped at his lips, but her movements slowed, her arms went slack, and weariness pulled at her.

He ended their kiss, grabbed the quilt from the chaise lounge, and spread it over her. How fast she fell asleep didn't surprise him; the heightened emotions of the day took their toll on her as she slipped into a deep sleep.

"My love for you goes beyond words, Leigh, you are my life." He whispered this, more for himself than for her as he kissed her forehead. He turned and walked out of their room in search of Edna.

Chapter Twenty-One

Garrett found Edna in the dining room. The fragrance of roses filled the air. An elaborate cake held the center spot on the table, rose petals and glitter lay scattered on the tablecloth.

"Wow! You've been busy," Garrett acknowledged the lady's efforts. "You didn't need to go to such great lengths for us."

"Nonsense. An actual engagement never happened here before. I'm so excited you'll share the joyous news with our other guests. Mr. Dane, there—"

"Please, call me Garrett."

"Garrett it is, thank you. The news coverage on TV discussed what I suspect was your afternoon. The reports didn't identify either of you, but I assume the news crews will dig up the information sooner or later. I would never talk with them, and neither would any of my staff." She completed her efforts with the table, stood back, and reviewed her handiwork. "Candles! We'll need lots of candles."

"Thanks for the heads up on the news coverage. Can I help with any of this?" Garrett waved at the extravagant display throughout the room. "We should cover the cost of this extravaganza you planned."

"Nonsense. Besides, I couldn't throw anything for my own daughter; she eloped after meeting her husband. You and Leigh are providing me an excuse for filling the void in my life left from her elopement." Edna couldn't contain her excitement. "You return with your pretty bride-to-be at five-thirty sharp. Okay?"

"We'll be here. Thank you so much." He wrapped her in a warm hug and gave her cheek a soft kiss. Flustered by his actions, she blushed.

"My, you're a smooth one; no wonder she said yes. Now you should be upstairs with your fiancée, not down here bothering me."

"Yes, ma'am." His deep chuckle drifted back to her as he walked away.

Being as quiet as possible, he let himself into the room. Leigh still slept; she lay on her back and a little snore escaped her. The time neared five o'clock, so he should wake her, giving her time for any preparations she needed before the party. He sat on the bed and for a moment reflected on her attractiveness and strength. He ran a hand through her hair.

"Leigh, you should get up." He leaned over and kissed her. "Wake up, darlin'. We can't be late for our party."

She stretched and opened her eyes. She smiled at him, and his heart skipped a beat. Her hands caressed his face and ran through his hair, settling at the back of his neck. "I love you so much. I'm glad you killed Klein. If he shot you—"

"Don't dwell on ifs, Leigh; playing around with ifs can drive you crazy. The whole thing is over and done. We can't hold any regrets at the end of each day."

"I'll try." She looked down at her state of undress. "Guess I should dress."

"You might consider putting a wee bit more on before we go downstairs. Oh, you'll love how the room is decorated. Edna never got to do anything for her daughter, so she put together quite the party for us."

"What happened to her daughter?"

"She eloped. You have less than a half hour."

He picked her up off the bed, carried her into the bathroom, and stood her in the middle of the room. After ensuring she remained standing, he backed out of the room, and shut the door behind him. While Leigh got ready, Garrett grabbed his cell and dialed Chief Martin's number.

"Martin here."

"Chief, it's Garrett. I thought I should update you on Klein."

"I'm listening."

"He's dead." His voice sounded cold and held no emotion.

"Did you shoot him?"

"Yes."

"A clean shoot?"

"Yes, he fired first, multiple times. I shot in self-defense and protected my fiancée."

"Fiancée?"

Garrett imagined the chief sitting up with interest.

"Ah, yeah, fiancée." Embarrassed for unknown reasons, his cheeks heated.

"Rather sudden isn't this?" Chief Martin's voice became fatherly, not the earlier brusque-business tone. He and his wife took Garrett under their wing after they learned of his being on his own with no family. Chief Martin became a father figure and mentor for Garrett over the last six years of his Air Force career.

"I fell in love with her the moment I saw her, and, fortunately for me, she feels the same way. This is right for both of us."

"Well, congratulations! I'm happy for you. You do realize Candace will be expecting a wedding invitation, don't you?"

"I understand. We plan on a small ceremony and hope we can finalize a date soon." Garrett's relief sounded in his voice.

"What do her parents think of all this? They must consider the engagement rather sudden." Always spot on, Chief Martin hit on their current dilemma.

"Leigh told them. Her mom hasn't fully accepted us yet, but her dad appears okay with the idea. We're meeting them this weekend." As he said this, Garrett realized how nervous the upcoming meeting with her parents made him.

"You'll do fine. Remember, be yourself. You're an upstanding young man who will take exceptional care of their daughter. You navigated through the difficult part already."

"The difficult part, sir?"

"You got Leigh to say yes!"

"I'm sure Leigh's acceptance would qualify as the easy part, Chief." Garrett ran a hand through his hair, anxiety over the weekend increasing at an alarming rate.

"I've got to go. Thanks for the update on Klein." All business now, the chief concluded the call, adding after a short pause, "Garrett, Tess would be proud of you."

"Thanks, Chief. I'll keep you posted on the wedding."

With the call ended, he plopped down on the bed. His head rested on the pillow, and he stared at the ceiling. He faced down armed criminals, deployed into war zones, and survived. Surely, he could survive a meeting with Leigh's parents, couldn't he? With the question echoing in his head, he turned as Leigh stepped out of the bathroom; his mind went blank when she entered the main room.

She wore a pair of black slacks and a deep maroon sweater with a neckline showing off her slim neck and shoulders. The golden locks he loved running his fingers through, had been pulled back and piled high with a few tendrils falling to her bared shoulders. Short black boots with a low heel and a silver chain as decoration covered her feet. Silver earrings dangled along the length of her neck. The silver matched the silver of her engagement ring, sparkling on her left hand.

"You look amazing!" He walked toward her as he eyed her up and down.

"Thank you. I decided I should dress extra special for you tonight."

She sauntered toward him, promises and love radiating from her. When she reached him, her arms circled his waist, and she settled against him. She smiled at him. Her eyes outsparkled her diamond.

He leaned down and kissed her, putting all his love and longing into his kiss. His arms wrapped around her, holding her close.

She responded with a tiny moan and melted into him.

After a couple of moments, she broke contact with him. "I heard you talking on your phone."

"I called Chief Martin and told him what happened today. I also told him we're getting married, and he said his wife would expect an invitation to our wedding. I figured out as much on my own, though. Candace would claim my hide if we didn't send them an invitation."

"Of course, they'll be here for it. Making a list of guests is one of the many things we'll be working on for the wedding."

"True, but a party awaits us. Are you ready?"

"I am." She took his arm, and they headed downstairs.

Chapter Twenty-Two

Candlelight illuminated the Aspen Inn's dining room. Votive candles and candles of all heights stood on every solid surface in the room. The table held a beautiful three-layer cake decorated with red roses and snowflakes. A buffet of Swedish meatballs, warm dips, vegetables, cheeses, and crackers awaited them. Fluted glasses filled with champagne stood ready for everyone.

When they walked into the room, all the other guests applauded. The rousing welcome overwhelmed them after the day they experienced. They stopped at the doorway unsure of what they should do next, but Edna breezed up and rescued them.

"Come with me. I told the other guests why you masqueraded as newlyweds, so no explanations on your part are necessary. We'll begin with a toast." She led them to the champagne and selected two glasses for Leigh and Garrett. She held a glass for herself and addressed the other guests. "Please, everyone take up a glass. Let's toast Leigh and Garrett."

The guests selected glasses and surrounded them. Edna raised her glass. "To our newlyweds turned newly engaged. We wish you happiness and ever-increasing love. To Leigh and Garrett."

A variety of responses echoed among the guests and the champagne went down easily.

Garrett cleared his throat, pulled Leigh close, and spoke for them both. "We appreciate Edna putting this together for us and apologize for masquerading as newlyweds. The reason we hid no longer exists, so let's party!"

Another cheer went up from the others, and they milled around for either food or refills of champagne. Leigh hugged Edna.

"Thank you for this. You are awesome! We can't wait until we return as real newlyweds." Leigh spoke so only Edna heard her.

"Call me when you're coming back, and I'll make sure all is ready for you two." Edna hugged Leigh back.

All the men surrounded Garrett.

"We're preparing to entrust you with all the wealth of our experience, so you'll be the perfect husband." Glenn spoke for all the guys. "But also, to ensure you don't screw things up for the rest of us."

Wrapping an arm around Garrett's shoulders, he drew him off to one side of the room for privacy from the women.

"I'm not sure—" Garrett attempted a response, but Glenn's wife, Mary, swooped in and saved him.

"Glenn! You leave the poor boy alone." Mary grabbed Glenn's arm and dragged him away from Garrett and the others.

Without their ringleader, the other guys drifted back to their wives. With intense relief, Garrett reached Leigh's side.

"I'm not sure what the guys planned on sharing with me, but I believe a guardian angel saved me." He kissed Leigh as he put an arm around her waist. "Mary is quite a force to be reckoned with."

She laughed and rested her forehead against his chest. She enjoyed the reassuring strength of his arm around her and the solidity of his body. Her wish for the future revolved around remaining in his arms forever.

"The early evening news included an exciting story about an escaped federal prisoner being killed at the local hospital. Did anyone else watch the coverage?" Connie asked. "The whole thing sounded frightening." Tom placed his arm around her as they joined the group.

"We were involved," Garrett admitted. Over the years, he experienced how people reacted after learning you killed someone, so he hesitated before saying more.

Leigh glanced at him, curious over his thoughts. She longed to sing his praises from the rooftops for anyone who listened. "Garrett spotted the man."

He flashed what he hoped Leigh would view as a warning of enough said, but he realized they never discussed this side of his work. She needed to understand the problem with being too free with information and possible social ramifications.

"Two U.S. Marshals as well as the local police force responded, too." Garrett tried deflecting the conversation from them.

"The report alluded to quite a shootout," Tom added. "They said the escaped prisoner held a young woman hostage and a young man saved her, so I suspect you two were the hostage and savior. Am I right?"

Garrett appeared uncomfortable, so Leigh spoke up.

"We can neither confirm nor deny any involvement. Would you excuse us, please? I need a moment with my fiancé." She flashed Connie and Tom a huge smile. She grabbed a hold of Garrett and led him out into the deserted lobby.

"What's up? You obviously object to letting anyone hear how you saved my life." She looked at him. "Please tell me what's going on inside your head."

His eyes met hers, but he turned away, focusing on the view of the barren snow-covered landscape out the front window. A long sigh escaped, but no words responded to her.

Torn by his retreating from her, Leigh tried to reach him again. "Garrett, please say something." Her pleading voice brought his eyes back to her.

"Leigh, in the past I've experienced how people react when they learn you killed someone. At first, they're okay with being around you because you're the hero and the other person deserved what happened. Once they deliberate over the danger and death surrounding you, your relationship ends. They aren't comfortable being around you anymore, and they avoid you like the plague. You represent everything bad in this world, and they detest being reminded of the ugliness."

"Garrett, I won't react like that."

"I hope not, losing you would hurt like hell."

When she locked eyes with him, his eyes reflected the fear he wrestled with. The thought of disappointing him haunted her.

"You'll never lose me, and don't worry about the others. I am proud of what you did today! I ache to tell everybody how proud I am of you. They should understand how well you did your job, how you showed up the U.S. Marshals and the local police, and what an excellent shot you are. Besides, after today we'll probably never meet these people again, except for Edna. Can we go back in now and tell our story if anyone asks us what happened?" Her eyes shone with pride for him. All she asked for was his agreement and belief in everything being okay.

"Yes, but don't say anything regarding showing up the marshals or the local police."

"Oh, alright, but I'll always know the truth."

She winked at him and led him back to the party. She searched for Tom and Connie and veered in their direction with Garrett in tow.

"Sorry we left so abruptly, but I needed to ask Garrett what details we could discuss. Plus, I learned my fiancé is rather shy over discussing his heroic feats." She beamed at Garrett.

Connie spoke up first. "So, the shootout did involve the two of you?"

The others in the room stopped talking, eager for the answer to Connie's question.

"Yes," Leigh confirmed.

"How long did he hold you hostage?" Diane asked.

"Only a few minutes."

"How frightening. Weren't you scared?" Grace's face paled.

"Klein terrified me when he first grabbed me, but I had complete confidence in Garrett. I believed in his ability to save me, and he did."

The amount of love in her words of praise for him embarrassed him, causing a blush across his cheeks.

"How did you save her?" Bob asked. He stood beside his wife, Grace, and wrapped an arm around her shoulders.

"I got a shot off and hit him in his right arm, so his grip loosened on Leigh. She broke away from him, dropped to the ground, and sheltered behind a vehicle. He shot at me again, but with Leigh out of the way, I gained a clear shot at him." Garrett described what happened with care because whatever he said could be repeated and misquoted.

"Wow, it sounds exciting! The news report made the whole thing sound like a long, drawn-out situation, but that's not what happened?" Bob looked impressed.

"No, the action ended after a few minutes. The local police rolled in along with the marshals, and we left." Garrett hoped for no additional questions. His shoulders sagged, when Larry's eyebrows raised, and his mouth opened for yet another question.

"Will you be interviewed by the news? They didn't share any names on the latest coverage."

"In all honesty, we hope they don't find out our names. We prefer putting this behind us. Besides, we need to plan a wedding!" Leigh intended for her answer to move the conversation away from the shootout. "We'd appreciate any advice on planning our wedding, such as locations for the reception, shopping for a dress, flowers, and music." The ladies gathered around Leigh, and their discussion rapidly centered on useful wedding tips.

With relief in his eyes, Garrett appreciated her quick thinking and ability at changing the topic. The men descended on him, and he braced himself for further questions on the shootout.

"You should rent a tuxedo unless you need one on a regular basis. A friend of mine rents them. I'll jot down his name and number for you," Tom offered.

Relieved, Garrett released a long breath and shrugged away the tension in his shoulders.

"I appreciate the information, Tom."

"If you aren't going real formal, a dark suit works well, plus you should always invest in at least one well-made, dark suit. With your build, you should buy a tailored suit. A good suit will show off your broad shoulders and keep Leigh firmly in the palm of your hand. Women love having a handsome, well-dressed man at their beck and call, if you understand what I mean." Larry winked at him and chuckled. "I use a guy who owns a nice shop. He'll give you a fair price on a suit." He pulled out a business card and wrote a name, address, and number on the back. "Here you go. Tell him I sent you."

"Thanks, Larry." Garrett relaxed further.

"How's your dancing ability? Can you waltz and foxtrot?" Bob dished up some food from the buffet, so he threw his question over his shoulder.

"I can maneuver around a dance floor fairly well." The thought of dancing in conjunction with their wedding never occurred to him, so he appreciated the topic being brought up.

"Well, you might consider brushing up, if your reception includes music. Trust me on this. When escorting your bride out on the dance floor, you need to be smooth because all eyes are on the two of you. Plus, you'll be dancing with Leigh's mother." Bob munched his food.

"Bob's right, you should brush up on your dancing skills. At our reception, I did perfect with Mary, but I let success go to my head," Glenn confessed. "When I danced with Mary's mom, I stepped on her dress. She tripped and fell, taking me with her!"

"No way!" Garrett tried not laughing at the picture developing in his head but failed when the other men chuckled with abandon.

"Yes. But wait until you hear the worst of what happened." With a glance at the ladies huddled around Leigh, he continued the story. "We bumped into Mary dancing with her dad, and they fell in a heap with us." Glenn laughed so hard, he struggled to complete his story.

The ending left all the men laughing hysterically. The ladies gaped at them.

"Oh, no!" Mary shook her head. "Sounds like Glenn told them the story of our wedding dance fiasco."

The ladies all raised their eyebrows at her, so she shared the story with them. By the end of her story, they laughed as hard as the men. The rest of the party passed with an abundance of shared wedding stories.

"Time for cake," Edna announced with a clapping of her hands. "Leigh and Garrett, you'll do the honors. Consider this practice for your wedding reception." She handed them a knife decorated with red roses and ribbons.

They each took hold of the knife and eyed the cake. With the knife poised over the bottom layer, they carved out a sizable chunk.

"Well done. Now, feed each other the cake," Edna completed her instructions. "Garrett, you can go first."

"Face! Face! Face! Face!" The men began a chant. They ignored the glares they received from their wives.

Garrett picked up a sizable piece of cake.

"Don't you dare," she warned him.

"Open wide, darlin'." He raised the cake near her face.

"You picked up way too much cake, Garrett." She backed away.

"Oh, I'm intimately aware of how much your mouth can handle." He said this quietly, for her ears only. "This should be no problem for you."

She blushed as she deciphered his reference and opened her mouth to protest. With perfect timing, he stuffed the cake into her mouth. He licked the frosting from his fingers, while she chewed through all the cake and swallowed.

"See? I didn't overestimate how much you can handle in your mouth." His voice remained quiet and only for her.

A deep blush flamed her cheeks at his words. Snatching up a much larger piece of cake, she wore an evil-looking smile.

The ladies began their own chant of "Payback! Payback! Payback!"

"Come over here, Garrett. Don't make me chase you down." Leigh beckoned him with one finger. He stepped toward her in anticipation of accepting his medicine. "As you told me, open wide."

Laughter prevented Garrett from opening his mouth wide, so little cake reached his mouth and most smeared across his face. He grabbed Leigh before she escaped his reach. His frosting and cake-covered face brushed against hers when he kissed her. Much of the cake and frosting transferred from his face to hers. Both the men and women whooped in appreciation of his maneuver.

Leigh kissed him; he tasted of almond flavoring. She leaned into him and licked some cake off his face. They broke out in laughter.

Edna handed them each a warm wet towel for cleaning their faces.

"You should do well at your wedding reception! You both put on quite a show. Congratulations you two." Edna smiled, while the others continued laughing.

"Thank you, Edna, for everything," Garrett said.

He finished cleaning his face and tried assisting Leigh. Too much cake and frosting clung to his towel, so she waved him away and used her own towel.

"I trust I removed every piece stuck to me." Leigh eyed the cake with apprehension. "I'm terrible at cutting cake, Edna. Would you finish, please?"

"Of course, I will. You both want a piece with a fork this time?"

Garrett stepped near Edna and Leigh. He reached for Leigh's neck, ran a finger along her neckline, and came back with a small chunk of cake. He licked the remains off his finger.

"Now all the cake is gone. I'll take a piece, Edna; I enjoyed what little I ate during the cake cutting."

Garrett gazed at Leigh as he spoke, his eyes an endless depth of warm brown. She didn't miss the promise in his eyes, and the dragons took flight in her stomach. She glanced at her watch and calculated how much longer they should stay at the party—way too long.

"I'll take a slice, and I'll serve the others," Leigh told Edna. She delivered cake around the room; as she dropped off cake, she exchanged a few words with each of the guests and returned for new slices of cake.

Garrett studied her, as she moved about the room. Each sway of her hips and every gentle laugh ignited a warm sensation through him. He turned away, before everyone noted the physical effect she had on him. He served up coffee for everyone, and when finished, he joined the others at a long table.

"What are you two doing tomorrow?" Connie asked, as he sat across from her.

"Nothing specific. We might wander around town and take life easy. We meet her parents on Saturday at their cabin for the weekend," Garrett said.

"Meeting the parents? Oh, boy! Best of luck with that," Larry said and stuffed cake in his mouth.

"Garrett shouldn't be concerned," Leigh commented as she joined them.

"No?" asked Larry.

"No. He faced down an armed escaped prisoner, so he should be capable of handling a meeting with my parents." Leigh winked at Garrett and ate a bite of cake.

"I understand what you're saying," Larry agreed. "Still, I wish you the best, Garrett."

"I'll take all the luck and best wishes I can get," Garrett admitted.

The conversation revolved around them while everyone devoured cake and coffee. As the evening progressed, Leigh and Garrett ached for the privacy of their room.

Minutes after seven o'clock, Leigh stood. "Thank you all for a much-improved ending to what started out as one horrendous day. Edna, thanks again for this spectacular engagement party! Now if you'll excuse us, I need some alone time with my fiancé." Before she finished talking, she gathered up Garrett's hands. He stood, said good evening, and followed Leigh out of the room and up the stairs.

Chapter Twenty-Three

As soon as the door closed behind them, Leigh spun and faced Garrett, backing him up against the wall. She looked deep into his eyes as she leaned into him.

"Garrett Dane, I love you." She took his lips in a hard kiss. Her tongue ran across his lips seeking entrance, at the parting of his lips her tongue darted in.

He greeted her enthusiasm and met her stroke for stroke.

She began undressing him with sheer determination. When he stood gloriously naked before her, she led him to the bed. Looking him over, she spotted a dark bruise on his right hip. She touched the center of the discolored area, and he winced.

"I thought your bruise disappeared, what happened?"

"I bounced off a vehicle when Klein shot at me today."

He eased into bed.

"Which time?"

"The first two times."

"Do you need some ice?"

"All I need is you in bed with me." Those bedroom eyes of his darkened with passion.

Her heart skipped a beat, and the dragons began dive bombing in her stomach.

"I'll join you as soon as I finish."

She turned off the lights and opened the drapes of their large window. The darkness transformed her into a silhouette against the moonlight streaming into the room.

His eyes followed her movements with the intensity of a wildcat following prey.

She rested one foot on a chair and slowly unzipped the boot. She sat, pulled off the boot and sock, and repeated the sequence with her other foot. With a glance at Garrett, she confirmed her planned foreplay captured his attention.

His quiet regard stimulated her need for him.

Her desire for him filled her, and she realized the enormity of her love for him. He completed her. Funny how she never felt incomplete, but now she comprehended how truly empty her life had been before him.

She entranced him, he couldn't look away, and he wouldn't if he could. He yearned for her; the need originated deep within his soul. Desire for her heightened with her every move.

She undid her pants, and they dropped, pooling about her ankles on the floor. She kicked them aside. Next, her sweater fell to the floor. She stood before him wearing beautiful, skimpy lingerie.

The vision she presented sent his blood racing. He couldn't distinguish her features because of the shadows, but his imagination heightened the desire building within him.

She reached behind her back and undid the clasp of her bra. She drew her arms out of the straps, and the wisp of material fell to her feet. With blistering speed, her panties joined the bra. She stood naked before him but covered in shadows. When she turned in profile, the moonlight kissed her body. She removed her hair pins and turned away from him as her hair cascaded over her shoulders to her waist.

Her beauty struck him speechless. He couldn't wait until she joined him. With a long ago learned stealth of movement, he rose and joined her before the window. He surprised her when his arms encircled her waist, thrilled her when he turned her in his arms, and took her breath away when he kissed her.

"Why aren't you in bed?" Leigh breathed against his lips.

"Impatience. I need you." He kissed her lips, nibbled an earlobe, and ran kisses down her neck. He loved her taste, her feel, her everything. "We should move this to the bed."

"Good suggestion."

Their lovemaking pushed the day's events far into the recesses of their memories.

"I love being this close to you." His hands drew small circles on her back. "Do you suppose our lovemaking will be super intense when we're trying for a baby?"

"I'm sure but ask again when we're trying."

"Okay. What should we put on the schedule for tomorrow, our last day here?"

"Sleep in first. The downtown area contains many interesting shops, so we can do some shopping."

"Shopping it is. Do you need groceries for the cabin?"

"I doubt it. Mom usually brings all kinds of stuff with her. I'll warn you now she's into gourmet cooking."

"Why does her gourmet meal require a warning?"

"The servings can be minuscule, covered in heavy sauces, and made of things you never heard of before, let alone eaten."

"Oh, so we may need late-night snacks." His voice suggested she might be on the late-night menu.

"Yes, definitely snacks." She kissed him, and he responded.

They laughed, kissed, and made love throughout the remainder of the night. Their lovemaking varied from slow and tender to frantic and demanding. Each cried out for the other as they found their release. Before exhaustion claimed them, she rolled over and nestled into him. His arm circled around her and drew her closer. She lay protected and safe in his arms. Falling asleep beside him for the rest of her life suited her and exceeded any past dreams of her future.

"Sleep well, Garrett. I love you so much."

"I'll love you forever, Leigh." He kissed her hair and settled in beside her.

The evening held no nightmares for him.

Chapter Twenty-Four

The morning light streamed in through the open drapes. Leigh opened her eyes and focused on Garrett beside her. His slow and steady breathing told her he hadn't woken yet.

The covers stretched over his hips and his sculpted chest moved up and down with each breath. She enjoyed the view. The length and fullness of his eyelashes amazed her. She laughed inwardly as she thought of a few women who would kill for such eyelashes.

He stirred but didn't wake. At least no nightmare interrupted his sleep last night; she hoped he wouldn't experience them anymore.

Throughout the evening their lovemaking had been tumultuous, so the fact any covers remained on the bed astonished her. A smile graced her face as she remembered the strength of his hands caressing her, the softness of his lips exploring her, and the solid length of him filling her. She should let him sleep, but his body called to her. Her fingers traced over his skin and circled his nipples, teasing until they tightened and stood erect. A yearning for him overwhelmed her and demanded satisfaction. By drawing the covers down, nothing hindered her from realizing her deepest desires.

Garrett slept until a sensation of coolness broke through his haze of exhaustion, but he didn't quite wake until something cold rubbed against his leg. He woke with a sudden jerk, surprising Leigh.

She sat up, a blush rising on her cheeks. "I didn't intend to wake you, I'm sorry."

"Darlin', how could I not wake up when your icy cold feet touch my legs?"

"They're not that cold, are they?" When he nodded, she flinched. "I'm sorry, and you were sleeping so peacefully, too. We can cuddle in bed awhile longer." She arranged the covers over them both. "After all your attentions last night, I may be incapable of walking today."

"We may never leave this bed, which is fine by me." He pulled her closer and rained kisses over her shoulders, his hands moving over her hips.

A sudden knock on the door surprised them.

She reached for a fluffy house robe and wrapped it around her.

He groaned and pulled the covers over his head in hopes of getting some much-needed sleep.

Leigh opened the door and found Edna standing in the hallway. She wore a worried look on her face.

"I'm sorry for coming up so early, but I thought you and Garrett should be aware of the reporters out front."

"Reporters? But how?"

"No idea, but I'm sure none of the guests or staff said anything. A couple of TV crews plus some reporters and photographers are camped out hoping they'll catch sight of you. A few came inside, but I directed them off my property. They're complying with my demands; however, once you step outside, they'll be on you like a pack of dogs. I'm so sorry." Edna gave Leigh's hand a squeeze and walked away down the hall.

"Damn!" Garrett got out of bed and stormed off for the bathroom.

"Why would someone leak our information?" Leigh called after him but received no response except for the sound of running water.

While staring out the window that overlooked the back lawn, a movement beyond the fence line caught her eye. A photographer aimed a huge telephoto lens at the inn. She jumped away from the window. Being hunted didn't set well with her. Closing the drapes, she curled into a chair. Edna's news surprised them, but Garrett's reaction concerned her. The way he stormed into the bathroom without saying a word signaled he stewed over something. She decided to await his return for an explanation rather than confront him in the bathroom.

Garrett headed for the shower. Under steaming water, his mind bounced over too many concerns. Having his picture plastered on TV or in newspapers jeopardized the undercover assignment for the BCA.

Damn! Damn! Damn!

With his eyes closed and forehead against the wet tile, the water cascaded over him. His thoughts ran amok. When Leigh's parents discover he placed their daughter in the crosshairs of a killer, they'd forbid her from marrying him.

Damn! Damn! Damn!

Anger flared at thoughts of life without Leigh and the loss of his treasured job with the BCA. A fist beat against the wall. Neither loss was acceptable.

Well, Dane, you can't feel sorry for yourself; you must consider Leigh now, he thought.

Memories assaulted him: Leigh making a snow angel, Leigh taking charge of their lovemaking, Leigh's passion on display in her eyes, and Leigh waiting for him in the other room because he left without saying a word to her.

Damn it all!

He turned off the shower, wrapped a towel around his waist, and searched for her. Only the light from the bathroom illuminated the room; he spotted her sitting in a chair near the cold fireplace.

"Leigh." He squatted in front of her. Their eyes met and held. "I'm sorry I walked off without a word."

"Oh, you said one word, before you disappeared into the bathroom. I believe it was 'Damn.' I expected some discussion, but I can forgive you for not talking with me right away."

"You can?"

"Well, you afforded me quite a luscious vision as you walked away; you have a fabulous butt, Mr. Dane." Her eyes twinkled in merriment as she teased him.

"I imagined news reports with our names and possibly our pictures. I can't be in any pictures, Leigh, because of the undercover assignment I'll work when I report to the BCA. More importantly, what'll happen when your parents learn of everything occurring up here? They won't accept your being with me or approve of us getting married, will they?" He reached for her hands, raised them to his lips, and kissed them.

Tears pooled in her eyes as she listened. She shook her head. "I don't care what they think; I will marry you, Garrett. Nothing can stop us because we belong together."

She placed her hands on either side of his face and kissed him; it was a soft, intense kiss.

He stood and pulled her up with him. He undid the belt of her robe, and his hand entered the warm confines beneath the thick material.

She loved the sensations building within her from the simple act of his hands roaming her body.

His hands grazed her body in a slow exploration of the many spots he kissed and feasted on the night before. Pushing the robe off her shoulders, he let it drop to her feet. His hands cupped her buttocks, and massaged up her back, along the nape of her neck, and into her hair. He tilted her head back and nibbled on her neck.

She moaned.

"You should take your shower, and we'll go downstairs for breakfast. Okay?" With reluctance, Garrett released her.

"Yes, I'll hurry."

Hazarding a glance out the window, he spotted photographers and a television camera crew farther back. While he straightened the bed, he smiled at the memory of their night together. The passion they'd shared surpassed any time before, and he credited the day's events as the reason. Taking down Klein ignited an adrenaline rush within both of them. The excitement of getting their rings and the joyous engagement party propelled the adrenaline to a higher level. But the zenith and most enjoyable stimulus occurred in the privacy of their room.

The bathroom door opened, and Leigh stepped out. A long braid hung down her back. She wore another wicked-sexy lingerie set; the combination of satin and lace made a return appearance. The rose of her nipples showed through the sheer material.

The vision of his fiancée startled his body into an immediate and fierce response. His erection grew and strained against the confines of his jeans. If he turned away, the effect may lessen, but he didn't have the will or desire to do so.

At the dresser, she pulled out a light blue turtleneck sweater and a pair of jeans. As she dressed, she took note of what he wore and took pleasure at how well they matched. He'd chosen a pale-blue Henley under a blue plaid-flannel shirt. His jeans clung to his muscular thighs. While focusing on the bulge in the front of his jeans, she blushed; she loved the physical display of his desire for her. Eat your hearts out, ladies, she thought. He's mine, all mine.

"I'm ready." She crossed the room and linked her fingers with his.

"Let's go." He led her out the door.

Chapter Twenty-Five

When they reached the bottom of the stairs, Edna met them.

"You're in time for breakfast. The food's still hot and so is the coffee." She walked with them toward the dining room. "A few of our guests are leaving today; however, I believe we're still full up." She winked at them as she turned back for the front desk.

"You gotta love that woman." Leigh chuckled as they perused the dishes in the buffet line. "I'm starved."

"Probably from all the exercise you enjoyed last night."

His smile and eyes radiated his love for her, so she couldn't harass him over his blunt, yet accurate assessment.

He set his plate piled high with food at one of the place settings and gathered coffee for them.

Leigh sat across from him and accepted a coffee with gratitude, hoping it would eliminate the last shreds of exhaustion clinging to her consciousness. Garrett settled across from her with his back to the window.

"What do you say we grab a couple of books from the library and bring them up to our room?" Garrett asked in between bites of food.

"A literary afternoon, snuggling by the fire and reading a few of the classics? Did you invent a stripping game for books we can play?"

He choked on his food. When he stopped coughing, his eyes locked on hers.

The innocence reflected in her eyes ended when she broke into a fit of laughter.

"What if we find a deck of cards and play a rematch of Crazy Eights?" Leigh suggested, and her smile heated his blood.

"I'm sure Edna has a deck around here somewhere. Are you sure you're willing to accept the risk? As I recall, I literally beat the pants off you." Finished with his food, he refilled his mug with piping hot coffee.

"Win or lose, it'd be a satisfying way to while away the hours." She enjoyed the sight of him walking to the coffee pot and back. His jeans fit snug over his butt and clung to his muscular thighs. "The library might contain a hot romance, and within the steamy pages some unique ideas on making love could be waiting for discovery by us."

She bit her lower lip and raised her eyebrows at him. His eyes darkened to the warm-brown color reflecting his desire for her. She downed the last of her juice and stood.

"I'm finding us a book." She made a dash for the room serving as the inn's library.

"I'll join you soon." Garrett's desire for her skyrocketed, and he feared losing control of his raging hormones if he followed her into the library right away. He decided on finding a distraction. A stop in the lobby for a talk with Edna may temper his desire for Leigh.

"Enjoy breakfast? Did I see Leigh hurrying off toward the library?"

Garrett leaned one hip against the desk as he nodded his head.

"As usual, your breakfast did not disappoint. With the circus outside, we decided on staying indoors today. We thought reading would be a relaxing way to pass the day. But just in case, do you have a deck of cards we can borrow? Oh, would you mind sending coffee or hot chocolate up to our room?"

"I'll send both and some cookies. Here's a deck you can use." Edna handed him the cards. "I'm sorry they found you; I'll make sure no one gets in here."

"Thanks, Edna. You're truly wonderful!" He leaned over and kissed her cheek.

"Oh, you! You're such a charmer." She slapped his arm and smiled. "You two are such a sweet couple; you deserve the absolute best."

"Well, we appreciate everything you've done for us. Tomorrow we're driving the snowmobiles back to Leigh's family cabin. May I leave my Jeep here?"

"Certainly. Leave your keys, and one of the staff can move it into the shed. When you leave, you can drive out through the back entrance. I'll ensure your machines are all gassed up for tomorrow morning."

"Super. Thank you." After handing over his keys, he pushed off from the desk and set off for the library and Leigh.

"There you are. What kept you?" She whirled around at the click of the door opening.

Her smile and the glint in her eyes stopped him in his tracks. She took his breath away. He held up the deck of cards in answer and entered the room.

"We can play cards, unless you found an interesting book."

"I found one, but we've tried almost everything described in it." Her smile brightened the room.

He strode toward a shelf of books and perused the titles. "Perhaps reading and talking would be the right thing for today."

Finding interest in a title, he pulled the book from the shelf. As he turned, his eyes locked on hers and cut through her. In contrast to what he said, his eyes relayed something different, and she understood their underlying message said I want you, and I want you soon. He dropped his gaze and continued perusing the books.

Her knees almost buckled. Desire for him overwhelmed her, so she surrendered to her instincts. She somehow reached the door and turned the key in the keyhole.

At the click of the lock, Garrett's head jerked toward her. An expressive eyebrow rose.

"What do you have in mind, Leigh?"

"I'm improvising, Garrett." She walked to the nearest bookcase, undid her jeans, and pulled them down, displaying her satin and lace panties.

Garrett couldn't take his eyes from her or move; he stood frozen in place by the delightful display before him.

When she recognized the raw hunger in his eyes, she turned back to the bookcase, facing away from him. She pulled her panties down, bent over, and wiggled her butt at him.

"Do you need a written invitation?" She tossed the question over her shoulder.

He dropped the book he held, and the cards fluttered out of his hand as he rushed toward her, reaching her in three strides. One warm hand embraced a hip, another kneaded a breast, and their quiet morning turned frantic. The public location threw an urgency into their actions as they made love and joined as one. Afterward, they leaned against each other, Garrett spreading warm kisses along her neck.

"Did we satisfy whatever you envisioned in your head?" His voice was husky with emotion.

The rattle of the doorknob interrupted her answer.

They stepped away from each other and worked on straightening and buttoning their clothes.

Leigh marveled at herself in provoking a sex act in a public area. How did loving Garrett change her? Free her? Inspire spontaneity? Whatever changed, she valued the difference. She glanced at him, standing all zipped up, buckled up, and looking as perfect and handsome as ever. Not flustered. Not mussed up. How did he do that?

Whereas she must look exactly as a recently loved woman should—a flushed hot mess.

On shaky legs, she walked to the door, turned the key, and swung it open.

"I'm sorry, didn't realize the door got locked."

"Don't worry, dear," Connie said as she and Mary entered the room. "Oh! Garrett, you're here, too."

"Yes, ma'am, we've been looking for a couple of books to help us pass the day." Somehow, he managed to pick up his book, but a few cards littered the floor.

"Did you run into problems with the playing cards? They can be tricky little things when your hands are full," Mary commented as she swept in.

"Uh, yes, we're playing cards later to…ah…break up the day." Leigh bent over and picked up the last of the cards.

"We didn't miss all the reporters milling around outside; guess they're looking for a story from you two. Are you poor things stuck inside until they leave?" Connie sympathized with them.

"This is our last day here, so we're relaxing today for a change. If you ladies will excuse us, we'll return to our room. Have a pleasant day." Garrett placed a hand on Leigh's back and pushed her out of the room.

"You enjoy your day, too," Mary called out after them. Her eyes caught Connie's, and the ladies shared a knowing moment. "Ah, to be young and in love."

Connie nodded her agreement.

They hustled out of the library. Not bursting into laughter proved difficult, but not impossible. They shot up the stairs and stumbled into their room.

"I cannot believe you did such a thing! Whatever got into you?" Garrett pulled her into his arms and gazed into her eyes.

"You did."

He grimaced at the obvious.

"I didn't mean that! My love for you frees me, so I'm exploring actions I never considered before. Before you arrived in the library, I decided adding a touch of risk in our lovemaking might intensify our enjoyment. I thought the library would be a perfect location; at least the door had a key."

"We're lucky it did; Connie and Mary didn't need a viewing of our private interlude. You surprised the heck out of me!"

"Ah, but you were up for the challenge."

"Well, I couldn't let a phenomenal offer go unaccepted," he replied. "Do we consider this useful practice for the weekend?"

"Honestly, I'm not sure how comfortable I am about us doing anything like this at the cabin over the weekend. I'm a grown woman but having sex when my parents are in the same house strikes me as wrong. Am I weird?"

His intense regard brought a pretty blush across her cheeks; he loved how she blushed. "I doubt your feelings are weird or unusual. Don't overthink the situation; your parents might surprise you." He hugged her close and kissed her.

"We'll find out soon enough, but don't hold your breath." She leaned into him. "Do I smell coffee?"

"You do. I asked Edna for some coffee while we spend our day up here. She sent up hot chocolate and cookies, too." He let go of her and scrutinized the contents left on a table. "Chocolate chip and snickerdoodles, alright!" He grabbed four cookies, munching them as he tackled the logs for a fire.

"You are too much. Thanks for ordering this." She poured a mug of hot chocolate, grabbed two cookies, and climbed into the chaise lounge. "Will you join me?"

"You bet." He got a mug of coffee, another handful of cookies, his book, and sat next to her.

Leigh nestled against Garrett's chest; she sighed as he wrapped his arms around her in a protective circle of strength and warmth. The fire crackled and blazed, battling the chill in the room. They settled into their books. For the longest time, the only sounds in the room came from the turning of pages, sipping of hot liquid, and the crunching sound of cookies being eaten.

"This is nice," Leigh said. "I never did this before."

"Read a book?" Garrett absently asked, caught up in his story.

"No, silly! Sit with a guy and read, with no talking, no TV watching, and no music."

"Proof positive how comfortable we are with each other." He kissed her hair. "I must admit I'm nervous about meeting your parents. What if they caught a news report and learned you were in harm's way because of me? They may never grant us their blessing, and they'll hate me."

She sat up and stared at him in shock. "Garrett, I love you. Mom and Dad will accept our engagement; besides we won't offer them a choice. We will be married. Stop worrying over this weekend."

"If you say so, I'll try. I thought we should drive the snowmobiles back to the cabin. Because of all the snow, the driveway won't be passable until I clear it. Plus, we can avoid the press by driving the snowmobiles. Edna will make sure the sleds are gassed up and ready for us tomorrow morning."

"What are we doing with your Jeep?"

"The staff will move it into the shed for me. If you drive me back for my appointment on Monday, I can pick it up afterward."

"No wonder you took so long to reach the library, you arranged our travel plans, too."

"Well, my delay gave you time to conjure up an entertaining indoor activity for us." He appreciated the blush rising on her cheeks. "Leigh, how soon do you suppose we can marry? After I report for work, I start the undercover assignment, so I won't be home at night or contacting you until the job is over. It'd be great if we're married before I leave on assignment."

"How much time does that leave for the wedding, one or two weeks?"

"More like one week, is that enough time?"

"For me, yes. Guess we should check on how we secure a marriage license and the timing for one. After this weekend, we'll be in Brainerd, and our first task is finding a house. Right?"

"Yeah, after my Monday morning appointment at the hospital, we can head out. I contacted a realtor in the area a month ago, and he's been searching for potential homes. I should check in with him and make him aware of the recent changes in my life. Would you mind if we hold off on looking for a storefront until later?"

"Not at all; depending on the house we find we may not need a storefront. Besides, we haven't researched how I'll work this photography career." She studied his eyes for a moment and hated herself for needing her next question answered. "May I ask you a question regarding your job?"

"You can ask me anything."

"How dangerous will this assignment be?" Her voice broke slightly with the question.

"There'd be some risk involved, but I don't know all the particulars yet. I've done undercover work before, and experience is always beneficial. Rest assured; I'll be as careful as possible." He worried his words may not ease her concerns.

"Earlier you said I won't see you or talk with you while you're on this assignment?"

"Probably not, but if I can contact you, I will."

"I won't lie. This won't be easy for me, and I'll worry for your safety. I realize that your job comes with risks, but…" Her voice faded off as she faced the reality of his career.

"Leigh?" Garrett's concern echoed in his voice.

"Don't worry. I can do this."

He wrapped his arms around her and held her close. "In the Air Force, the unit members and their families supported one another during similar times of separation. The BCA may act in the same way for families. Keep in mind, I'm well-trained and experienced. I'll try to be extra careful because a cherished and adored lady is at home waiting for me." He gave her a squeeze. She smiled at him, and he relaxed. "Would you care for a refill of your hot chocolate?"

"Yes please and a couple of cookies."

"For you, darlin', anything."

He refilled their mugs and handed her an assortment of cookies. Before returning, he tossed another log on the fire. Back to cuddling with Leigh, he grabbed his book and drew her close. The serenity he experienced with her proved unexpected, gratifying, and worth waiting for.

Leigh drank her hot chocolate and devoured her cookies. She abandoned her book and nestled in closer against Garrett. With him, she never doubted or questioned his love for her or whether he cared for her. Embracing the sense of peace gained from him, she drifted off to sleep, content and happy.

When Leigh's full weight pressed against his side, he glanced down at her. With her eyes closed and her soft breathing, she appeared so peaceful. He spread the quilt over her, warding off any chill. A lock of hair lay across her cheek, so he swept it behind her ear with the lightest touch. A new mission consumed him, convincing her parents he loved her, cherished her, and needed her in his life. He drew her closer and abandoned his book as thoughts of meeting her parents barraged his concentration.

***

Leigh blinked herself awake. Warm and comfortable, she snuggled closer against Garrett. The logs glowed as mere embers in the fireplace and darkness cloaked the room. Regular sounds of breathing and the steady up and down of his chest told her he slept.

What a day! The exhilaration of their library experience turned to terrifying when Connie and Mary almost caught them in a compromising position. She wondered if the ladies guessed why they found the library door locked. A chuckle escaped. Of course, they figured out what she and Garrett had been up to as soon as they walked into the library.

As thoughts often ramble, hers jumped to the upcoming weekend at the cabin. Where would they sleep in relation to her parents' room? Would they expect her to sleep in her room alone? Would they be surprised/shocked/disappointed if she and Garrett shared a room? Once they arrived at the cabin, Garrett's things should be deposited in Alex's room, the one farthest from her parents' room. What should she do with her things? The expected or what she wanted? Does this need to be complicated?

She fidgeted with the quilt while her mind ran in tangential patterns of thought. Okay, sleeping arrangements were a decision for later. If sleeping together became impossible, their sexual activity moved outside of the cabin. In the shed? No, too cold. If they went for a drive in her car, would the backseat accommodate them? No, not enough room. Her brow furrowed and her lips pouted as she thought further. A deep laugh startled her.

"What are you plotting?"

"I am not plotting." The blush racing across her cheeks contradicted her denial.

"Why am I not convinced?" he countered, with a knowing look on his face.

Obviously, she would never hide anything from him.

"Fine, I was plotting! I tried imagining having sex in the backseat of my car." When he feigned surprise, she amended, "With you, of course. Oh, I did some plotting earlier regarding the how and where we can be together at the cabin while my parents are there."

"You did? So, you'll be comfortable having sex while they're with us at the cabin?"

"Considering our actions this morning in the library, I guess so. I'm sure Connie and Mary either immediately knew what happened between us before they entered or figured it out later. How much worse will the suspicions be with my parents?"

He laughed. "I'm sure Connie and Mary knew what we did behind the locked door; they're bright ladies. What are your thoughts for the cabin and our love trysts?"

He pushed aside her braid and attacked her neck with kisses.

"We'll put your things in Alex's room before they arrive. Would you stop, this is important." She swatted at him, so he sat back and listened. "As I was saying, Alex's room is the farthest from my parents' bedroom, so his room would be the best location in the house for our love trysts. If you recall, their room is next to mine, so a tryst in my room is ridiculous to even think about. The plan is I sneak out of my room late in the evening and return before they wake up in the morning. If meeting inside doesn't work, I haven't come up with an alternative. The shed would be too cold, and my car is too small for parking. That's as far as I got, when you interrupted my plotting on how and where we can be together for, you know, sex." She blushed with her confession.

"I think we can survive a weekend without having any sex, as long as we're together." He pulled her on his lap and kissed her. "Doesn't a chance exist they won't consider our sleeping together a big deal, so we can stay together in a bedroom? We are engaged after all, so they must suspect we're having sex. If you're thinking about sexual liaisons with them in the house, why not be forthcoming with them?"

"Openness with them would be the grown-up approach, but how comfortable will a discussion of our sexual activity with my parents be for us?" Leigh nibbled on her lower lip.

"Not much. Won't they expect intimacy because of our engagement?"

"One would think. I'll consider your position, but no promises. Sorry I fell asleep. Did you finish your book?"

"No. I bookmarked my spot, so I can finish it when we're back for our honeymoon."

"What makes you suppose you'll have time for reading on our honeymoon?" She turned and pressed her lips against his. She could feel his smile and chuckle.

"Should we go downstairs for supper?" Garrett asked as his stomach rumbled.

"Guess we should feed the beast before it devours me!" Leigh joked with him as she stood.

He swatted her bottom as she walked past him.

"I'll devour you later, darlin', and that's a promise."

Chapter Twenty-Six

Leigh and Garrett were the first ones down for dinner. They had just seated themselves when the remaining guests, Connie, Tom, Mary, and Glenn, entered the dining room. It became apparent their supper would turn into an interesting meal.

"Hello. Heard a tale of you two reading in the library this morning, behind a locked door. Read any good books?" Larry stopped putting food on his plate and raised his eyebrows at them.

"Yeah, ever find out how the door got mysteriously locked from the inside?" Tom almost choked on his laughter as he sipped his soup. "The doors in these older buildings can be tricky or else the inn's haunted."

"Haunted? No, but we ended up reading in our room. Much cozier if you catch my drift." Leigh surprised herself by dropping an innuendo as if asking for a comment from anybody.

"I'm sure reading in front of a fireplace would be a huge improvement over a cold library." Mary added such emphasis on the word 'reading' everyone understood her true meaning.

"A fireplace is a rather warm setting for reading," Leigh agreed.

Tired of skirting around the topic, Glenn tossed out a gruff, "Aw, hell, we all know what you're talking about, Leigh, and it sure as heck ain't reading!"

Everyone shared a long laugh.

Garrett tried redirecting the conversation with a diversion. "With all the reading we did, keeping up our energy was critical, so Edna sent up some coffee, hot chocolate, and cookies. She makes the best cookies."

The ploy met success as the conversation turned away from their escapades in the library and to the excellent quality and variety of food at the Aspen Inn. The conversation flowed around them during the remainder of the meal. They spoke up on occasion, but mostly they listened and enjoyed both the company and the meal. Coffee and dessert came out and soon the meal ended. They wished the other couples a good evening and sought sanctuary in their room. The last of their bottle of wine came up with them along with two wine glasses.

Once inside, Leigh sat on the braid rug in front of the fireplace. She patted the space beside her.

"Over here, Garrett. Time for my revenge."

"What, time for Crazy Eights?" After building up the fire, he sat opposite her and handed her a glass of wine.

"We're playing Strip Crazy Eights," she corrected. She shuffled the cards and dealt out two hands. She flipped over the top card, the three of clubs. "Your play."

"Okay." He played a club.

"Unbelievable." She pulled off a boot and drew a card. After emitting a frustrated noise, she pulled off the other boot.

"Problems so soon, darlin'?" Garrett queried with a raise of an eyebrow as he sipped his wine.

"No worries. I'm sure I'll gain a play with this next draw."

She drew a card and sighed. Off came a sock and she drew again.

"Where are the clubs and the eights?"

"Still nothing?" He sipped his wine, waiting on her next play. He considered throwing the game but dismissed the idea. She would kick his butt for trying such a stunt.

"Mighty astute observation, Mr. BCA Special Agent, still nothing!" She tossed aside the last sock and drew again. "Aha! Finally, a club." She snapped the card down, sat back, and drank her wine.

"A club or a two, huh? How's this?" Another club dropped on the pile.

"A seven, a seven..." Leigh studied her cards and glared at him.

"No seven, huh?" He struggled at containing his laugh.

"No." Off came her sweater, gracing him with a beautiful view of her breasts held in a minuscule satin and lace bra. A hearty curse came from her after she drew a card. Standing; she pulled off her jeans.

He had to admit her selection of lingerie left him speechless.

She drew a card and laughed. An eight plopped down. "Spades." She sat back with defiance in her eyes.

He spotted goose bumps on her arms. This game needed to end before she caught a cold. He laid down an eight. She scowled at him.

"Clubs."

"Of course, you'd select clubs!" She pulled off her panties and drew a card. "Argh!"

He couldn't contain a hiss of laughter.

She glared at him, as her hands undid the clasp of her bra and bared her breasts.

"There's still hope. I could win a piece back." She sat before him, trying not to shiver. The chill in the room hardened her nipples.

"You go with that, Leigh." He choked back his laughter, as she drew another card.

"Ha!" She slapped down an eight. "Spades."

"You must hold most of the spades in the deck by now, huh?"

"Guess you'll find out."

"Maybe and maybe not, darlin'." He pulled a card from his hand and played the fourth eight! "Clubs."

"Unbelievable, and I dealt these hands! Obviously, you are the Strip Crazy Eights champion and to the winner goes the spoils."

She threw herself at him. He fell back and gathered her into his arms.

Her lips pressed against his. His tongue grazed her lips, and she opened for him. Their tongues met in an explosion of love and passion. He rolled her beneath him.

"Frankly, Leigh, you should find another card game." His hands roamed over her body, warming, and exciting her.

"Garrett?"

"I'm here for you, darlin'."

Her phone rang. He paused and she moaned.

"They'll call back, Garrett. I need to be with you, as close to you as possible. Make love to me."

"My pleasure."

His answer rumbled through his chest and caused vibrations wherever her body touched his. The vibrations increased her feelings of love for him as they continued directly to her heart.

Their world exploded as they made love. Unable to remain in one place, they moved around the room with the ebb and flow of their passion. Much later they found themselves in bed, exhausted and glowing in their love for one another. Garrett managed to stagger to the bathroom. Returning with warm washcloths and towels, he cleaned and dried Leigh with a provocative slowness and gentleness. When he finished, she reciprocated with equal care and attentiveness. Refreshed, they lay together.

"I love you, Leigh Ramsey." A gentle kiss on her hair punctuated his reverent declaration.

"And I love you, Garrett Dane." She nestled closer to him and, with thoughts of their love, fell into a blissful sleep.

He held her close, but thoughts of meeting her parents followed him into a fitful sleep.

Chapter Twenty-Seven

He awoke before dawn. With Leigh cuddled in his arms, he extricated himself slowly away from her, so she wouldn't wake. Wasting no time, he went straight into the bathroom to clean up and dress. He packed his things and hauled his duffel bag to the door. Nervous energy coursed through his body. Anxious to depart, he knew they should wait for daylight before leaving on the snowmobiles. He turned on one of the smaller lamps in their room, sat in the nearby chair, and opened the book he'd been reading.

Leigh reached for Garrett but touched cold sheets instead of his warm body. The emptiness shocked her, and she bolted upright. "Garrett?"

"I'm right here, Leigh." His deep, calm voice cut through her fog of sleep. She found him as she wiped away the sleep from her eyes.

"What are you doing?"

"Couldn't sleep, but you should stay in bed."

"But if you're up—"

"Leigh," Garrett interrupted her. "The hour is too early to leave, so you may as well go back to sleep."

"Why are you up and dressed?"

"Honestly? I'm too nervous to sleep; figured I'd read a little to relax."

"Ah, Garrett, you shouldn't be nervous. How could they not love you? No way will I allow my parents to come between us. Whatever happens, I will do everything within my power to ensure we survive this weekend. We're soul mates and will be together forever. Be sure to wake me a half hour before we need to leave, so I'm not rushed." She stretched and plopped down, pulling his pillow into her stomach.

"I promise," he vowed, crossing his heart. He watched, as she flopped around getting comfortable. He realized the ridiculousness of being nervous over meeting her parents, but he still couldn't relieve the anxiety growing within him. Picturing an inquisition didn't ease his anxiety. Soon her soft, regular breathing filled the quiet, so he returned to his book.

After a couple of hours, he set the book down and walked to the bed. Curled up, Leigh still hugged his pillow to her chest. Her hair draped over her shoulders, rendering her a soft, angelic appearance. Her long lashes lay against her cheeks. He leaned down, with his lips by an ear.

"Time to rise and shine."

"Is it morning already?" She blinked her eyes open, stretched, and smiled at him.

"Yes. While you clean up and dress, I'll pack for you. We'll eat breakfast and check out afterward. If we wear our helmets out, the reporters hanging around won't be able to snap a picture of our faces."

"Perfect plan, and you'll pack for me? I'm such a lucky woman." She kissed him on the lips, before entering the bathroom.

"Actually, I'm the lucky one," he said to himself as he regarded her naked form as she disappeared into the bathroom.

In half an hour, Leigh was dressed and ready to go. Garrett picked up their bags and followed her down the stairs.

An empty dining room greeted them due to the early hour. After a delectable meal, they stopped at the front desk to check out.

"Edna! Do you ever escape from this place?" Leigh asked when they spotted her manning the desk.

"On a rare occasion but being here is a labor of love for me. So, what's next for you two?"

"Ride the snowmobiles back to my family's cabin and prepare for my mom and dad to show up," Leigh explained while she messed with her bag. "They're going to love Garrett almost as much as I do."

Edna nodded her head in agreement, but Garrett's eyes reflected his apprehension.

"Time will tell. I'm sure the driveway will need to be cleared. I intend on blowing all the snow out, so they can drive right up to the cabin and not wade through snow to reach the front door. Hoping my skill with a snowblower may earn me a few brownie points," Garrett confessed. As Leigh rummaged through her bag, he frowned. "Did I forget to pack something?"

"Nope, searching for these." She held up house keys.

"We should check out and be on our way." He handed over his credit card. "Thank you for everything, Edna. We look forward to returning as actual newlyweds."

"Helping you through this time and celebrating your love has been my pleasure." She completed the payment transaction, before stepping around the desk to give each of them a hug. "You take care. Garrett, we'll watch over your Jeep until you pick it up."

"Thank you."

With their helmets on, they walked out the back door. Fewer reporters stood along the property line but plenty of them remained. Garrett and Leigh walked to the shed without being accosted. Once in the shed, Garrett strapped down their bags.

"That proved easy enough," Leigh called out over the roar of her machine's motor.

Garrett gave her a thumbs up, started his machine, and indicated for her to lead the way. They roared out of the shed and disappeared out the back entrance of the inn. A pack of reporters remained behind without a clue their quarry eluded them.

The solitude of riding across snow-covered fields failed to sooth Leigh's nervousness over her parents meeting Garrett. Confident in her dad's acceptance of her fiancé, her anxiety centered on her mom's reaction. The wild assumption Leigh's good news involved David didn't bode well regarding her mom's acceptance of her fiancé. In her mom's opinion, David's social connections, his money, and his profession assured a successful marriage. In comparison, Garrett lacked all those, so she would consider him disastrous husband material. A horrendous weekend loomed ahead of them.

Her frustration ramped up as she thought of her mom's ability for caustic, hostile words and deeds. The call they missed last night had been from her; her fury over an ignored call was legendary in the family. As Leigh's frustration increased, so did her speed. Suddenly, Garrett blasted past her and careened to a stop, shooting snow skyward. She stopped beside him.

"What the heck is up with you?" Garrett yelled over the engine noise.

"Nothing. Why?" she lied to him.

"You're driving as though hell hounds are on your tail."

"Well, we need plenty of time to prepare the cabin before my parents arrive." Her voice quivered, but not noticeable over the engine noise. "I need to do some laundry and start supper. You have snow blowing to complete. All our tasks take time. Can we go again?"

"Sure but slow down a bit."

"Okay."

She took off in a cloud of snow. Garrett shook his head and gunned his engine to chase her down.

They made the trek to the cabin in record time. When they drove across the three- to four-foot drifts covering the driveway, they were glad they rode the snowmobiles. Snow drifts stretched across what remained of the path Garrett had cleared between the shed and garage four short days ago. They parked the snowmobiles by the shed. Garrett handled their bags and broke a trail for Leigh to the back door. She opened the door, and he dumped in the bags.

"I'll start working on the driveway."

"There should be gas in the shed. I'm sure you'll refill the snowblower a couple of times before you're done."

"I'll bring in firewood before I start."

"Thanks. Will you eat some lunch later?"

"Don't need anything; I'm still full from breakfast."

After Garrett brought in firewood and started a fire, he disappeared into the garage.

Soon streams of snow arced across the front yard, so she admired his skill and progress for a while. With a sigh, she turned away and gathered dirty clothes to start laundry.

With thoughts of their conversation from last night, she decided on the grown-up approach and hauled their bags toward the bedrooms. Feeling less than confident, she dropped both bags in Alex's room and moved in some items from her room. Surely her parents wouldn't say anything negative. After all, she and Garrett were engaged.

To distract herself from further negative thoughts, she tore apart the beds and remade them with fresh linens. With the last load of clothes in the dryer, she dumped a roast and vegetables in a crock pot. Not up to her mom's gourmet standards, but the simple, hearty supper would suffice.

The back door burst open, and Garrett stomped his way into the cabin. Cheeks red from the cold and his eyes sparkling, he struck her as having a Viking quality, strong and bold.

"Snow blowing agrees with you." She met him at the door and helped him pull off his cold weather gear.

"Call me crazy, but I missed this while stationed in Georgia." He grinned at her as he pulled off his boots.

"Why don't you pull off all your clothes and take a shower? The water should warm you up. I'll wash your clothes, so everything will be clean for the weekend. Our things are in Alex's room." She noted his eyebrows rising. "Rather than assume we can't stay together, I put us together."

"You're going with the grown-up approach?" He peeled off his shirt and reached for his belt.

"Ah, yes, and you shouldn't remove your clothes here."

"Why? Don't you believe I could reach the bathroom before they walk in?"

He continued with his stripping.

"I'm sure you're capable; however, your actions are distracting me."

He dropped his jeans, pulled off his socks, and removed his shorts.

"So, are you distracted?"

With legs spread and hands on his hips, he stood gloriously naked before her.

She gulped and looked him up and down.

"Am I what?"

He laughed, kissed her, and departed for the bedroom. She admired his athletic and powerful build, as he walked away.

"Definitely distracting," she muttered as she picked up his clothes.

With all his clothes in the washer, she wandered into the bathroom. Finished with his shower, Garrett stood in the center of the room toweling himself dry.

"They ought to arrive soon. I'm going to put out some munchies to tide us over until the roast is done."

As he wrapped the towel around him, she admired how well the damp plushness rode about his trim hips. If she stayed any longer, sex would happen in the bathroom regardless of the impending arrival of her parents. A sudden mental image of herself sitting in the sink with her legs wrapped around his hips instead of a towel jarred her into action.

"Gotta go!" She hastened out of the bathroom, leaving a bewildered Garrett in her wake.

"Can't wait to find out what drove her out of here," he said to himself as he toweled his hair dry.

Leigh busied herself in the kitchen and prepared a platter of cheeses and meats with a basket of crackers for when her parents arrived. Rummaging through her wine bottles for one to open, she didn't hear Garrett come up behind her.

"Anything I can do?" Garrett asked her.

"Crap!" She fell back; one hand went over her heart. "You startled me! Can't you make some noise or something?"

"Stealth skills keep me alive, Leigh. I need to stay sharp." He offered her a hand and helped her up. "What's with you? You're acting different."

His eyes appeared bluer than brown. She felt as though they pierced through her, as if he glimpsed into her soul and learned all her secrets.

"I realize I keep telling you not to worry over meeting my parents, but I'm not sure what to expect when they arrive. I believe Dad will be okay with us, but Mom may be difficult. She really, really adored my ex-boyfriend, David. I never understood why she thought so highly of him."

"So, you don't expect I'll measure up in her eyes?"

"In all honesty, I'm not sure. Sorry, Garrett."

"Well, we'll find out soon. I just heard a car door."

A momentary panic froze her in place before she reached for his hand and led him to the front door. Upon opening it, sure enough, her parents had arrived.

"Mom. Dad!"

Garrett stepped outside and, in a few strides, he stood by her dad at the car's trunk.

"I'll handle those, sir. Leigh's anxious to see you." Garrett grabbed their two suitcases and took them indoors. He passed Leigh being crushed by her mom's hug, and he smiled at the snippet of conversation he caught as he walked by them.

"Leigh, are you okay? Are you sure about him?"

"His name is Garrett, Mom, and I'm way beyond okay. I'm so happy I could burst."

"You know I always worry."

"Let's go inside, and we can talk. Did you eat anything?"

They walked inside, and Leigh helped her mom remove her coat. She caught sight of her mom looking over the cabin as if searching for signs of something awry. She led her mom to the kitchen away from the chill entering through the open front door.

"No, we didn't stop for lunch. The food I brought needs to come in."

"I'll bring everything in for you, ma'am." Garrett walked past as he returned from dropping off their bags.

"He's extremely polite."

"Mom, he's way more than polite." She turned as a hand touched her shoulder. "Dad!" Her arms flew around him, and she hugged him close.

"Leigh. We're happy to join you. Did Garrett clear all the snow?"

"Yes, he blew snow for a long time. In fact, he finished cleaning up moments before you arrived."

She relaxed against her dad, hoping for an ally.

Garrett walked into the kitchen carrying all the grocery bags. He sat them on a counter.

"Mom, Dad, this is my fiancé, Garrett Dane. Garrett, my parents, Frank and Lois Ramsey." She moved to Garrett's side and wrapped an arm around him.

"Mr. Ramsey. Mrs. Ramsey. I'm pleased to meet you." Garrett shook hands with each of them.

Her dad spoke up first. "Garrett, we're happy to meet you. None of that Mr. and Mrs. stuff. You'll need to call us Frank and Lois. First things first, I'm tired from driving, so let's grab something to drink and sit down."

Sweet old dad, thought Leigh, trying his best to put everyone at ease.

"I prepared snacks, so make yourselves comfortable in the family room, and we'll bring the food in." She pressed for her folks to head to the other room and collapsed against Garrett when they left the kitchen area. "Let's put this stuff away. Then we'll pour a white wine for Mom and bring Dad a beer."

They went through the bags trying hard not to laugh over the bizarre items they came up with. Dinner à la mom promised to be interesting.

"There's a Pinot Grigio in the chiller for Mom and me. Do you want wine or a beer?"

"Tonight's a beer night for sure."

Garrett opened the bottle of wine Leigh mentioned and poured two glasses. She finalized the snacks and pulled out beers for her dad and Garrett.

"Here goes nothing." Leigh lifted the tray of food.

"We'll be fine."

He kissed her rather passionately, leaving Leigh unsure whether her legs would hold her up. With a wink, he encouraged her to lead the way. Fortunately, they reached the family room without incident.

"Here you are. Something to snack on before dinner. A beef roast is in the crock-pot and should be ready around five-thirty."

She sat the food on the coffee table; Garrett handed Lois a glass of wine and Frank a cold beer. Everyone fixed themselves a plate of snacks and settled back in their respective spots. Garrett took a swallow of beer and steeled himself for the start of an inquisition. Leigh's mom didn't disappoint.

"So, where are you from?"

"I'm originally from Graceville, Minnesota, a small farming community in western Minnesota. But I haven't been back in years."

"Oh? Not close to your family?"

Leigh rolled her eyes and gritted her teeth. Why did her mom go in the forsaking family direction? Garrett squeezed her knee, a gentle reassurance he could handle this.

"I don't have any family, Lois. My parents died in a car accident when I was twenty years old. The last time I went there was for their funeral."

"Oh, I'm sorry. And what kind of business are you in?"

"Law enforcement. I'm starting a new job with the BCA out of the Brainerd office."

"A rather dangerous job, wouldn't you agree?"

"At times, yes, but the danger is lessened with training and experience. Having worked in law enforcement for years, my skills are well honed. Thanks to my experience and a knack for investigations, the BCA hired me."

"Where did you gain your experience?" Frank joined in on the questioning.

"In the Air Force." Garrett's pride in his military service showed in his face and in his tone. "Right after high school, I joined the Air Force and went in the Security Forces career field. I eventually became a special agent with the Air Force Office of Special Investigations."

"So, you never attended college?" The haughty tone of her voice made Lois's question sound like an accusation.

Surprised at such a negative reaction by Lois, Garrett forged ahead. "No, I never went to an actual college campus, but I earned a BS in criminal science as well as a master's degree while serving my country."

"Oh." Lois tried to disguise her dismay in his education accomplishments by drinking her wine.

"Impressive resume, Garrett. I'm sure the BCA is lucky to include you in their ranks." Frank raised his beer to Garrett in salute and downed a long swallow.

"Thank you, Frank."

Leigh realized what her mom tried to do to Garrett and how miserably she failed.

"Garrett's remarkably talented and skilled at what he does, Mom."

"Your father received a call the other day from a reporter asking us for a statement concerning our daughter being held hostage during a shootout by a hospital. Imagine our shock at her request. You didn't bother telling us, instead we learned about your escapade from a reporter." Lois glared at them, her eyes as cold as an Arctic blast. "If he's so remarkably talented and skilled at his job, why did he allow you to be in harm's way?"

Like a gauntlet thrown down in a challenge, Lois tossed out her accusation. This took them by surprise. They hadn't anticipated anyone obtaining their names and contacting her family.

"Garrett didn't want me going with him, but I insisted. I wasn't in any real danger, Mom." She decided stretching the truth a bit might calm down her mother. "Garrett was with me and stopped the guy before anything bad happened to me."

"'Stopped the guy?' What does that mean? Did he kill this man?" Lois spit out her questions in a louder voice than necessary for the room.

Garrett tried not to flinch at her words. During their engagement party at the Aspen Inn, he explained to Leigh this exact reaction.

"The guy shot at Garrett, Mom, so he defended himself and saved me. Let it be." Leigh's voice rose in volume to match her mom.

"Lois, calm down." Dad to the rescue. "I'm sure he did what he could to ensure Leigh's safety. She shouldn't have been involved, but you know as well as I do how obstinate and headstrong she can be. Tying her up would have been necessary to keep her away."

"Thank you, sir. I admire those qualities in Leigh. They are what make her so unique and desirable." Garrett hugged her to him and kissed her cheek. She melted into him, so thankful for her dad's commonsense and for the man holding her close.

Her mom huffed in frustration. She sat back and took a large swallow of wine.

"What are you two planning for your wedding? Being the father of a daughter, I always figured on paying big bucks for our only girl's wedding."

"Dad, we want to marry before Garrett starts his BCA job. If you remember, I never asked for a big wedding." With her mom pursing her lips, reddening, and almost squirming in her seat, she sped forward. "A small wedding at the house or at the Aspen Inn would be enough for us. After spending a few days at the inn, we discovered how wonderful it is, and we're fond of the owner. The location is beautiful."

"Leigh, a wedding cannot happen in such a short space of time. Getting a dress can involve months between the initial sewing and subsequent fittings. Invitations must be selected and mailed out. People aren't able to drop everything and come to your wedding."

"But Mom—"

"I will not allow my only daughter to be married in such a hasty fashion. You will have a proper wedding. Frank, surely you won't agree with Leigh's wedding being a cheap, sordid, little affair."

"Lois, I think 'cheap' and 'sordid' is going a bit too far. A small wedding sounds exactly what Leigh would want, not the lavish church wedding you always envisioned for her."

Leigh breathed a sigh of relief, and her mom looked ready to bite off her dad's head.

Her dad continued. "Leigh, surely you prefer an elegant wedding with friends and family in attendance. What woman doesn't want to feel like a princess on their wedding day?"

Leigh stared at her dad in disbelief. How dare he side with her mom on this? It would be her wedding, not theirs.

"We could always elope." Leigh spoke of elopement as a last-ditch effort to force their agreement.

"You will *not* elope!" Her mom slapped her hand down on her chair's arm for emphasis. "Leigh, you are not thinking this through rationally. You should give yourself additional time to become better acquainted with each other. Why do you need to get married so quickly? Are you pregnant?"

Garrett and her dad almost spit out their beer with her question. Leigh blushed deep red.

"No, Mom! We love each other and intend to marry. No ulterior motives, no pregnancy, only our love for each other. Why can't you accept the simple fact we're in love? I need to check on dinner." Leigh stormed off to the kitchen. Cabinet doors started slamming, pots and pans rattled.

"Our preference is to marry before I start my job with the BCA. My first assignment will keep me away for an unknown length of time, so we're unsure of when we could schedule a wedding if we waited. I love your daughter, and I will do everything I can to ensure her happiness." Garrett tried to further explain their situation to her parents. "Excuse me, I'm going to check if Leigh needs any help."

"Nicely done, Lois. You face an uphill battle now."

Frank made a mock toast to his wife and drained his beer.

Lois glared at him.

"She's too caught up in the romance of the situation. I'm going to freshen up." Lois added wine to her glass and carried it down the hall. On her way to their room, she glanced into Leigh's bedroom and made note of the lack of a suitcase or any of Leigh's things.

Frank watched his wife walk away. He had faith this wedding dispute would resolve itself, but not without some butting of heads. Apparently, his little girl found herself a deserving-young man. He filled up his plate, turned on the TV, and relaxed in his recliner.

Garrett walked into the kitchen and wrapped his arms around Leigh. He pulled her close. She rested her head against his chest and breathed in his outdoorsy scent of fresh air, pine, and cedar.

"I didn't expect their reaction would be this bad or this meeting so difficult and trying." As she spoke, she relaxed into him, and he held her tightly against him. "At least it's only for the weekend."

"I told them why we planned to marry so quickly. I didn't tell them anything about the undercover aspect of my assignment, only that I'd be gone for an unknown amount of time." He spoke quietly, his words for only her. "I like the idea of having our wedding at the Aspen Inn."

"I think it would be a beautiful location. Gonna help me with dinner?"

"Helping you is my new mission in life and why I'm here. Well, moral support and dinner for now. What can I do?"

"Set the table?"

They were busy with dinner when Lois walked into the kitchen.

"Leigh, why are your things in Alex's room?"

"Garrett and I are staying in there." Leigh stopped dishing up the food to return her mom's stare.

"Unacceptable." Lois glanced at Garrett as he set the table.

"Why unacceptable, Mom?" Determined to win this debate, Leigh decided to challenge her mother head-to-head.

"You only met him a few days ago. I firmly believe you're moving way too fast, so the two of you staying together in one bedroom is unacceptable." Her mom lowered her voice trying to keep their conversation private.

"Mom, we've been sleeping together and will continue to do so." Leigh spoke evenly and turned away from her mother.

"Leigh! Do not turn your back on me." Lois increased the volume of her voice so both Garrett and Frank heard clearly. Frank came into the kitchen, but Garrett hung back in the dining room. If necessary, he'd rush to Leigh's aid, but he wouldn't barge into a family argument.

"What's going on in here?" Frank's eyes bounced back and forth between his wife and daughter. "Lois?"

"I told Leigh they're moving too fast."

"Oh, you didn't stop there, Mom. You don't believe we should sleep together. We're engaged, for Pete's sake! What do you think we do at night, play checkers and sleep in separate beds?" On a roll, Leigh readied for her mom's response.

Her dad stepped in between them before Lois retaliated.

"I don't consider anything wrong with them sharing a bedroom, Lois. Leigh's a grown woman; you can't treat her as though she's still in high school."

Leigh sent up a silent thank you for her dad.

"I'm in agreement with your mother regarding how fast you two are moving on marrying. I believe waiting a few months on the wedding would be beneficial for you. Once Garrett's back in the area, you can plan for the wedding. In the meantime, you can get to know each other better."

"But Garrett—" She understood the message in his sharp look and shake of his head and realized she almost disclosed his undercover assignment. Adjusting her original thought, she continued. "And I don't need extra time."

Garrett's exhale was slow and shaky. Leigh recovered nicely without disclosing the details of his upcoming assignment.

"We simply prefer getting married sooner rather than later, but we can discuss the timing further." Garrett's words supported her and hopefully bought them time to build their case and win this timing argument.

He walked behind her and spoke quietly in her ear, "You're turning me on with how feisty you're getting." A deep kiss accented his words.

She willed herself not to blush as the proof of his words pressed against her back.

"Garrett's right, we can discuss the wedding timing later; after all, we have the whole weekend." Her dad's agreement virtually called a truce to the debate, at least for the time being.

"Dinner is ready. Why don't you two sit down? Leigh and I will bring in the food," Garrett suggested.

"Good thinking, Garrett. Come on, Lois." Frank escorted his wife to the table. "I could go for another beer."

Dinner turned out to be an extremely stiff and uncomfortable meal. Both Garrett and Frank made multiple attempts at conversation, but the women offered no more than one-word responses, making for difficult conversation. Finally, the meal ended.

"We'll clean up," Leigh said as she stood.

She and Garrett cleared the table, put leftovers away, and loaded the dishwasher. When they finished, he swept her in his arms.

"I love you, Leigh Ramsey."

His lips gently caressed her brow, he moved to her nose and lips. He ran his tongue along her lips in search of entry, and she responded with a welcoming sigh. Their tongues twirled and explored each other.

His hands roamed down to cup her butt, and he pulled her closer against him. His mouth muffled her moan.

Her hands went into his hair. She kissed him urgently. Her hands roamed over his back and downward, massaging and pinching.

A groan came from deep in his throat.

She leaned back and stared into the now warm-brown eyes she loved.

"I love you, Garrett. Thanks for tempering me or trying to. I'm sorry I got so crazy with my mom." Leigh sighed against his chest. "I suppose I should apologize to her."

"A heartfelt apology couldn't hurt." Garrett gave her a kiss and a pat on the butt. "I'm sure she'd appreciate it."

They walked out of the kitchen and joined her parents in the family room. Garrett sat on the couch. Leigh stood by him.

"Delicious dinner, honey," her dad said from his comfortable recliner by the window.

"Thanks, Dad." She walked over to her mom and knelt beside her. "Mom, I'm sorry for being so touchy as to the timing of the wedding and sleeping arrangements."

"Thank you, Leigh. I appreciate your apology. I still believe the wedding needs to be later, much later, maybe next spring or summer or the following year. A year delay will allow us time for planning a proper wedding. His friends invited to the wedding will need time to make travel arrangements."

"Garrett, Mom. His name is Garrett. Why can't you remember?" Frustration over her mom's attitude put an edge to Leigh's words.

"The suddenness of the engagement shocked me, so I'm having difficulty processing this change in your life." Her mom touched her shoulder.

All Leigh experienced in the touch was insincerity. She abandoned her mom and plopped onto the couch beside Garrett.

He overheard the conversation with her mom, so he knew the odds were highly in favor of Leigh being upset. His arm went around her, and he pulled her close.

She relaxed against him. His gentle kiss placed on her head grounded her and ended her dwelling on her mom's words. The support of his solid body provided the strength she needed to move beyond her mom's opinions.

"Leigh, how 'bout we play a board game? I don't imagine Strip Crazy Eights would be appropriate with your parents here unless we play in our room later." His quiet words were heard only by her.

She glanced up and recognized the humor in his eyes.

"A game sounds fun and safer than other things around here."

The evening dragged along with them playing a game, while her parents sat in their recliners and watched TV. One more day of this drama, and they escaped the accompanying aggravation. After Garrett's follow-up medical appointment early Monday morning, they planned on a swift departure for Brainerd and their future. If not married, at least they'd be together.

"You won again! Are you skilled or lucky?" Leigh looked at him in disbelief.

"All skill, darlin'. Luck has nothing to do with it."

At his smile, a throb of desire coursed through her.

She yawned. "Let's put this away. I'm tired and ready to put today behind us."

"And no telling what tomorrow holds for us, so bed sounds perfect." He tossed the board game pieces in the box with more speed than precision. "Okay, all put away. Shall we go?"

"Mom. Dad. We're going to bed. See you in the morning," Leigh called to her parents.

"Good night, you two," her dad called back.

But her mom didn't respond, she simply frowned her displeasure.

Leigh followed Garrett down the hall and into the bedroom. She closed the door behind her and leaned against the hard wood.

"Could the evening have been any worse?" Leigh pushed away from the door and began undressing as she walked toward Garrett.

"Well, they could have kicked me out or demanded we sleep in separate bedrooms." Garrett stripped with abandon, tossing clothes in all directions, before he hopped into bed. "What is taking you so long?"

"You got in here before me, plus I wear more clothes." Leigh pulled off her lingerie and crawled in with him. The bed squeaked under her.

"Uh-oh! This bed's too noisy."

"Too noisy for what?"

"Having my way with you."

"You claimed to be tired."

"I am tired, but my hands ache for you and I miss touching your body; I'm going through Garrett withdrawal."

She cozied up to him. One of his arms came around her, and she moved closer to him. She started to relax in the strength of his embrace.

"We can forego any sexual activities for one night; I'm beat. Snow blowing is tough work, and I shoveled a lot, too. Plus, the mental and emotional exercise all evening took its toll. Let's rest tonight and let tomorrow unfold on its own."

"You're right." Leigh's memories of the evening raced through her head. "Mom didn't say anything after you rattled off your degrees; silencing Mom doesn't happen often. I'm sure Dad likes you."

He yawned in response. "I received positive vibes from him, but your mom…I doubt I'm anywhere close to getting her acceptance. Did she ever say my name?"

"Don't get me started on her and your name. I don't understand what her problem is toward us." She punched her pillow, before settling back against him.

"Let it go, Leigh," Garrett advised. "Maybe tomorrow will be different, although one thing concerns me about tomorrow."

Her blue eyes searched his face. "What?"

"Whether I can fake my way through her gourmet dinner if I don't care for the flavors of her concoctions."

She slapped his stomach.

"You're terrible! I thought you had something important to worry over."

"Well, dinner is important to my stomach, which you so viciously attacked." He laughed and started tickling her.

"Garrett! Don't!" She doubled up trying to prevent his fingers from succeeding in his quest to make her laugh. Her laughter came out loud and long.

"Since you're in a better mood, let's get some shut-eye. Morning will be here before we know it." He hauled her close, and soon they were both fast asleep.

Meanwhile, Leigh's parents discussed them.

"I don't care for this farce. Their relationship isn't right." Lois glared at her husband as soon as the bedroom door closed.

"Lois, she's a grown woman. Surely, you realize, as a young woman, she's sexually active. I'm sure she and David slept together." He reached for his newspaper, shook out the pages, and began reading.

"Not the sleeping arrangement, Frank. What's not right is them as a couple and this wedding they're clamoring for so quickly. The entire situation is what's not right."

"So, they aren't interested in a big wedding. Leigh's reaction doesn't surprise me; she's never shown an interest in fancy and huge events. Small and intimate sounds like our girl. Besides, he loves her."

"Hah! How did you figure out his devotion for her so soon?" Lois crossed her arms and sat back in her chair.

"By the way he looks at her and touches her. By the way he says her name. That young man is both infatuated and in love with her; his adoration of her warms my soul. She deserves someone who treasures her as Garrett does. So what if they met a week or two ago? When love's right, it's right, and no amount of time or effort on your part will turn their love less right."

"Leigh should be marrying David. The two of them together were a perfect match."

"Not perfect. Thank God she figured out how imperfect a couple they were before you married them off."

"But—"

"Not another word regarding David. This is Leigh's life. I believe she's made a sensible selection this time and on her own, too." As Leigh's muffled giggles reached them, he smiled at the joy he heard. "Garrett makes her happy, and that's all a parent can hope for. We should go to bed, too. Come on."

Chapter Twenty-Eight

Garrett woke with a start. What the hell woke me? he wondered. Small cold feet grazed his legs in answer. The coldness brought Lois to mind. Quite forceful with her opinions and attitude, her animosity confused him. Why did she prefer this David character so much? He couldn't understand Lois's disbelief of Leigh regarding David's mistreatment of her. You would imagine a mother would be supportive of her daughter. How could he help her settle this disagreement with her mom, when the disagreement centered on him?

He pulled Leigh closer. No telling what today would hold for them, but at least they had each other and their love for one another. Leigh stirred but didn't wake. He held her close and drifted back to sleep.

***

"Leigh, are you awake?" Garrett's voice broke through her dreams. A frown creased her brow as she tried to ignore him. "Come on, darlin', you should get up now."

She rolled away from his voice, tossing a pillow at him. "Let me sleep in this morning," she mumbled as she burrowed under the covers.

"What's this? We weren't up late last night." He pulled at the covers and dragged them down but stopped abruptly. Uncovering the naked, luscious body of his fiancée didn't make for a sensible idea. His body automatically reacted to the sight of her curled on the bed, sleep-tousled hair falling around her shoulders and down her back. He flipped the covers back over her to save himself.

"Maybe sleep is the problem; too much sleep and not enough extracurricular activities." She turned back to face him, pulling the covers close to her body. She opened one eye to see him, the second eye opened quickly to view the vision before her. He wore jeans and flannel. "You have a lumberjack thing going for you this morning. Why?"

"Your dad got it in his head to replenish the firewood and run the snowmobiles for a bit this morning." He sat on the bed and ran a gentle hand down her back.

"Oh, well, I can be ready in no time." She attempted to rise, but he held her down.

"You're not invited."

"Why not?"

"Because your dad asked for me alone. He announced the snowmobiling offered him 'bonding time with his future son-in-law.' Your mom threw a fit."

"Glad I slept in. When are you leaving?"

"In ten minutes. I thought to say good morning and goodbye before we left. Will you be okay?"

"Yeah, I'll be fine. Hopefully, Mom will be easier to talk with today. She'll work on her gourmet dinner and cooking usually puts her in a pleasant mood. If not, are you leaving your SIG behind?" She gave him a sly smile.

"I planned on leaving it, but maybe I shouldn't." He leaned down and kissed her, a smile evident on his lips. "You'll be fine. Remember, tomorrow they go home, and we head out."

"Tomorrow offers no relief for today. Toss me my robe, please." She sat up and let the covers fall to her waist. He groaned as his body responded to her again; he tossed her the robe.

"I need to leave before I join you in bed."

Leigh laughed as she covered herself with the robe. "You do need to go outside; Dad isn't in the habit of waiting."

"Okay. I'll see you whenever we get back." He gave her a long hot kiss before walking out the door. Leigh decided she needed coffee before her shower. She reached the kitchen in time to catch a flurry of snow as Garrett and her dad barreled out of the yard on the snowmobiles. Her mom sat at the counter with a cup of coffee and her recipes. Leigh poured herself some coffee and sat next to her.

"Morning, Mom. Are those recipes for dinner tonight?"

"Good morning, Leigh. Yes, this will be dinner." She sipped her coffee and eyed her daughter. "Care to be my sous chef?"

"I'd enjoy cooking with you again." Leigh hoped this indicated her mom might be coming around to accepting Garrett and her as a couple. Maybe today would be easier than yesterday, she thought to herself as she drank her coffee.

"You slept late this morning," her mom observed.

Alarms went off in Leigh's head.

"I'm exhausted for some reason; maybe I got too much sleep. If Garrett hadn't come in, I'd probably still be sleeping."

"Are you sure too much sleep is the reason?"

"Yes, Mom, we went to sleep shortly after we went to bed. We didn't wake up during the night; before you ask, I'll tell you we didn't have sex at all last night." Leigh tried to cut off her mom's thoughts before she voiced them.

"Really?"

"Yes, really. I'm off for a shower. When I return, I'll review the recipes with you." Leigh grabbed her cup and wandered to the bathroom. Doubts of having an agreeable time with her mom crept into her thoughts. Hopefully, Garrett would have a more enjoyable time with her dad.

***

Frank's desire to bond with him had surprised and pleased Garrett this morning. As he followed Frank on the snowmobile, tearing across fields and flying over hills, he knew exactly who taught Leigh to snowmobile. They finally stopped at a small house. Frank pulled off his helmet and motioned for Garrett to follow him.

"Jake is my source for firewood; he cuts, delivers, and stacks all the wood for a reasonable price," Frank confided to Garrett. "Trust me; this is the easiest way to stock up on firewood. If you find a place in Brainerd with a wood-burning fireplace or stove, find yourself a Jake." He winked at Garrett as he walked up to the house. A knock on the door brought Jake out. After a hearty greeting, Frank turned toward Garrett. "Jake, this is Garrett. He's going to marry my little girl."

"Pleased to meet you." Jake offered his hand and smiled broadly. "You're getting a one-in-a-million kind of gal."

Garrett shook the man's hand, while realizing how much he enjoyed Frank's introduction of him. "A pleasure meeting you, sir. I agree, Leigh is one-in-a-million."

"Jake, I need extra firewood for the cabin. I'm thinking a cord should do me."

"Sure. I can deliver the wood later this week."

"Perfect. Thanks, and send me your bill as usual."

"You betcha. Give my best to Lois."

"I will. See ya." Frank shook Jake's hand. As he walked back to the snowmobiles, he shared sage advice with Garrett. "By buying wood already cut saves you time for other pursuits."

"'Other pursuits,' sir?"

"Beer and pool, Garrett, beer and pool. You do shoot pool, don't you?"

"I've been known to shoot pool and drink beer, sir." Garrett settled back on his snowmobile and put on his helmet.

"Excellent, and Garrett? Call me Frank, not sir."

"Okay, Frank."

"Let's go."

Another ten minutes found them parking their sleds with other snowmobiles behind a country bar. Many of the men greeted Frank, after they walked in. He talked with each as they worked their way to the bar. Continually introduced as 'Frank's future son-in-law,' Garrett received congratulations, claps on his shoulder, warnings to treat Leigh right or else, and multiple offers of drinks.

Upon reaching the bar, their first draft beers waited for them. The frosted glasses shimmered and beckoned to be hefted and drank from. A stack of credits for more beers sat beside each glass. Garrett glanced at the clock behind the bar, only minutes after ten in the morning; this appeared to be a long day in the making for him.

"Garrett, come over here. We're taking on these two in a game of pool," Frank called for him from across the room.

Garrett pushed off from the bar, hoping his pool skills were up to snuff. So far things were going great with Leigh's dad. He hoped her day brought similar success with her mom.

***

Leigh delayed going back to the kitchen as long as she could, but her excuses ran out. She trudged back to the kitchen to join her mom.

"There you are. Whatever took you so long?"

"I tried something different with my hair, but the style didn't work for me." Leigh shrugged as she poured more coffee and then leaned against the counter opposite of her mom.

"We'll start looking at hairstyles for your wedding." Leigh rolled her eyes. "We will do this. Depending on your veil and dress, certain styles may work better. Wearing your hair up will be best, I'm sure, but we'll meet with my hairstylist for her ideas. She works miracles with long hair." Her mom eyed Leigh's hair critically. "After we find you a dress and veil, we can schedule an appointment."

"Mom, we don't have time for all that. Remember, we're getting married in a week."

"If you recall, your father agreed with me about you two waiting to schedule the wedding. I believe next spring or summer a year from now would be preferable. We're only asking to give you the wedding of your dreams, Leigh."

"My dreams or yours?" Leigh muttered under her breath.

"What?" The recipes distracted her attention.

"I said my dreams or yours, Mom? I don't want the size of wedding Tina and Alex had when they got married. They barely had time to visit with family and friends during the reception. I prefer small and intimate. Why can't you accept my preferences?"

"Because I'm afraid you'll regret your decision later. As your friends marry and you attend their weddings, you'll regret not having a larger one."

"I couldn't care less about any of my friends' weddings, so they can be as lavish and outrageous as they desire. We're looking for small and simple. Garrett and I each plan on asking one friend to stand up with us, so there won't be a huge wedding party of multiple bridesmaids and groomsmen. Wouldn't you and Dad be happy not spending a fortune on my wedding? I remember how much you paid for Alex's groom's dinner. You could have fed a small nation for the money you spent!"

"You're exaggerating. This is something we want to do for our only daughter."

"Well, your only daughter would prefer you spend the money on yourselves, go on a cruise or a trip somewhere. You could do a California wine tour or go to France or Italy." Leigh pounced on the idea because her mom valued wine and fine dining. "Haven't you been looking at trips with gourmet cooking schools included?"

"Yes, but—"

"But nothing, Mom. Why not spend the money on something for you and Dad? Besides, Garrett and I can pay for the wedding; we don't need your money." Pleased with what she assumed were winning points, Leigh changed the subject. "What can I do to help you with dinner?"

"Chopping these items would help. I'll start the risotto."

Lois threw herself into her cooking, feigning interest in Leigh's suggestions. She spent the morning calculating how to pull off a spectacular wedding for her daughter with the groom of her choice instead of Leigh's. David Walker would marry her daughter, not Leigh's current fiancé. Somehow, she'd delay this wedding and furnish David time to snatch up Leigh. She smiled to herself at the thought.

During the time they worked together, Leigh began to relax. She and her mom discussed past meals they'd cooked together, both successful and disastrous. They laughed and joked together as they got things ready for the evening's dinner. As Leigh washed her hands from cleaning all the vegetables, her mom struck.

"Is that your engagement ring?"

On the surface her mom's statement appeared as a simple observation.

"Yes! It's beautiful, don't you think?" Leigh extended her hand, giving her mom a clear view of the ring.

"Isn't the diamond rather small?" Her mom's voice sounded hollow and full of contempt. "Couldn't your fiancé afford a proper ring?"

Leigh jerked her hand back. "This ring is perfect for me. I don't want a ring with a huge rock or a cluster of diamonds. I love this ring, as I love the man who placed it on my finger." Anger at her mom seethed within her.

Thankfully, Garrett missed hearing her mom's denigration of their ring choice and her implications regarding his finances. "I'm going to lie down for a while."

"Leigh, we need to discuss your wedding in greater detail," Lois called out as her daughter walked down the hall. "Well, if you don't wish to help, I'll do all the planning myself."

The composure she maintained in the face of her mom's negativity of anything Garrett-related amazed Leigh. She walked down the hall rather than run as a tragic heroine in a romance novel. When she closed the door behind her, tears flowed down her cheeks. She flopped on the bed and grabbed Garrett's pillow. Drawing in a deep breath, his scent comforted her. With the cool softness crushed against her face, his pillow captured her sobs and tears. She willed Garrett to return as soon as possible and cried herself into a fitful sleep.

***

Two o'clock and activity started slowing down at the bar. Ecstatic over Garrett's pool skills, Frank rehashed each game with him. They won every time, and now they sat at the bar with the last of their beers and the remainder of a pizza.

"Garrett, you must have hung around pool halls rather than go to school as a kid. I never witnessed anyone executing shots like yours!"

"I enjoy the geometry of pool." Garrett downed the last of his beer. "Guess understanding angles helps my shots."

"Whatever helped your shooting, I'm thankful for it." Frank raised his beer glass to him. "Now, on a more serious note, I need to let you know something."

"What's that, Frank?" The sudden change in tone instantly concerned Garrett.

"Regarding Leigh, I want you to know she's been hurt in the past by a young man. If you ever hurt her or cause her to suffer, I won't be gentle with you." Frank leveled his eyes at Garrett in what he hoped would be taken as a warning glare.

"She told me all about David and what he did to her." Garrett's eyes held Frank's. "I hate how he hurt her, but I'm selfish enough to be glad he did."

"What the heck do you mean?" Clenched fists warned he was ready to swing a punch at Garrett's head.

"If they hadn't broken up, we wouldn't be sitting here drinking beer, and you wouldn't be threatening me, because your exquisite daughter and I would have never met. The opportunity for me to experience her capacity for love would be lost. I'm grateful she's willing to take a chance on love with me." Garrett took a deep breath and tried to calm himself. "Leigh means more to me than my own life. I cherish every moment I spend with her and foresee us building a successful life together."

"When you put it like that, guess I'm happy for her breakup. You're a far cry from David Walker, a true waste of manhood, by the way." Frank relaxed on his bar stool and clapped Garrett on the back. "You'll do. You'll do just fine! Welcome to the family."

With those words, his fate was sealed; thank you, God. Gaining her father's acceptance capped off a perfect day. He had a fun time with Frank today, but now a strong need to return to Leigh's side overtook him. "As much fun as this has been, Frank, I should get back to her."

All the men sitting around them hooted and guffawed over his statement. Frank hushed them all. "He's still young, guys, give him a break. After ten years of marriage, he'll be staying longer." In total agreement, the other men nodded and laughed in honest amusement.

On their way out, Garrett accepted further congratulations on his engagement. When they got outside, Frank clapped him on his back.

"You did awesome! I waited a long time to win their money, but not a word of this to Lois. Understand?" Frank settled his helmet on his head.

"You can count on me; I won't say a word to Lois," Garrett agreed as he sat on his snowmobile. Because Lois wouldn't search him out for conversation, it'd be easy to keep his word.

They sped away in a spray of snow.

In a half hour, they walked into the cabin.

"We're back!" Frank called out as they stomped in.

Lois came out to greet her husband. "Back so soon? I didn't expect your return for a couple more hours."

"If left to me, we would still be out and about, but Garrett wanted to get back to Leigh. Where is she?" They stood in the entry pulling off winter gear and hanging up things.

Garrett also noticed Leigh's absence.

"She laid down an hour ago. I'm worried about her. She slept late, and yet she needed to lie down after being up for a few hours."

"Excuse me; I'll check on how she's doing." Garrett walked past Lois, who glared at his back as he walked down the hall.

"So, how did your bonding excursion go with him?" Lois asked.

"First-rate! We had an amazing time, and the guys all liked him. Did your time with Leigh go well?" Frank grabbed a beer and sat in his recliner. Lois followed him, a glass of wine in her hand, and sat in her matching recliner.

"We discussed wedding hairstyles, and she helped me with the prep work for dinner. We laughed and remembered other dinners, but right after we discussed her engagement ring she went to lie down."

"Did you say something about her ring, Lois?"

"I merely commented on the size. I believe she's embarrassed over it."

"Why would she be embarrassed?"

"Because the diamond is so small, way too small. When I remember the rings David had considered for her, tsk, the simplicity of her ring is shameful."

"You didn't say anything so negative to her, did you?"

"No, of course not. Seriously, David would be so much better for her." Lois clucked her tongue to emphasize her opinion and sipped her wine.

"Leigh doesn't agree with your opinion on David Walker, and I doubt she'll change her mind. Besides, I approve of Garrett; he's a nice guy."

"A nice guy isn't sufficient for our daughter. Her husband should be someone of influence, and someone with money who can ensure she lives as we raised her. If she doesn't marry David, she needs to marry someone David's equal. He falls short in comparison." She motioned with her glass toward the bedroom where Garrett had joined Leigh. Recognizing the edge in her voice, Frank didn't say anything further. Lois would not be easily swayed from her position.

***

As Garrett passed Lois on the way to the bedroom, the coldness of her eyes rivaled the temperature outdoors. He tried suppressing an involuntary shiver but failed.

Glad he insisted on returning to the cabin, his concern for Leigh made him uneasy. Could she be sick? Pregnant? No, it'd be too soon to cause a problem, wouldn't it? They should talk about the possibility.

He found her curled up on the bed with his pillow clutched to her chest. In the dim light, a dried trail of tears on her cheeks was visible. When his hand touched the pillows, dampness from her tears wet his fingers. She had cried a long time before falling asleep.

"Leigh, I'm back." His fingers ran gently through her hair, as he kissed her cheek. "Darlin'?"

After her eyes opened, she flung herself into his arms. "You're back!"

"What happened between you and your mom that resulted in you crying yourself to sleep?"

"I tried, Garrett, I did try." Her tears started flowing again. He held her closer and wiped away her tears. "First, Mom talked of hairstyles for the wedding, and we moved on to a long talk regarding the size of the wedding. I explained our reasons against a big wedding, but our preferences conflict with her dream for an extravagant spectacle. Since my thoughts were also on cooking, I suggested they spend the wedding money on themselves and go on a cruise or a wine and cooking trip. But I'm certain she humored me and pretended to consider them. Thinking we finished on the topic of our wedding, I focused on food prep for her meal plans, and we even laughed over stories of past dinners."

"What you describe doesn't sound too bad." He spoke quietly, caressing her back and holding her close.

"It's been a long time since I acted as her sous chef. The fun ended abruptly when Mom spotted my engagement ring." She paused to catch her breath and wipe away some tears.

"What'd she say?"

"She said the diamond is too small. What I like didn't matter; nothing I say ever matters to her." The tears rolled down her cheeks. "I told her I loved the ring and you. Before I lost my composure, I came in here to lie down. Once I got behind the closed door, I started crying and couldn't stop. I ached so badly for you to be here with me." Red-rimmed eyes gazed up at him.

His heart broke over the pain and hurt in her eyes. He hated how she experienced all the turmoil and unpleasantness, because of her mother's biases.

"I'm here now." His lips gently kissed her damp eyes and cheeks. He worked his way to her lips. When his lips brushed across hers, she automatically opened them. His tongue found hers and rolled, plunged, and skimmed within her mouth. He deepened the kiss, and she leaned further into him.

He drew her on his lap and trailed kisses along her jaw, to her ear, and down her neck. His hands moved under her sweater to her breasts, and he massaged them until she whimpered.

She forgot the altercation with her mom, all the hurt replaced by the love of the man holding her. She reached for his belt.

"Slow down, darlin'. Let's take our time."

"I need you now, Garrett, so don't expect me to wait. Do me a favor and take off your clothes."

Their clothes ended in a pile on the floor. He lifted her, and her legs wrapped around his hips. With her back against the outside wall, they made slow love to each other. The power of their physical connection replaced the pain she experienced with the sweetness of their love. Afterward, she rested her head on his shoulder. He held her against the wall with her legs still around him.

"Don't you ever leave me alone with my mother, Garrett. Promise me, never again!"

"Not sure I can promise you that; after all, she is your mother." He kissed her as they came apart, and he made sure her feet hit the floor in front of him. "All better?"

"Much better. Thank you."

"Totally my pleasure. We need to join your parents. Your mom suggested you might be sick, and I worried about you. I wondered if you might be pregnant, but I suppose it'd be too soon for morning sickness. Besides, we're in the afternoon." He handed clothes to her and started putting on his own.

"I'm not sick, other than being sick of Mom and her attitude. I got so mad. I needed separation from her." She stopped pulling up her pants and gave him a mischievous smile. "If I were pregnant, we could get married faster."

He smiled back at her as he pulled up his jeans. "The thought crossed my mind, too."

"Mom would hate you for spoiling all her wedding plans. Even though making a baby requires two people, she'd place all the blame on you," Leigh confessed with a sigh. When she finished dressing, she wrapped her arms around his waist.

"I could handle her hating me. After all, she doesn't care for me now, so what's the difference?" He shrugged his shoulders. "Ready?"

"I'm going to freshen up first and meet you out there." She gave him a quick kiss on the cheek. "Thanks again."

He walked back to the kitchen, opened himself a cold beer, and proceeded to the couch in the family room. Two pairs of eyes followed him: one pair friendly and warm, the other suspicious and cold.

"How's my girl?" Frank asked him with an honest interest in Leigh's welfare.

"She fell asleep. She's fine and will be out soon." He sipped his beer and watched Lois, as she stayed busy perusing a magazine. "Leigh said she enjoyed doing all the prep work for dinner tonight, Lois."

"Yes, as did I." Lois coolly set down her magazine to glare at him.

"I'm looking forward to your dinner tonight. I don't have much occasion for eating gourmet dishes." He returned her glare, accepting her unspoken challenge. He didn't have a clue what she had against him, but he wouldn't allow Lois's prejudices to hurt Leigh. "Did Leigh cook with you often?"

"Yes, she started as my sous chef once she reached the countertop."

"Once we're married, she can be our gourmet chef, and I'll be her sous chef."

"You'll be my what?" Leigh asked as she walked in, looking rested and happy.

"Garrett said he'll be your sous chef after you two are married, so best take him up on his offer. I never ever offered to do that for your mom." Her father checked Leigh over with his eyes as she walked into the room.

"Which is a good thing, because you are hopeless in the kitchen." She threw her arms around her dad's shoulder and gave him a kiss on the cheek. "Does anyone need something?" She meandered into the kitchen.

"I'll take another beer," her dad called out.

Leigh came back in, handed her dad a beer, and cuddled next to Garrett on the couch. She held a glass of red wine.

"So, what did you guys do all day?" Leigh asked looking from Garrett to her dad.

"Your dad took me all around the countryside." Garrett took a long drink of his beer, leaving the rest of the story up to Frank.

"We ran the trails and visited with Jake regarding firewood." He debated with himself before he added, "Then we stopped in for some pool with the boys and beat the pants off all of them." He chuckled, relishing the memory of them beating his friends.

"So, you're saying my fiancé and you hustled your old friends at pool?" Leigh couldn't hold back the laughter in her voice.

"Well, hustled might be too strong a word." Frank laughed with her. "But not too far off! Leigh, it wouldn't surprise me if Garrett spent time in pool halls while growing up. You two ought to buy a pool table for your house."

"I didn't spend much time in pool halls as a kid. I will admit to spending time in the rec centers or clubs on base, and they usually had pool tables," Garrett confessed.

"Aha, I knew your shooting required practice. The guys won't be such easy pickings next time so keep those skills polished." Frank picked up his newspaper.

"A pool table might be fun," Leigh considered as her eyes bounced between her dad and fiancé. "We'd need a big room for one."

"We could consider—" Garrett started, but Lois's icy words interrupted him.

"Well, if you'll excuse me, I have dinner to make." Lois got up and walked into the kitchen.

In silence, they watched her leave. Leigh settled back against Garrett and drank her wine. She relished the strength of his body and the hardness of his strong thighs against her legs. She put a hand on his nearest leg and rubbed up and down, over and over. Eventually, he placed a hand over hers to still the movement.

"Need to stop, Leigh, or your folks will be sorely aware of what you do to me."

His deep voice sang directly to her heart.

He wrapped an arm around her and held her close. She fit perfectly against him, around him, and with him. Yet again, he marveled at his good fortune at meeting her. His belief that everything happened for a reason took a strange twist this time. Anxious to begin his life with Leigh, he ached for the end of the weekend. He hugged her close and planted a kiss on the top of her head.

"Any particular reason for the kiss?" Leigh raised her eyes to his, and immediately got lost in the warm-brown depths.

"Just considering how fortunate I am and how much I love you," Garrett whispered in her ear.

He lowered his head to give her a deep kiss.

Her hands came up to his face, and she leaned into his kiss.

"I love you, too." Breathless from his kiss, Leigh managed to gasp her words out.

"You two need to either stop making out or get a room!" Her dad threw a section of newspaper at them. "Oh, wait! You have a room!"

Garrett deflected the paper before the flying projectile hit Leigh. They both laughed at her dad, but his acceptance of them as a couple warmed their spirits.

"Okay. Okay, we'll stop." Leigh laughed. She grabbed the paper and settled back to read the section. Garrett read over her shoulder.

Soon a spicy meat aroma drifted into the family room. The sounds from the kitchen became erratic. The slamming of cupboard doors and major rattling of pots and pans grew louder. Finally, her dad couldn't cope with the harsh noises anymore.

"Leigh, would you please go out there and ask your mom if she needs any help?"

Not wishing to disappoint her dad, Leigh replied, "Sure thing, Dad."

Garrett thought she resembled a martyr headed for execution, as she walked to the kitchen.

"Mom? Would you care for some help setting supper on the table?"

"Yes, thank you, Leigh. I could have used you an hour ago."

Not planning to fall into that trap, Leigh didn't respond to her mom's comment. "I'll start setting the table. Would you prefer a tablecloth or placemats?"

"Placemats. So, are you feeling better?"

"Yes." Leigh thought of how Garrett helped her forget the anguish of dealing with her mom and made her feel loved and protected. The memory of their lovemaking put a secretive smile on her face as she walked away from the kitchen.

Her mom stopped stirring a pot to watch Leigh walk away. Her eyes narrowed as she wondered what her daughter could be thinking.

Leigh helped with the table and plating the food. Her mom outdid herself in the number of dishes she cooked for them.

"Dinner's ready!" Lois announced from the dining area, so Frank and Garrett walked in from the family room. Leigh placed Garrett next to her dad, and she braved sitting by her mom.

"So, Lois, what are we eating tonight?" Frank asked as he eased into his chair. Garrett held Leigh's chair for her before he sat.

"For an appetizer, figs with goat cheese and almonds. The main course is veal scaloppini with mushrooms and peppers, a wild mushroom risotto, roasted root vegetables, and mango chutney. And a pumpkin cheesecake for dessert later." Lois smiled as she rattled off her menu, visibly pleased with herself.

Leigh glanced at Garrett. She could have sworn she heard him say "Shit" under his breath while her mom had recited the menu. His eyes caught hers, and she noted they appeared bluer in color than brown. Not a comforting sign.

Garrett reached for the roasted root vegetables and loaded up. He passed the bowl to Leigh.

She attempted to ask him about his reaction to the menu, but her dad passing Garrett the veal prevented her from asking her question.

Garrett put some sauce on his vegetables and passed the platter to Leigh without taking any veal. As he accepted the risotto from Frank, Lois attacked.

"What? You're not having any veal?" Again, she didn't use his name, but Garrett sensed she directed her question at him.

"No, I'm not." He added a healthy amount of risotto to his plate.

"Don't tell me you're a vegetarian! It would have been appreciated if either of you informed me of your preference before I cooked all of this." Lois glared at him. She craved a fight, and her preferred target provided her ammunition she wouldn't hesitate to use. If she demonstrated how this man didn't fit into Leigh's lifestyle, perhaps they would break up. That would be perfect, and then she could work on forcing David back into Leigh's life.

"I'm not a vegetarian, Lois; however, I don't eat veal. I take issue with how the calves are raised." Garrett spoke in a forceful, even cadence, directly to her. A blue firestorm flashed in his eyes.

"I never heard of such a thing." Lois directed her glare at her daughter. "Leigh, you should have told me of his aversion to veal."

"Why the hell should Leigh be aware of my distaste for veal? Discussing our food preferences never occurred to us over the last few days, we learned more important preferences." Garrett verbally battled Lois to prevent her from making Leigh the scapegoat. Swearing at his future mother-in-law didn't strike him as a brilliant move, but defending his fiancée blinded him to niceties.

"Oh. So, how many other things is she not aware of?"

The challenge in Lois's words caught him off guard, but he wouldn't be intimidated by her. Again, he wondered at the origin of the antagonistic attitude she held for him. Why did she oppose Leigh being with him? All because of this David, who had been foolish enough to squander his two-year relationship with Leigh? The man had been a fool of gargantuan proportions.

To sacrifice the fledgling relationship he and Leigh had forged was inconceivable. As unfortunate as the looming confrontation may be, he wouldn't allow his future mother-in-law to destroy their being together. He'd fight Lois for a future with Leigh.

"There are plenty of things we still have to learn about each other, but we have a lifetime to discover them." Garrett wrapped his hand around Leigh's and propped their joined hands on the table as a symbol of their resolve.

"Let it rest, Lois," Frank pleaded. "If he doesn't eat the veal, there's more for me. Look at his plate, he's eating the rest of your meal."

"Yes, of course you're right, Frank." Lois agreed with her words, but neither Garrett nor Leigh missed the tone of her voice or the glare she leveled at Garrett. Her final words struck Garrett hard. "I just don't understand how someone who kills people has problems with how an animal is raised."

A dead silence fell over the room. Frank's mouth fell open at his wife's cruel words. Leigh reached for Garrett, but he was already standing.

"Excuse me, I need some air." Garrett's polite words cut through the tension like a knife. With six strides, he walked out the front door.

"Lois! I'm shocked at how inexcusably rude you acted toward Garrett," Frank admonished his wife. "As soon as he comes back in, you will apologize to him."

Leigh stared at her mom, unable to respond. Her thoughts fled to Garrett; he stood outside alone and probably hurting from such a vicious attack. Her mother sank to an unprecedented low with her harsh sentiments. Without saying a word, she left the table to join Garrett outside.

"Leigh, I'm sorry." Lois called out to her daughter, who didn't look back, but slammed the front door behind her. "Frank, I—"

"I believe you said more than enough already, Lois," Frank interrupted.

Leigh stepped outside in search of Garrett. He stood in the driveway, facing away from the house. She rushed over to him.

"Garrett." Her mind had difficulty processing what happened at the dinner table. At a loss for words, she wrapped her arms around him.

Certain Leigh would be the one to join him, Garrett didn't bother turning around when the door clicked, whooshed open, and slammed shut. Afraid the overwhelming hurt and despair assaulting him would be on full display, he couldn't bring himself to face her. Staring instead at the darkness of the nearby pines, his eyes closed when her arms came around him.

"Can we do this, Leigh?" He choked out his words. "If your mom dislikes me that much..." Unable to complete his thoughts, he ended with a sigh.

"Yes, we can. This is our life together, our future," Leigh's voice pleaded with him. "My mom was way out of line; in fact, she crossed a line tonight. If I never talk to her again, it'll be okay with me, as long as I'm with you!"

He turned to her, holding her at arms' length. "Leigh, I want to fight for us, but I can't come between you and your family."

"You aren't. Mom's doing it all on her own."

"But I'm the reason she's doing it." The haunted expression in his eyes broke her heart. He turned around to once again stare at the trees.

Her voice trembled. "Look at me, please." She grabbed an arm.

He slowly turned to face her. The fury reflected in her eyes twisted his stomach, because he was the ultimate impetus for the fury and angst tearing her from her parents.

"Leigh, we can't—"

"Yes, we can. Don't let her win." Her words became sobs. "Please, do not let her win."

He responded with a deeper sigh than before. His eyes closed for a moment. When he looked at her, a firestorm of blue raged in his eyes. He pulled her into his arms.

"I'm sorry, Leigh." He held her close; his eyes filled with tears. "I'm sorry our love is causing this, this...ah hell, I can't figure out what this is."

Leigh's laughter lightened the mood. "I have no idea either, but nothing will block us from being together. I love you, and we are getting married." She held up her left hand, the diamond caught the moonlight and sparkled. "This is our promise for that to happen, and a sign of our love for one another. Now, let's go back inside before we catch pneumonia."

He hesitated and pulled her in his arms. Uttering a deep growl, he devoured her lips. Her hands crunched his sweater and pulled him closer, deepening the kiss. Molded together they escaped for a moment the pain of her mom's attitude and words.

"Thank you, Leigh. While I stood out here, I worked my way into a dark place of life without you. I convinced myself this rift between you and your mom will hurt you, all because of me, and I can't do that to you. I imagined walking back in there, saying goodbye, and leaving tonight without you, because I love you so damned much. Leaving you behind would devastate me, but I thought I should give you up for your family's sake."

"I wouldn't let you leave without me." Leigh's hands were on either side of his face. "You are my family now." She reached up to kiss him. "Come on; let's go back in and finish our supper." She led him inside the cabin.

As they entered the dining room, Frank cleared his throat and glared at Lois.

"I'm sorry for upsetting you." Lois spewed out a lackluster apology.

Frank and Leigh looked at her with the expectation of her expressing further apologetic sentiments, but they were sorely disappointed.

Garrett met her cool gaze with his own icy-blue regard.

"Lois, my job may require me to kill someone, but I don't take a life lightly. Whenever I fire my weapon at someone, they're either trying to kill me or hurt someone under my protection. I don't apologize for what I do." He continued, his voice steady. "When a calf is raised for veal, it probably lives a restrictive life in a veal crate. They typically have limited mobility, their feed is limited, they only get a few hours or a few days with their mother, and they're slaughtered anywhere from eighteen to twenty-six weeks of age. Everything involved in the production of veal is abhorrent to me, and why I don't eat the meat."

Lois stared, at a loss for words. Frank smiled as he turned to his plate. Leigh gave Garrett's leg a squeeze.

They completed the meal in silence and without further incident. With major relief, they all laid aside their silverware marking the end of the disastrous supper. Lois received none of the typical compliments on her meal and culinary skills.

Leigh stood by her chair. "Garrett and I will clean up."

"Thanks, honey. That's considerate of you two," her dad answered with a smile for them.

After her parents were out of earshot, she stood behind Garrett and massaged his shoulders. "You did great. You made me extremely proud when you spoke up to Mom after she had been so rude to you."

"Is this what you experienced earlier today?"

"Not quite as bad as your experience, but yeah."

"No wonder you escaped to the bedroom. Your mom doesn't always act this way, does she? I mean, damn, I don't know what I mean. I bring out the...what's the word? Oh, yeah, bitch. I bring out the bitch in her. Is it only me, or do others bring out her inner bitch as well?"

"Hate to tell you this, but you're the only one I ever witnessed who brought out her inner bitch." Leigh whispered the b-word and laughed.

"What the hell did I do to make her dislike me so much?"

Leigh cringed at the torment in his eyes, and she ached for him. She became certain she understood why her mom had developed such an instant animosity against Garrett, so she forged ahead with her theory.

"You made me love you." At his questioning look, she continued. "Remember I told you how she adored my ex-boyfriend, David?"

"Yes, but you broke up with him over four years ago." Confused, he stumbled over the words.

"I told you how Mom never accepted our breakup. Because they are close friends with his parents, Mom learns what's going on in David's life. While I lived in Chicago, she kept trying to push me back into his arms. Got the picture?" He nodded, so she continued. "Now you come along, totally out of the blue so to speak. You're a huge threat to the happy ending she envisions for David and me. If I know my mom, this isn't over."

"Great! I'm at war with my future mother-in-law." He jabbed at remnants of vegetables on his plate with his fork. "Geez, could it be any worse?"

"Don't ask because you might get an answer you can't handle. Come on, we offered to clean up."

They took their time in the kitchen. When they finished, Leigh started a pot of coffee to go with their dessert. They joined her parents in the family room. A movie played on the TV, but no one paid attention to it.

"If you're not watching this, could we put on the hockey game?" Leigh asked as she and Garrett sat together on the couch.

"Hockey? The Wild plays tonight? Sure, we can put it on, right, Lois?" With controller in hand, her dad searched for the game.

"Leigh, you never showed interest in sports on TV before. What's changed? Is that since you two got together?" Her mom looked up from her magazine and radiated her disapproval.

"I watched more sports over the last year, Mom. Football, hockey, golf, baseball, and some NASCAR."

"Really?"

"Yes, I admire the competition. I don't pay close attention all the time, so I multi-task while watching."

"That's my girl, always figuring out the angles." Frank chuckled. He found the game and tuned it in.

"I started the coffee for the dessert course, Mom."

"Why, thank you, dear. I'll go pull out the cheesecake, so it's at room temperature for us."

"Already done. Garrett and I will serve up dessert when the coffee's finished." A priceless look of surprise crossed her mom's face. Leigh snuggled close to Garrett ready to enjoy the rest of the evening.

They completed dessert without glares or verbal daggers. Leigh breathed a sigh of relief when Garrett closed the door to their bedroom.

"Garrett, I am sorry Mom put you through so much. The attacks and attitude toward you made me cringe, so I can imagine how uncomfortable the entire evening had been for you." She wrapped her arms around him, hugging him close.

"Your mom definitely knows how to make an evening interesting; I'll give her that. Because she's your mother, I'm sure there will be other such occasions; although I prefer not experiencing a repeat performance." Leigh cringed at the accuracy of his words. "As long as you're on my side, I can handle anything she dishes out." He hugged her back and kissed her. "All I'm looking to do is climb in bed and allow this day to end." He stepped back from her and started undressing.

The loss of his body against her stripped away warmth and physical support. She decided she had a responsibility to aid in his recovery from the battering he received from her mother all evening.

She hurriedly undressed and climbed in bed with him. As she cuddled close to him, a hand roamed down his body, encouraging the growth of an erection.

"You do know how much I love you, don't you?"

"I believe I do." His hand drew slow circles on her back.

"Tonight I need to show you exactly how much." With that said, she dove under the covers.

Surprised at her sudden action, Garrett reached for the covers.

"Leigh, what the hell—" He didn't finish, when the moist warmth of her mouth held his enlarged flesh hostage. A deep groan completed the sentence, as she eased the tension he experienced all evening.

After Leigh satisfied him and Garrett reciprocated for her, they lay relaxed in each other's arms. The darkness of the room cloaked them in a blanket of stillness.

"I love you, Leigh, and will forever. I'm determined to marry you now, not months from now." He traced kisses down her throat.

She couldn't find her voice to respond right away but sighed in pleasure. His attentions tonight had carried her to heights she never experienced before and given her an evening of sexual bliss. She needed to tell him what his love meant to her, and how much she loved him.

"Garrett," Leigh started in a voice softened by their lovemaking, "they mentioned us waiting a whole year, but I can't wait. We need to be firm and persistent on the timing of our wedding."

Garrett nodded. "I agree; I had to be bold and determined in the past when up against difficult circumstances. Determination in the face of adversity. I believe that's called resolute, Leigh."

"Yes, resolute describes our love and us," Leigh agreed. "When we reach Brainerd, we'll make all our marriage arrangements. Mom and Dad will have to accept our plans; they can decide to show up or not."

"Your mom couldn't possibly dislike me any more than she already does, so I'm in." He drew her close and kissed her.

"If all else fails, we can always tell them I'm pregnant. We'll marry for the sake of their future grandbaby." The laughter in her voice gave her joke away.

Garrett chuckled as he settled back in the pillows. "I need sleep; don't forget you napped today. I spent a lot of time out with your dad, and he plays hard. I can't remember the last time I drank so much beer."

She laughed. "You can't be a lightweight around my dad."

They snuggled together, each with their own thoughts regarding their shared future. They drifted off to sleep, lost in their separate dreams, but each with the same last thought: tomorrow we're out of here and off to our future.

Chapter Twenty-Nine

The morning dawned bright and clear, a promising omen for them. Leigh and Garrett had been up for a couple of hours, and they'd packed all their things in her car. Their bedding and towels had been washed, the bedding dried, and the towels were in the dryer.

Leigh stood looking out the kitchen window and saw Garrett's reflection as he walked up behind her. His arms wove around her waist and drew her back to him. She breathed in his woodsy scent as she settled against his chest.

"The bed's all made." He kissed her cheek.

"I love how you do house chores without coercion; that'll come in handy when we move into our house."

She leaned her head to one side, giving him access to her neck. He wasted no time to rain kisses down it.

"Can you wait for breakfast until we reach the town?" Kisses muffled his words.

"Yes, if you buy me breakfast."

"Okay, but no stealing food from my plate this time."

With slow, delicious progress, he kissed and tasted his way up to her ear. When his tongue circled around the ear, she released a soft sigh. A noise in the hallway jolted them upright and a step away from each other.

Leigh glanced down the hallway to find her dad yawning and stretching his way toward the kitchen.

"Morning, smelled coffee," he greeted as he made his way to the counter.

"Good morning." Leigh poured him coffee. "We're leaving soon. Garrett has an early doctor's appointment in town, and afterward we leave for Brainerd."

Frank sipped his coffee and woke up further. "You can't wait for your mother to get up? She expected to say goodbye before you left."

"No, Garrett can't be late for this appointment. Besides, this visit hasn't been too pleasant because of Mom."

"Understand. Garrett, I'm sorry for how she acted toward you. She didn't handle the news of you two awfully well. Remember how much she valued your relationship with David, Leigh? Her dream for your future always centered on you and David being together. Your engagement to Garrett threw her off kilter, but she'll come around in time."

"Sure she will, Dad." Leigh didn't expect her mom would ever accept Garrett as a son-in-law, and she didn't propose waiting for her to 'come around.'

"Garrett, it's been a pleasure. I believe you're going to do your utmost to care for my little girl." Frank extended his hand to Garrett, who accepted it, and they shook.

"I promise, sir," Garrett replied solemnly.

"Well, I'm sure we'll be seeing you soon. There's a wedding to plan, right?"

"I don't imagine we'll need anything from you for the wedding, other than giving me away."

"Well, we're here for you. We always thought we would pay for your wedding, so we can help cover the costs." He looked from Leigh to Garrett.

"We appreciate your offer, and we'll keep your generosity in mind," Garrett acknowledged his soon-to-be father-in-law's proposition. Leigh and he hadn't discussed finances; yet another unknown between them.

The dryer buzzer sounded.

"That's our towels. The bed linens are all cleaned in our bedroom, Dad. Please remember to tell Mom all our things are washed, so she doesn't rewash everything." She started toward the laundry room, but Garrett stopped her.

"I'll fold the towels. You say goodbye to your dad." He walked away with long, fluid strides, her eyes drawn to his blue jeans encased butt as he walked away. He turned her on simply walking away and with her dad standing by her no less. She heard her dad's soft chuckle, so she turned to him.

"I can see he loves you, honey. I totally approve of him." He wrapped his arms around her and placed a fatherly kiss on her cheek.

"I love him, Dad; I truly do love him." She hugged her dad.

"I'll say your goodbyes to your mother."

"Thanks, Dad, love you."

"I love you, Leigh. Now go help him, so you can leave before your mother wakes up."

Leigh hurried after Garrett. By working together, they folded and stowed away the towels. With a last hug for her dad, they found themselves in her car driving to town.

"Are you sure you should leave without saying goodbye to your mom?" Garrett looked at her as if he could read her thoughts. He detested coming between her and her family, and a division appeared certain.

"Yeah, I'm sure." She glanced at him. "Trust me, this is the safest way, so don't feel bad. I've left without saying goodbye to her before; our relationship fractured a while ago."

"All right. Breakfast first, my appointment second, followed by a stop at the Aspen Inn for my Jeep, and then off to Brainerd."

"Yes! I'm so excited. This is the start of our future together, Garrett."

"It is, Leigh, that it is." He settled back in the car seat and watched the woman he loved drive them toward their future.

The End

About Elaine M. DeGroot

Originally from Minnesota, I now live in Upstate South Carolina and enjoy retirement. My husband, Mike, is a retired US Air Force Chief Master Sergeant and is loving life with the year-round golfing! We have a pup, Missy, a Belgian Malinois-German Shepherd mix, who keeps us busy and entertained. They are an inspiration, a distraction, and my life.

I served 12 years active duty in the US Air Force. Ultimately, I worked in the federal civil service, beginning with the Department of Veterans Affairs, on to the US Air Force, a fun stint with the US Fish & Wildlife Service, and ending back at the VA. All told, serving thirty years in federal service and loved every minute of it.

I write romance stories...rather steamy ones. Some with a touch of suspense. I've found inspiration in where I've lived, what I've done/experienced, and hobbies I enjoy. In the midst of writing a story, I love it when my characters take hold of the plot and own it!

Social Media

Website: https://www.romance-degrootified.net/

Facebook: https://www.facebook.com/RomanceByDeGroot

Acknowledgements

First, I need to acknowledge Kathi Sprayberry, Editor in Chief, at Solstice Publishing, for seeing something in my work and offering me my first publishing contract. I appreciate your taking a chance on me. To my editor, Brian Cavit, time zones and distance may separate us, but we've

267 • Resolute Love (Consequential Love Series #1)

overcome the separations. Your skills have ensured *Resolute Love* is a stunning story and ready for the readers of romance and romantic suspense books. Thank you.

To my local friends who read, enjoyed, and ferried my stories between each other, even though they were contained in bulky three ring binders. Thank you. You bolstered my confidence as an author and in pursuing a publishing contract. Stay tuned for the next stories.

Finally, to the love of my life, Mike. As my husband you support and encourage me. As my best friend, you make me laugh and enjoy life to the fullest. You have always believed in me. I love you forever and a day.

Made in United States
Orlando, FL
21 May 2022

18061342R00146